THE HOLY GRAIL OF ERIS

2

T0054356

©Yu-nagi

Salvador

Shoshanna's older brother, an easygoing young man. Kidnapped a child from an unknown location.

Shoshanna

Currently in a secret hideout, caring for the kidnapped child as per Salvador's instructions.

Rufus May

Timid-looking assistant to the vice-comptroller of the treasury. Has two black dots in his eye.

©Yu-nagi

Lily Orlamunde

Scarlett's friend, she committed suicide two years ago. Left behind a mysterious message and key.

Kyle Hughes

Randolph's deputy at the Royal Security Force. Looks like a playboy, actually a workaholic.

Lucia O'Brian

Abigail O'Brian's precocious adopted daughter. Able to see Scarlett.

Characters

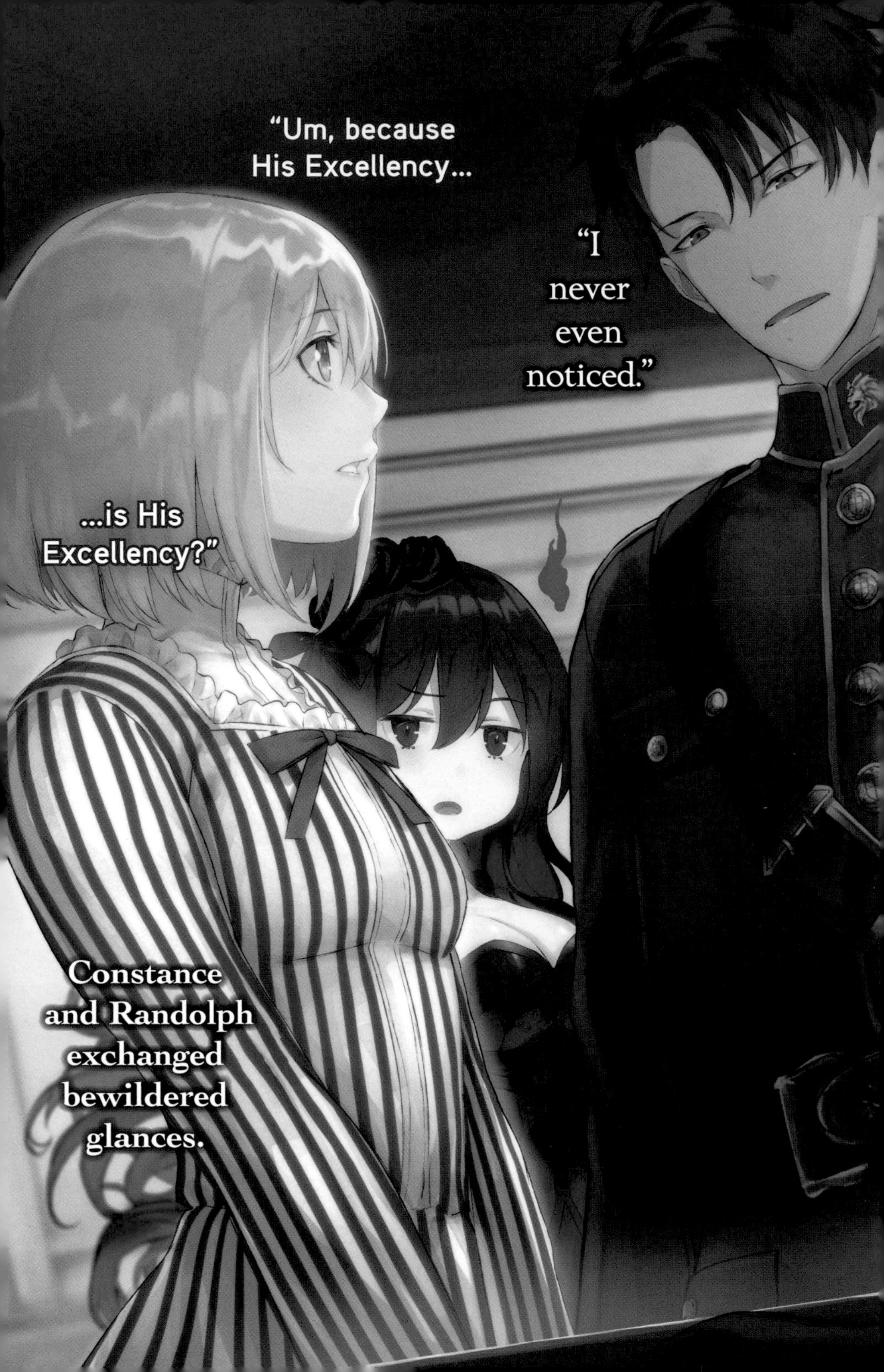
"Um, because His Excellency...
"I never even noticed."
...is His Excellency?"
Constance and Randolph exchanged bewildered glances.

"Why do you call him **Your Excellency**? You two *are* **engaged**, aren't you?"

©Yu-nagi

Contents

The Holy Grail of Eris

author Kujira Tokiwa
illustration Yu-nagi

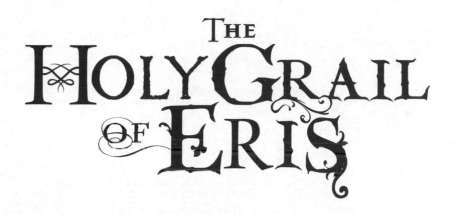

The Holy Grail of Eris

2

KUJIRA TOKIWA

ILLUSTRATION BY YU-NAGI

YEN ON

NEW YORK

THE HOLY GRAIL OF ERIS

2

KUJIRA TOKIWA

Translation by Winifred Bird
Cover art by Yu-nagi

Eris NO SEIHAI Vol. 2
Copyright © 2020 Kujira Tokiwa
Illustrations copyright © 2020 Yu-nagi. All rights reserved.
Original Japanese edition published in 2020 by SB Creative Corp.

This English edition is published by arrangement with SB Creative Corp., Tokyo
in care of TUTTLE-MORI AGENCY, INC., Tokyo.

English translation © 2022 by Yen Press, LLC

Yen On
150 West 30th Street, 19th Floor
New York, NY 10001

Visit us at yenpress.com • facebook.com/yenpress • twitter.com/yenpress •
yenpress.tumblr.com • instagram.com/yenpress

First Yen On Edition: July 2022
Edited by Yen On Editorial: Emma McClain, Anna Powers
Designed by Yen Press Design: Wendy Chan

Yen On is an imprint of Yen Press, LLC.
The Yen On name and logo are trademarks of Yen Press, LLC.

Library of Congress Cataloging-in-Publication Data
Names: Tokiwa, Kujira, author. | Yu-nagi, illustrator. | Bird, Winifred, translator.
Title: The holy grail of Eris / Kujira Tokiwa ; illustration by Yu-nagi ; translation by Winifred Bird.
Other titles: Eris no seihai. English
Description: First Yen On edition. | New York, NY : Yen On, 2022.
Identifiers: LCCN 2021060246 | ISBN 9781975339579 (v. 1 ; trade paperback) |
ISBN 9781975339593 (v. 2 ; trade paperback)
Subjects: LCGFT: Light novels.
Classification: LCC PZ7.1.T6223 Ho 2022 | DDC [Fic]—dc23
LC record available at https://lccn.loc.gov/2021060246

ISBNs: 978-1-9753-3959-3 (paperback)
978-1-9753-3960-9 (ebook)

10 9 8 7 6 5 4 3 2 1

LSC-C

Printed in the United States of America

Shoshanna sighed. Annoyingly enough, the "pet" her brother Salvador had stolen was no fool. He showed obvious fear only on the day he arrived. After that, he studied his new surroundings with a thoughtful, observant gaze. Yes, his perfect face would go pale and his hands would shake at times, but he never once lashed out at her, or even cried or struggled.

Shoshanna let out another theatrical sigh. *Oh, what a pain.*

"Thank you," the boy said.

She didn't know who his teacher had been, but they must have been quite skilled.

Whenever she served him his simple meal of grains cooked in a broth made from vegetable scraps and chicken bones, he invariably fixed his violet eyes on hers and thanked her politely. Those eyes held neither servility nor rebellion. Yes, his behavior truly was exemplary.

The first thing a hostage had to do to survive was remain calm. The next was to observe their surroundings. The third was to make their captor realize they were a person, not an object.

Still, the boy was young. No matter how good a student he was, the only way he could possibly remain so calm in his current situation was if he had complete trust in his teacher.

"My name is Uly—" he started to say.

"You're just a pet."

But Shoshanna had been trained, too—since she was old enough to remember. She had learned many methods of guarding her heart from attachment.

She flipped around the knife she'd been playing with and pointed it at the boy's throat.

"And clever pets don't talk. Got that?"

She had realized a while back that her current situation was not a good one.

She had no idea why her brother had kidnapped this boy and pushed him into her hands, but for once, he had made a bad choice.

No matter how thoroughly Shoshanna had been trained, she didn't have the sun tattoo. Strictly speaking, she herself belonged to Salvador and was not a member of the organization. Even if she could turn a knife on an enemy who tried to attack her, she had never yet harmed a complete stranger. Plus, the boy was a mere child, younger than her.

"...Why are you so calm?"

It was Shoshanna who gave in first, several days later. Shackles were fastened to the boy's feet, with a chain connecting them so he could not move freely. But this hardly seemed to affect him. Every day he thanked her for his food and found chances to talk to her. Honestly, it was hard to fathom.

For a second, he blinked in confusion but then quickly nodded, understanding.

"Because I have faith."

There was strength in his clear eyes. When Shoshanna looked into them, she realized she had forgotten the most important thing. The thing a person had to do no matter what if they wanted to protect their heart.

"I have faith that my sister will come rescue me."

They must never lose hope. This boy was certain on the most fundamental level that things would turn out all right.

Shoshanna was still searching for words when a cold voice interrupted her thoughts.

"Oh, you mean Princess Alexandra?"

Startled, she looked around. A shabbily dressed man was leaning against the wall, watching the two of them with apparent interest.

"You're awfully attached to her, considering you've got different mothers."

Shoshanna didn't recognize the man's face. But she knew the voice all too well. Goose bumps rose on her arms.

She had fastened both locks. She had set several other traps as well. Still, he had managed to slip through them all without making a sound.

"…Krishna."

They said he had a hundred faces, and today he wore that of an emaciated vagrant. His sole identifying feature were the two black dots in his eye, but to see those, you had to get close enough to touch him and look very closely. If he could change his voice as well as his appearance, Shoshanna thought, no one in the world would be able to see through his disguises.

Krishna glanced at the boy and smiled cruelly.

"My, my, Shoshanna, you seem to be treating the boy very well. You talk to him, you give him home-cooked meals—and I see you even offer him a damp towel to wipe his hands with. Whatever did your trainer teach you? Oh, that's right—if I recall correctly, Salvador doesn't believe in hitting children. He could have advanced so much further if he didn't have that little quirk."

"Why are you here?" Shoshanna asked in a strained voice. She didn't like this man. Her brother instinctively disliked him, too.

Krishna was far more brutal than he needed to be.

"Oh, just to have some fun."

He walked silently over to the chained-up boy.

"I have some good news for the captive prince."

He brought his lips close to the boy's ear and whispered to him, as if he were delivering a special gift.

"That big sister you love so much? She's locked away in your native land."

The boy's eyes widened.

"She's in the Tower of Sorrow. In two weeks' time, she'll burn at the stake for a crime she never committed. Even the most popular among us fall on hard times, I suppose."

"You're lying!"

For the first time, Shoshanna heard emotion in the boy's voice. Krishna's lips curled upward in satisfaction.

"A lie? I've heard the third princess's supporters are planning to rescue her, but they'll never succeed. No one ever leaves that tower once they've gone in. You ought to know that, considering you've got royal blood in you."

"You're lying…"

She could see the light fading from his eyes. So much for his strength.

"No one is coming to save you. You'll be a captive until you die."

"…Kendall will come, I know he will."

"You honestly expect an upstart commoner to save you? I'm sorry to inform you, but the old fox has decided to cover up your kidnapping. Personally, I wish he hadn't. We've had to change our plans because of it. Our employer is simply livid about the situation."

Despair seeped into the boy's eyes. Shoshanna turned away, unable to bear watching anymore.

"Anyhow, that's not why I'm here. Your party are the ones who poisoned the Fifth Prince, Jerome, aren't they? To tell you the truth, it's made a wreck of my plans. So if you want to stay in one piece, I suggest you answer the question I'm about to ask."

The boy grimaced, but Krishna did not lighten the pressure.

"What in the world is Kendall Levine up to?"

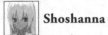 ## Shoshanna

Going through a rebellious phase that makes her want to scream that humans are not pets. She is like an honor student: good at studying for tests but not so good at practical skills. Possessed of common sense, she has been taking diligent care of the child her brother kidnapped, only to be criticized for it by Krishna. When her brother gets back, she'll probably vent her anger to him.

Ulysses

A handsome young boy with violet eyes. Thoughtful and observant. Kept his chin up longer than most kids his age could have, but he finally broke down when a childish adult harassed him. Seems to share some kind of secret with Kendall Levine. Loves his big sister a lot.

Krishna

Tops the list of childish adults. Very good at disguising himself and seems to have many identities. Can change his voice if he wants to. Unless you have an insanely good memory, you'd have a hard time seeing through his disguises. The only characteristic he can't hide is the pair of black dots in his eye, but they're only visible from very close-up. Despite saying sensible things about wanting to know the bald man's plans, he was probably just looking to bully the weak. Most likely hates children.

CHAPTER 1

The Deceivers and the Deceived

Kate Lorraine got her first taste of noble society at the tender age of six. It happened at the birthday party of a girl her own age.

The Lorraine family had attained noble status only in Kate's grandfather's generation. On top of that, her mother was a commoner from the castle district. It goes without saying that she was excluded from the nobles' social circles. That was why Kate had never had a friend her own age.

So when the invitation arrived, the Lorraine family erupted in a flurry of excitement.

The truth was, Kate was elated. Even her mother was acting as if the Moirai had specially blessed them. She baked a batch of her most delicious cookies, the kind she normally made only on very special days, for Kate to take with her. Kate couldn't help smiling. Once everyone tasted the cookies, they would be so envious, they would all want to come to her house. Then what would she do? Would her mother bake another batch for them? It would be hard to make enough for so many people, so maybe everyone could help. Yes, that was a good idea. It would be so much fun!

Her head filled with silly dreams about the future, she ever so carefully packed away the bundle of baked sweets.

It was the first time she'd ever been to a baron's house, and it was much finer and bigger than her own. There were glittering chandeliers and gaudy, gilded decorations. There was also a stomach-turning scent of perfume.

"You stink!" The cute birthday girl scowled as soon as Kate had recited her greeting. "What is that smell? It's gross!"

Little Pamela Francis was wearing a white dress and had her white-gold hair braided in a grown-up updo, just like a princess in a fairy tale. When Kate heard such contemptuous words from the mouth of such a delicate, kind-looking, beautiful child, she felt terrified. The crowd of other little girls surrounding Pamela instantly piled on. "She stinks, she stinks!" "Ewww!" "That's how commoners smell!"

The chorus of mean, giggly voices jeered at her. She squeezed her fists tight and thought about how glad she was that her mother wasn't with her. The Francis family had invited her, but she had turned down the invitation, saying a former kitchen maid like herself didn't have the proper manners for society, and she wouldn't want to ruin the party by making some blunder. Instead, Kate's aunt on her father's side had offered to go along.

Pamela Francis was dressed in more beautiful clothes than anyone else at the party, and she had a charm that drew all eyes to her. Flanked by the group of other little girls, her presence was absolute. Kate trembled to think what might happen next.

Pamela's eyes glittered with an awful light as she smiled.

"Don't you think she stinks?" she said, suddenly turning her haughty gaze on another noble girl.

There probably wasn't any deep meaning behind her actions. She simply did as she pleased, calling out to a girl who happened to be passing by.

She had no doubt the girl would agree with her.

"What?"

But against all expectations, the girl did not agree. She simply stood still and looked at Kate. She had hazelnut hair, green eyes, and a very ordinary face. Her dress was plain.

She stepped closer to Kate, a completely calm expression on her face.

Everyone else was watching in surprise. Kate froze, too. But the girl just sniffed indifferently and looked over her shoulder.

"No, she doesn't stink at all," she said.

Pamela suddenly looked embarrassed. The other girls tensed, then all in unison turned their critical eyes on the one with the hazelnut hair. But she didn't seem to care one bit. Instead, she seemed to be puzzling over something.

"I think…," she said, before breaking into a smile. "It's the smell of cookies!"

She looked very excited. Kate stared at her in surprise. It was as if a balloon that had been on the verge of popping were suddenly deflating with a soft *whoosh*. Pamela arched her eyebrows and glared at the other girl with a terrifying expression, then spun silently on her heels. The other girls ran after her.

The one with the hazelnut hair seemed to find all this very strange.

"Everyone left," she said.

"Y-yes…," Kate stuttered.

Who was this girl?

Just then, she heard a sound like a little animal. When she blinked in confusion, the girl pressed her hands bashfully over her stomach.

Kate hesitated for a few seconds, then pulled out the prettily wrapped bundle she'd brought.

"…Do you want some?"

"Can I?!" she asked, her green eyes glittering. She looked around, then untied the bundle and threw a cookie into her mouth. Right away she pressed her hands to her cheeks in surprise.

"Yum!"

A happy smile lit up the kind girl's face. Without realizing what she was doing, Kate opened her mouth and spoke.

"My name is Kate…! Kate Lorraine…!"

The girl paused, her hand already reaching for a second cookie, and widened her eyes. Then she pointed happily at her face and said, "I'm Connie!"

*　　*　　*

Kate slowly opened her eyes. Cold wind tickled her cheek. The dusty room she was in must have been some sort of shed.

She seemed to have lost consciousness with her face down on the cold floor. Fortunately, she was alone in the dim room. When she tried to stand up, she realized her hands were tied behind her back. No wonder she felt so sore. She wriggled over to the wall, leaned against it for balance, and sat up.

The room was nearly bare. There was one chair and one table. The small amount of light filtering in from outside was still bright. Peering quietly around, Kate heard no sounds of people going about their daily lives, which made her think she must be beyond the city limits—and sure enough, the scene she could see through the lone window suggested a forest.

Presently, the door opened, and Kate froze. A muscular, middle-aged man walked in. The look in his eyes was chilling.

"So you woke up, eh?"

Kate retraced her memory. She had been returning from the Grail house. She remembered someone attacking her from behind, then some sort of chemical being pressed over her nose before she passed out.

The man sank heavily into the chair and curled his lips back over yellowed teeth.

"Kate Lorraine, is it?"

She didn't answer, waiting for his next move.

"Do you know anything about *Lily Orlamunde's key?*"

"...What?"

"Tell me where it is, and I'll let you go. Constance Grail had it, didn't she?"

Kate gasped. So they were after Connie.

That made it easy. Kate narrowed her eyes and smirked.

"I don't know anything about that—and if I did, I wouldn't tell you."

The man dropped his smile and raised his hand. Before she had a chance to dodge, she felt the impact on her cheek. Her vision wavered, and she collapsed to the floor under the merciless force of his blow. The taste of rust filled her mouth.

He stepped toward her and grabbed her chestnut hair. A cry of pain escaped her throat.

"Then trick her into giving it to you."

Kate's grandfather had started out as a mere petty officer in the border police. She'd heard that he'd been awarded noble rank through a series of fortunate coincidences. Lower nobles and commoners alike had scoffed at his half-baked success. At best, they showed barefaced malice and contempt. Some could not accept the upstart nobles and went as far as trying to eliminate them by force. For that reason, children in the Lorraine family were taught from a young age the physical and mental skills necessary to protect themselves—including what to do if they were kidnapped.

Kate knew very well that she shouldn't have taken a rebellious attitude toward her captor.

But this man hadn't blindfolded her. He'd made no effort to hide his identity at all, in fact. Plus, he was after Connie, not Kate. That meant he saw no special value in his hostage. She glared at him.

"Never."

This time, instead of exploding, he calmly pulled a knife from his breast pocket and sawed through the handful of hair he was still holding. The chestnut locks that Connie always praised scattered to the floor. Kate glanced down at her suddenly shoulder-length hair, then slowly closed her eyes and steeled her will. There was only one conclusion she could draw.

This man had never intended to let her go alive.

※

One night had passed since Kate's abduction.

Although their daughter was missing, the Lorraine family had appeared to be going about their normal routines when Connie stopped by. Nobody had mentioned filing a missing person report with the Security Force. *Maybe...*, Connie thought to herself. *Maybe they also got a message like the one that was thrown into my courtyard.* In other words, it was possible they'd been told to keep quiet if they wanted to save their daughter.

Baron Lorraine, Kate's father, had stayed in the family's domain this year to work on a new business venture, so he wasn't in the city. Her brothers worked for the border police and were also away.

That left the baroness alone in the Lorraine house.

"...His Excellency," Connie mumbled, sitting on her bed and hugging her knees. "...I'm sure His Excellency will help."

She thought of the forbidding figure dressed all in black.

The letter had said not to tell anybody. Still, it was the best strategy she could think of.

From now on—

She thought back to what he had said to her in that low, serious voice of his as they returned by carriage from the Folkvangr.

From now on, when you're going to take action, it would be helpful if you could let me know in advance.

It was a kind thing to say, and she wanted to do as he'd asked.

"Well, well. I was certain you were going to be an honest idiot as usual and do exactly as you were told."

Scarlett, who until now had been sitting next to Connie looking bored, snorted scornfully.

Not long ago, Connie probably *would* have done that. She used to believe that sincere deeds brought sincerity in return. She had always used sincerity as an excuse when she didn't want to do something. But sitting around waiting for sincerity to save her wouldn't help this time.

Think! Connie told herself. Thinking was the solution. What was the best thing to do?

If the answer went against "sincerity," so be it.

Connie knew now that if she wanted to find a way out, she had to act.

She got ready to go see Randolph right away and slipped out the back gate.

"May I speak with you for a moment?"

A figure stepped out of the shadows, where they seemed to have been waiting for her. Connie looked over in surprise. It was a woman with curly red hair and gray-green eyes.

"Amelia Hobbes?" Connie moaned. No doubt about it, that infernal reporter from the *Mayflower* was here.

She stepped out to block Connie's path and began cross-examining her in the rude way Connie remembered all too well.

"It's been quite a while since we talked, hasn't it, Constance Grail? I've been wanting to ask you about something."

"I-I'm in a hurry…," Connie said, her face tensing. Amelia raised one eyebrow.

"I see. So you can't be bothered to talk to a commoner like me?"

That sounded awfully familiar.

"Not at all," Connie replied, pressing her fingers between her eyebrows. Of course, Amelia completely ignored her.

"Tell me, what entertaining event is the viscount's daughter sneaking off to participate in today? If need be, I can ask the question more loudly."

That would be a problem. Connie had wanted to avoid drawing attention to herself. Her anxiety must have shown on her face, because Amelia smiled with satisfaction.

"You met with Crown Princess Cecilia at the Elbaite Detached Palace the other day, didn't you?"

Connie didn't reply. This did not seem to bother Amelia, who kept right on talking.

"How impressive, to be invited to tea after meeting her for the very first time. She must have liked you. Let's make a deal. I'll pay you if that's what you want. Or would you prefer that I write up another article to bring you some attention?"

"I'll thank you not to do that."

"Ha! Why don't you take that chip off your shoulder? I'd like you to get some information from the crown princess for me. Some nasty rumors are going around about her."

Connie considered going back into the house and trying again later, then thought better of it. Amelia had been waiting for her. Connie wouldn't be surprised if before long she knocked on the door and asked to be invited in. If it came to that, maybe Connie could force her way—

As Connie was considering these possibilities, she heard Amelia say something disturbing and looked up.

"The word is, Princess Cecilia is the daughter of a whore."

That couldn't be. Her maiden name was Luze. She was the eldest daughter of Viscount Luze. Her mother was a noble from Melvina, an ally of Adelbide.

"A few months ago, a man from the palace who was posted at city hall happened to notice signs of falsification on the Luze family register."

Amelia must have been pleased by Connie's shocked expression, because she began to speak with increasing gusto.

"The man who discovered it is real high-strung, and he couldn't leave it alone. He started investigating on his own and soon enough found out that Cecilia Luze wasn't the viscount's legitimate daughter, but instead his daughter by a prostitute. His wife's child had died sometime before from an infectious disease. I'm sure that girl was the frail one. In other words, Viscount Luze switched the birth certificates of his two daughters."

Connie gasped.

"The man tried to make the truth public. After all, it was a clear betrayal of the royal family and the people of Adelbide. He came to us at the *Mayflower*. What a scoop! …But suddenly he couldn't be reached, and then we heard he'd become a junkie and was recovering at a sanitarium. Not to mention his wife ended up killing herself after an affair gone wrong. Poor Kevin Jennings!"

Connie's heart thumped unpleasantly. *Jennings?* Then his wife must have been—

The image of a certain woman flitted across her memory—the woman who had announced her infidelity at Emilia's ball and ended up getting slashed across the cheek by Margot Tudor. Amelia must be talking about Teresa Jennings's husband.

"Sadly, the prostitute thought to be the crown princess's mother died in childbirth. The baby, it seems, was given to a local orphanage. But that orphanage burned down fourteen years ago, just around the time the birth certificates were switched. The orphanage's records were all incinerated, but I managed to track down someone who had been there at the time and confirmed that there had indeed been a child with rose-colored eyes at the orphanage."

Rose-colored eyes were common in the Luze family. Cecilia had them, too.

"The girl seems to have pledged her love to a boy at the orphanage. I think the name was Sarsy or Cici, something like that. I'm sure you've heard the famous stories about the crown princess going out in secret among the common folk, right? They're all beautiful tales about how she plays with poor children in the slums and visits the sick at the public hospital. But what if all along she'd been arranging secret trysts with her old love? How romantic!"

Amelia's gray-green eyes glittered. A chill ran down Connie's back.

Amelia must have taken her silence for agreement, because she concluded by instructing Connie to gather any information she could on the topic before striding off in a hurry.

"...Did you know?" Connie timidly asked Scarlett. Scarlett shook her head, frowning.

"It's news to me."

If it was true, it was a scoop indeed. But this was Amelia Hobbes. Considering what she'd written about Connie, who knew if she was telling the truth?

Frowning, Connie started walking again, but no sooner had she taken a step than a boy came running up to her. "Are you Constance?" he asked. She nodded in surprise. He handed her a letter.

"Someone over on that corner asked me to give you this," he said, then ran off. She looked down at the paper, wondering what it could be. The following words were written in a hurried script:

Go back to your house. This is your last chance.

Connie gulped. She glanced over her shoulder, then whispered shakily, "…I'm being watched."

To cut to the chase, she wasn't able to meet with Randolph Ulster. Someone was tracking her, which limited what she could do even more than she'd expected. She was at a loss.

She sat helplessly as time passed. Soon, the hour arrived for her to do as the mystery letter had instructed, so she slipped out of the house again.

On her way, she noticed the outline of someone outside the gate. She thought it might be Amelia again and readied herself, but this figure was of a very different size. She gaped in surprise.

"Your Excellency…?"

"Are you stepping out, Miss Grail?"

As usual, he was in all black except for his sky-blue eyes. Also as usual, his expression was stern and his posture vaguely intimidating.

"You look poorly. Did something happen?"

For some reason, though, he no longer scared her.

Randolph peered at her curiously. She opened and closed her mouth like a goldfish gasping for air.

"Wh-why are you here…?"

"Remember the Daeg Gallus case I mentioned the other day? I wanted to ask Scarlett if anyone at the ball other than that injured woman had been using Jackal's Paradise."

Connie was sorry to say she absorbed less than half of that sentence. She was too busy listening to the cold, low voice that used to make her feel so uneasy—and instead felt incredibly soothed by it.

"It's Kate…!" she blurted out pleadingly, only to freeze a second later. The street was full of people. Women, elderly men, children. They looked completely ordinary, with nothing at all to make her suspicious. Nevertheless, their presence silenced her. Right now, someone was most likely watching. That possibility had gotten into her head and wouldn't leave. They might even be listening in on this very conversation.

Next time it's her finger you'll get.

That lock of cruelly sheared chestnut hair flickered across her memory. Randolph looked at Connie, who had suddenly fallen silent, and frowned. She panicked. If she didn't do something, he would become suspicious.

Just then, Scarlett let out a dramatic sigh.

"*Norman Holden,*" she said. "*I'm sure he was there. I didn't get close enough to smell him, but he used to love Jane. Randolph knows him.*"

Connie grabbed gratefully on to this unexpected lifeboat and conveyed the message to Randolph.

"Norman?" he asked, blinking in surprise. "Are you sure?"

"Y-yes."

He thought for a moment.

"…I see. I'll look into it." With that, he started to walk off.

"Wait!" she couldn't help crying out, but he didn't hear her. She reached her hand toward the rapidly receding black figure.

Before she had finished the gesture, however, she changed her mind and squeezed her palm into a fist. Randolph quickly vanished from sight. She took a deep breath, refocused her mind, and looked up.

There was Scarlett Castiel, smiling at her with the same haughty expression as always.

The sight brought Connie some semblance of calm.

"Let's go," she said with a nod.

※

Kate's cheek hurt. It was throbbing with heat. If she didn't watch herself, she would cry, so she stayed curled on the floor biting her lip.

The man who had abducted her seemed to have underlings. They were guarding the shed and most likely the Grail house. They appeared to be delivering regular reports, because she'd heard them telling the man inside several times that they'd seen nothing unusual.

She wondered how long she'd been in the shed. Her sense of time was gradually fading, along with her strength.

Suddenly, she heard a commotion near the door. What was going on? She shifted her gaze slightly. The man looked tense as he pulled a gun from his breast pocket.

After a few moments, silence returned as if nothing had happened—a second later, the door creaked open.

The man put his finger on the trigger.

Seemingly unbothered by the tense atmosphere, a lanky young man with brown skin walked in.

"What the hell are you doing in a place like this, José?" the young man asked in a tone far too casual for the situation. The man—José, apparently—was obviously upset by this turn of events.

"Salvador?! How did you find…?" he squawked.

Instead of answering, the younger man sauntered farther into the room. He glanced down at Kate lying on the floor and sighed theatrically.

"Don't tell me you kidnapped this girl? And look, her cheek is swollen. Did you hit her? Man, that's too much for me. Anyway, looks like you went off on your own again, eh? I thought your job was to sell Paradise. Just do your job, man. If you don't, I'm the one who'll hear about it from that asshole Krishna."

"…I can't sell on Rosenkreuz Street anymore. Abigail O'Brian made sure of that. There aren't many people crazy enough to touch Paradise when they know she's paying attention."

"O'Brian doesn't control that street all by herself. I'm sure there are ways to go about it. I'm no genius myself, but come on, man, use your brain."

This exasperated statement from the younger man seemed to infuriate José.

"Gunter…was my partner! And that woman's hound killed him…!"

These were heated words. José squared his shoulders indignantly. The atmosphere grew tense again.

"…And?"

But the young man simply smiled and tilted his head. His expression was neither provocative nor astonished nor sympathetic. Kate shivered at his profound lack of concern over the situation.

"Don't pretend you don't know! His job was to look into Lily Orlamunde's key! When he started getting close to Constance Grail, he was killed…! That ass went off and died without telling me a word of what he knew, but I'd bet my last coin Constance Grail knows something!"

"Oh, so that's why you went and did this?"

"Gunter was offed, and the Paradise sales aren't what the ones up top are hoping for. If I don't at least get that key, I'm done for!"

The younger man looked coolly at José, who was closing in on him with a harried expression.

"Hey, if you're getting results, then do what you want. But I've gotta say, your way of doing things is…" He paused. Although he seemed to be reproaching José, his tone remained as casual as ever. "Just like the guys outside, you're always hiring random thugs off the street to work for you. It's really sloppy, you know?"

José remained silent, maybe because the words hit home.

"Anyway, you've been warned. Clean up your own messes from here on out, old man."

The younger man shrugged carelessly. Then, seeming to remember Kate was there, he looked down at her. She froze in fear.

"I do feel sorry for you. This is a hell of a thing to get caught up in."

She turned away, but the young man squatted down next to her and forced her to return his gaze. His eyes, the color of a red-gold setting sun, sparkled with amusement.

"…Do you hate Constance Grail?"

"…No." She snapped her head up, unable let his words go unanswered. "Not at all. Meeting her was the best thing that ever happened to me, and being her friend is what I'm most proud of. Hate her? You must be joking."

She glared at him. He widened his eyes for a second before letting out a laugh.

※

It was a clear, sunny day.

The pale purple flowers carpeting the hillside rippled, their distinctive sweet smell wafting on the breeze. The banks of Lake Bernadia were famous for their abundant lavender. The scenery when they were blooming was magical, but ordinary people were not allowed in the area. This was because poisonous monkshood flowers were mixed in among the gorgeous field of lavender. The flowers, the stems, the leaves, the roots… even the pollen was said to be poisonous and had killed quite a few people in the past, leading to the regulations. Partly for that reason, hardly anyone visited the area anymore.

As instructed, Connie had come alone. Scarlett, who usually had plenty to say, was quiet for once.

After a while, a group of muscular, armed men appeared, seemingly out of nowhere, and approached Connie. One of them held a knife to her neck, and she forced down the scream that tried to escape her mouth. They brought her to a shed beyond a grove of trees, where one of the armed men said something toward the door. A girl bound with rope was then brought out, with a man behind her holding a gun to her back.

"Kate!"

The relief at seeing her friend alive lasted only an instant. Kate's right cheek was horribly swollen. She must have been hit. The sight of it made Connie's heart feel like it was being crushed.

Suddenly, Kate jerked her face up.

"Why did you come?! You're so stupid!" she yelled angrily at Connie.

"Why? Because…"

"Listen up! I won't be the tiniest bit happy if you sacrifice yourself for me!" Kate pursed her lips in a familiar pout. "You always mess everything up at the last minute."

Connie stood rooted to the spot. She'd thought Kate hated her. It was Connie's fault she'd been kidnapped. It wouldn't have been strange for her to blame the whole thing on Connie. Instead, she was the same old Kate Lorraine. Connie's chest grew hot, and her nose tingled. She bit her lip, trying not to cry. *Don't cry. Don't cry. You have more important things to do right now.*

Connie turned to the man with the gun.

"...As you requested, I came alone. So let Kate go."

She had to at least save Kate. She was trying not to think about what would happen after that.

"Fine," the man said, smiling so his teeth showed. "You, take her over there."

He gestured with his chin toward one of his apparent underlings and pushed his gun into Kate's back. She stumbled forward. The underling grabbed her arm roughly.

"Constance Grail!" Kate shouted. She locked eyes with a surprised Connie and broke into a gentle smile. "Walk your own path."

Her chestnut eyes were completely calm.

"What...?"

She sounded like she was saying good-bye forever. As suspicion entered Connie's mind, the man laughed hideously. "Take care of her," he said to one of the underlings, handing over his pistol. Connie stared in disbelief.

"What are you doing?!"

"Shutting her up, of course. Dead girls don't talk."

The two men dragged Kate into the woods. Connie's face went white as the meaning of the words sank in.

"But you promised...!" she screamed. "You promised to let her go!"

"My apologies, little lady," he said, throwing her a pitying glance. "But it's your own fault for letting yourself be tricked."

Connie stared at him, holding her breath.

"Please, stop!" she pleaded, her voice trembling. "I'll tell you everything! I'll do anything, anything...!"

Kate's figure was receding by the second, until finally Connie couldn't see her. Connie's heart pounded. She clung to the man, shaking her head again and again to clear the horrible sense of doom.

"Please, stop, make him stop…! I'm begging you…!"

"She was far calmer than you. She knew what was coming. She knew we would kill her, but she wouldn't say a word against you. She has my respect for that."

In her mind, she could see her friend's chestnut eyes, smiling softly.

It was awful. Too awful. This couldn't be happening. There had to have been a mistake. She tried to run, but someone grabbed her shoulder. She tried to shake off the hand, but it pushed her into the dirt. She kept struggling, but they slapped her cheeks over and over. She started to lose consciousness, but she bit her lip and struggled as hard as she could to break free.

A gunshot echoed dryly across the cloudless blue sky.

Connie screamed, and she felt as if all the blood in her body were about to boil. She screamed and screamed, but when she realized it would do no good, she collapsed to the ground as if the thread holding her up had been cut.

The man walked toward her, smirking. She no longer had the strength to resist. Something cold ran down her cheek and fell to the ground. Unable to think, she closed her eyes in resignation.

At that very moment, a forceful voice rang out.

"Don't move."

She heard a number of footsteps running toward her, then guns being cocked. The intimidating metallic sound shook the air.

That voice… It can't be.

Connie lifted her face and slowly looked over her shoulder.

Yes—there were the cerulean eyes, like pieces of the sky.

"…Your Excellency."

Randolph Ulster's pistol was pointed at the kidnapper. Behind him, several men in military uniform stood on guard. They were holding long-barreled rifles.

The man at the end of the pistol swore, then glanced into the woods, evidently hoping for backup.

"I regret to inform you that we've already arrested all of them," Randolph said in a businesslike tone.

Instantly, a torrent of curses so foul Connie wanted to cover her ears flooded out from the man's mouth. He glared spitefully at her.

"You tricked me!"

Connie heard someone burst into laughter. It was a sweet sound, like a ringing bell.

Scarlett, who had been silent until this point, floated into the air and peered at the man's face.

"My apologies," she said. *"But..."*

There was not a hint of guilt in that breathtakingly beautiful face. The amethyst eyes grew round with amusement.

From the high, clear sky, blindingly bright sunlight poured across the land.

"...it's your own fault for letting yourself be tricked," Scarlett concluded, smiling as brilliantly as the summer sky overhead.

"The Marquess Norman Holden died thirteen years ago. There's no way he could have been at that ball."

They were in a lounge at the Royal Security Force headquarters. Connie blinked at Randolph, pressing an ice pack to her cheek.

Norman Holden?

"Oh, now I remember!" she cried. That was the name of the man Scarlett had said was at the Earl John Doe Ball when Connie bumped into Randolph outside her house. She glanced at Scarlett. She was giggling proudly, her chest puffed out.

"He was a mean old man, deeply devoted to the Moirai," she explained. "Preaching was his hobby. He used to endlessly lecture bankrupt nobles about the virtues of poverty, and one day someone got so mad about it, they stabbed him to death. His last words were, 'Gods, save me!' Everyone was talking about how he stayed true to character up till his very last breath."

"Save me"—ah, so Scarlett had brought up the dead man's name to convey the message that Connie needed help. Connie hadn't noticed

©Yu-nagi

what was happening, but Scarlett's quick wit had prompted Randolph to call for backup.

I'm so grateful, Connie thought, finally relaxing.

The kidnapper had been arrested by Randolph's security unit, and Kate was alive. At the moment, she was being treated in a different room for bruises and exhaustion.

The Security Force had planned to bring the criminal back to their headquarters, but they ran into an unexpected obstacle on the way.

For some reason, a unit of Royal Knights had been stationed near the lake. Normally, the knights were charged with guarding the royal family, but when the Security Forces crossed their path, they requested custody of Kate's kidnapper. They said he was wanted in connection with a trader who had been visiting the Elbaite Palace under a false identity. Randolph did not look happy about the request but apparently sensed that he would not be able to reach an agreement with the obstinate Knights. In the end, he let out a pained sigh and agreed, on the condition that he be present during the questioning.

Connie and Kate were also supposed to be questioned after they'd recovered. That had been a point of contention as well, but Randolph refused to give in to the Knights, and in the end, they agreed on the condition that he would take down a report.

"I knew that if Scarlett was insisting a dead man was at the ball, it must mean something," he said. "After all, everyone who was around back then knows the last words of Marquess Norman. Also, like I said before—you're awful at lying."

Those blue eyes zeroed in on Connie. His tone wasn't scolding, and his eyes appeared calm. And what was that she glimpsed in his face? Relief?

"…I'm sorry."

The apology slipped out as soon as she realized what he must have been feeling. He gave her a puzzled look.

"For what?"

"I'm afraid I must have made you worried…"

He widened his eyes as if she'd said something completely unexpected.

Flustered by this unusual display of emotion, Connie scrambled to take back her words.

"Oh no, of course, I didn't mean that…! I'm sure you weren't worried…! You were only doing your job, after all…! I was so careless to say so…! I—I got carried away…!"

How embarrassing. She felt like her face was on fire. As she sat there squirming at the unbearable awkwardness, Randolph mumbled, "…Oh, you're right."

He sounded a little surprised—but also convinced.

"I think I *was* worried."

"You were…?"

Connie stiffened. As his words sank in, she felt heat rising steadily from her neck to her head. This time, her face was on fire for a different reason.

An attendant came to tell them that Kate was ready to be seen, so Connie headed to the infirmary. Kate was sitting on the bed, a large gauze patch covering her cheek.

"Connie?"

Kate turned to her in surprise. The color had returned to her face. What a relief! Connie felt the tension drain from her body. She ran to Kate, on the verge of tears. Kate held her arms out and hugged her tight. She was so soft and warm.

She was alive.

"…So I was saved in the end," Kate said, shivering slightly. Connie couldn't imagine how terrified she must have been. She had tried so hard to keep Kate out of danger, but ultimately, she had been pulled in all the same. In the worst way possible.

Connie wanted to apologize right away, but she was certain her brave, kind friend would say she didn't need to. Apologizing would only make Connie feel better, not Kate.

Instead, she looked into Kate's chestnut eyes and said, "I want to tell you something."

Then she related everything that had happened since the moment she met Scarlett at the Grand Merillian.

"You've really gotten dragged into a load of trouble, haven't you?" Kate said when Connie had finished. "Though I've got to say, it doesn't seem entirely out of character for you."

Connie blinked, caught off guard by Kate's nonchalant tone.

"You believe me, then?"

Her story was true, but it was also absurd. She had been ready for Kate to call her a liar or fear that she had lost her mind.

But Kate was the same old Kate. To top it off, she was giving the stunned Connie a mischievous look.

"I know you very well, Constance Grail. If you say something is true, then no matter what happens or what anyone else says, I know it's true," she declared.

With that, she looked straight at Connie and smiled like she wouldn't let anyone tell her otherwise.

※

José was in an interrogation room on the palace grounds with his hands and feet restrained.

The room had almost nothing in it, not even a window. Fortunately, the interrogation hadn't yet begun, and no one else was in the room. But there was no doubt that with a guard outside the door, shackles on, and rope tying him to the chair, he would have a hard time escaping on his own.

He heard a key turn in the lock. A woman wearing a maid's uniform entered. He gave her one glance and then, with no change in his expression, mumbled, "Kiriki kirikuku."

The woman stepped silently toward him, raised her expressionless face slightly, and replied in an even tone.

"Lie low and stay calm."

José finally let out a long breath. Escaping alone would be impossible. But the situation was different if he had outside help.

"...What about the guards?" he whispered, glancing at the door.

"They've been removed."

Very nice. Daeg Gallus did indeed boast the greatest organizational strength on the continent. It seemingly bestowed its grace on even the lowest of its servants like himself. A smile spread over José's face at the thought.

"How much did you tell them?" the woman asked quietly.

He had heard that the organization's operatives had infiltrated the palace. According to the rumors, they had wormed into even the higher levels. This maid must be one of them.

Her face was attractive but as cold as a doll's. José shook his head bitterly.

"Relax, I haven't said anything yet. But Earl Ulster was the one who arrested me, wasn't he? I know all about his interrogation techniques. To tell you the truth, I'm worried I'll crack. You've got to get me out of here quick."

Ulster was no mere subsidiary title of Duke Richelieu's family. In Adelbide, that appellation had a profound and enigmatic meaning. It wasn't that the current Earl Ulster didn't intend to take over the Richelieu dukedom—it was that he couldn't.

The woman replied calmly to José's desperate plea, "I understand. Relax."

I'm saved. No sooner had he let out a sigh of relief, however, than he felt a cloth being pushed over his mouth.

"?!"

A sweet scent tickled his nose.

As soon as he realized what it was, the blood drained from his face. He didn't want to die. He twisted his head, struggling desperately, but he was powerless to do anything more than clatter his restraints against the chair. *Please, somebody, hear me! Anyone!*

The woman's grip grew stronger. She shushed into his ear as if she were soothing an infant.

No! The light gradually faded from his vision.

No. No! His hands shook. Sweat poured from his body. His chest tightened.

I can't breathe.

And just like that, the cloth was removed from his mouth, but it was too late. José was twitching like a beached fish. All the same, he managed to glare into the woman's face.

"Y-you—"

The last thing he saw was a pair of cold, rose-colored eyes staring down at him.

Having dispatched her former associate without a moment's hesitation, the woman left the room and walked innocently down the hallway. At this time of day, no guards or patrolmen were around. Just as she had planned. After she had been walking for a few minutes, she heard a voice behind her.

"Hey, you, what are you doing?"

She almost cursed at the guard's earlier-than-expected return, but wanting to avoid the annoyance of a scene, she stopped obediently. She silently placed her fingers on the dagger hidden at her breast.

"This area is currently off limits. Why are you here?"

As she turned slowly around, the guard gaped in surprise.

"Y-you…I mean, Your Highness—"

The man was wearing the familiar maroon uniform of Johan's knights. Which meant he would be very familiar with her face.

"Crown Princess Cecilia…?!"

"Oh dear, I've been caught." Cecilia's rose-colored eyes glittered as she smiled. "I had some personal business to take care of, so I had an acquaintance let me in. Security is quite heavy, I see. Did something happen?"

"We've arrested a heinous criminal. Please return to the detached palace right away, since his associates may well attempt to break him out."

Cecilia lowered her head, acting cowed by the guard's stern tone.

"I see. I thought I would go into town, since I haven't been in a while… but I suppose in this case I must return. Don't tell Enrique," she added with a teasing wink.

It was an open secret that the crown princess disguised herself as a maid to visit the castle town. The guard nodded. He seemed to suspect nothing.

"Shall I call an escort?" he asked, but before she could reply, a scream echoed in the distance. A moment later, pandemonium broke loose.

"Where did the guards go?!"

"Call the doctors, quick!"

"It's too late, he's already dead! Shit—he's been poisoned!"

As Cecilia headed toward the Elbaite Detached Palace, a lanky young man emerged from the shadows of the trees.

"Hey there!"

Cecilia glanced at the man, then turned her back on him and strode off at a rapid pace.

"You're ignoring me?! Cess, how could you?"

The man ran after her. He had pale skin. Cecilia's favorite trader had brown skin, and he wrapped his head in cloth that concealed his face. Few people would have recognized this as the same man.

Cecilia walked into the guards' blind spot, then spun on her heels. The man laughed carelessly. She gave him a withering stare.

"Man, you're in a shitty mood today. That time of the month?"

"Go to hell, you third-rate salesman."

"Whoo, fierce. Don't tell me you're still sulking about the pregnancy drug thing?"

Cecilia sighed. "And who was it that said I didn't need to worry about anyone finding out because it didn't smell very strong?"

"Yeah, that was me. But most people really wouldn't notice. What wild child figured it out anyway?"

"Constance Grail."

"Her again?" Salvador's reddish-gold eyes flashed wryly. "She does get in the way," he muttered, then switched to a cheerful, unbothered tone. "But maybe it's a good opportunity. Why not give His Royal Highness a little rug rat? Haven't the higher-ups been pressuring you to have a kid anyway? I can't believe you've managed to put them off this long."

"...I think I'd have a hard time getting around with a full belly."

Caught off guard by Salvador's casual comment, Cecilia couldn't help missing a beat before she answered. In response, he shrugged playfully.

"Fine by me. I hate using kids myself."

Ignoring his comment, she changed the topic.

"What about Jackal's Paradise?"

"The client wants to get more out there, but it'll be hard. Abigail O'Brian has a close eye on Rosenkreuz Street. Things are totally different now compared to ten years ago."

So they are, Cecilia thought. *Nothing is the same, and all our plans have gone awry. All since the day that fool Scarlett Castiel got herself executed.*

"Oh, I meant to ask you. Did you hear the news from José before you offed him? Actually, I've known for a while. But I was banned from the castle over the pregnancy prevention incident. Though you're the one who banned me, actually."

"I didn't have a choice. You kept jabbering about drugs in front of maids and guards."

"...You think that girl is really a noble and not some wild monkey?"

It was true that Constance lacked a noble's touch for subtle communication. Cecilia hadn't thought her terribly threatening, but for some reason, she couldn't get those idiotically direct green eyes out of her mind.

"...Who knows? Anyhow, I killed that useless man before he could say much of anything."

"Figures. You've always been quick to act. Anyway, there's a message from headquarters."

He smiled his usual careless smile and narrowed his eyes very slightly.

"The Holy Grail of Eris is being revived."

Constance Grail

Sixteen-year-old with a reputation for being deceived. Ready to start doing the deceiving, but unfortunately lacks the skills. ←**new!**

 Scarlett Castiel

Eternal sixteen-year-old with a reputation for deceiving. Publicly stated that the fault lies with the one who is tricked but doesn't yet realize that statement will come back to haunt her.

 Randolph Ulster

Twenty-six years old. Functions as a living lie detector for Scarlett. Ten years ago, that skill got him pigeonholed as her natural enemy. His (fake) fiancée is always getting into trouble, which makes him nervous.

Kate Lorraine

Most girls would have had a mental breakdown after being kidnapped, beaten, and given an involuntary haircut, but not this stalwart. More of a heroine than the actual heroine. BFF of Constance Grail.

 Cecilia

At first, appears to be a mere juvenile delinquent from the boonies; turns out to be a player in a sprawling criminal organization. On second thought, given that she blatantly ignores orders from her superiors, takes drugs without permission, and disposes of colleagues without asking questions first, she may be a juvenile delinquent after all.

 Salvador

Used to come and go as he pleased at the Elbaite Palace, using the ridiculously obvious pseudonym Vado, but thanks to a certain pair, is now banned from the premises. Not particularly loyal to Daeg Gallus; for instance, overlooks José's recklessness and supplies Cecilia with drugs. For some reason, his little sister chewed him out when he got back to his hideout.

Scarlett was skipping innocently through a field of yellow flowers. Gentle sunlight spilled from the pure blue sky, so clear you'd have never guessed there had been a storm the day before. A carpet of freesias as tall as her head rippled in the soft breeze.

Someone was calling to her from behind to wait, but she ignored them and kept running forward, shouting excitedly.

"Oh!"

Her foot caught in the mud and sent her flying forward. Unfortunately, there was a puddle exactly where she landed.

"Scarlett!" the voice cried anxiously from behind, followed by running footsteps. But her mind was elsewhere. This was a disaster. Her brand-new dress was ruined, and the adorable face that everyone praised was covered in mud. Her pride, however, would not allow her to break down in ugly tears, so she simply looked up sullenly.

She saw someone with pale golden hair and magenta eyes approaching. Her brother, who was quite a bit older than her, peered down with concern. But when he saw her mask of mud, his lips twitched. He quickly frowned in an attempt to remain serious, but his shoulders were shaking. Finally unable to hold back any longer, he fell to his knees in a fit of laughter. Scarlett stared at him, indignant.

"You're awful."

"I'm s-sorry. But I told you to wait, didn't I? It's your fault for not listening, Lettie," Maximilian said with a terribly kind smile, wiping the tears away with his finger. He held out his hand toward her. She paused, then timidly took it.

Lettie. He called her that a lot.

As if he was pouring all his affection into those six letters.

When Scarlett awoke, the first things she saw were Connie's green eyes peering worriedly at her. She blinked. Connie drew her brows together anxiously.

"Scarlett, are you all right? I could see you, but your eyes wouldn't open, so I thought—"

She must have been dreaming. Dreaming about the Castiel domain, back when she was only five years old.

Lettie.

She missed that voice so much. She shook her head, trying to dispel the pain deep in her chest, and shrugged casually.

"I'm fine."

Usually, if she said that and gave someone a cold stare, they would be too scared of getting on her bad side to bother her with any more questions.

However, this girl with the idiotic look on her face was different.

"Really? You're really all right? Should we forget about our plans for today?" she asked, hovering around Scarlett like a puppy. The sight melted away Scarlett's resolve. Sighing softly, she gave in.

"I don't know why you're so worried. I see nothing wrong with going. After all, we went once before, to get the mask."

A few days earlier, Randolph had invited Constance out with him, saying an old friend wanted to meet his fiancée. Something very similar had happened not too long ago, but it did make sense. Not only had that incomprehensible man with an apparent inability to form facial expressions gotten engaged to a girl a decade his junior, but said girl was currently the talk of the town. Who wouldn't want to know all the details?

He'd told Connie she should feel free to decline the invitation and then named the friend in question. And it had been, of all people, Scarlett's own brother—Maximilian Castiel.

He was the oldest son of the house of Castiel, who shared a father but not a mother with Scarlett.

Scarlett glanced down. No doubt that was why she'd had the dream about the field of flowers.

"It's fine."

She snorted, hoping to clear her head, then looked down at her worried accomplice, put one hand on her hip, and pouted.

"Don't you know who I am?"

※

Randolph Ulster was on his way back to the Security Force headquarters from the office of the Royal Knights, having just been informed that a spy who had been dispatched to Faris was back.

Kate Lorraine's kidnapper had died of poisoning a week earlier. It had happened soon after his arrest, and the conclusion—arrived at without much of an investigation—was that he'd killed himself. Apparently the corpse had a sun tattoo. A Daeg Gallus man, then. Suicide wasn't out of the question, but if that had been his plan, he probably would have done it at the time of his arrest. More likely someone had killed him to shut him up.

Randolph had requested records from the Royal Knights on security at the time and other details but hadn't received a reply. Rumor even had it Crown Princess Cecilia was seen in the vicinity of the crime.

"Did you find anything out?" Randolph asked the instant he walked into the investigations office of the Security Force headquarters.

Kyle, who had just received a report, flicked a couple of small objects toward Randolph. He caught them in one hand and looked them over. They were two silver coins. The Goddess of Victory was engraved in profile on one side, and a shield and sword on the other. Money from Faris.

"What do you think of those?" Kyle asked, resting his jaw in his hand with an ironic smile.

They didn't look different from one another at first glance. And coins minted in different years varied slightly in appearance anyway. Nevertheless, Randolph squinted at them, then pulled a knife from his breast pocket and tapped them in turn with its handle.

The sound he got back from each coin was different.

"…They're using less silver?"

One was probably silver plating over a bronze core. Faris must be recasting coins to make more money.

"Correct! I'm having Morie test the silver content right now, but he thinks it's less than a third of what they originally were. We've been hearing about the financial problems of our esteemed neighbor for quite a while, but this is bad."

"How much are they worth?"

"They intend to circulate them for the same value, no doubt. Doubt it'll pass muster with people on the ground, though. The report says the prices of commodities are already starting to rise, and I hear exchanging currency unofficially has been outlawed. Which means their foreign trade connections are probably dead. Even inside the country, this expansion of the money supply is starting to make life hard for ordinary people."

He handed Randolph a fat stack of papers. Randolph took them silently and started to skim through them.

"By the way, that's the industry report. There's one strange thing in there. The mints in Faris had been going at a breakneck pace until very recently, but now they've eased up—and the production of money is stagnating."

Randolph stopped turning the pages.

"…Is Faris issuing government bonds right now?"

"Hmm? Oh, yeah, I did read something about that. Makes sense, if the economy is in a slump…"

"No, this is different…" .

According to the report, while production of almost all everyday items was falling, the output of certain other items was skyrocketing. That was probably what they were spending the money from the bonds on. Gunpowder. Steel. Large horse-drawn wagons. Factories along the rivers.

Randolph narrowed his cerulean eyes.

"They're preparing for war."

※

His Excellency was acting strange—at least, Connie thought so.

She kept glancing at her fiancé, who was sitting across from her in the carriage as they headed toward the Castiel residence. His face was as blank as always, but he seemed stiffer than usual, lost in thought.

Scarlett was talking less than usual, too. She'd laughed off Connie's worries about the visit, but the last time they snuck into the mansion, they'd only bumped into Maximilian by accident. This was completely different.

"By the way," Randolph said. "The woman you saved at the Earl John Doe Ball—Kiara Grafton's her name—I looked into her and found that she owns several wharves outside the city. There's a possibility she was involved in smuggling Jackal's Paradise."

"...You mean the drug that was popular ten years ago?"

According to Scarlett, the woman had been a user of the hallucinogen nicknamed Jane. Scarlett had said it was safe, without many side effects, but...

"Strictly speaking, one several iterations after that. These days it's so strong, you can't even compare it to what people used back then. My research suggests that the drug going around now is a refined product made by isolating the biologically active compounds in the Jackal's Paradise from ten years ago. It's highly addictive and has powerful physical and psychological effects. Even the older variety, if pure enough, could be used as a neurotoxin. That's one reason they banned it ten years ago."

How frightening, Connie thought—and then remembered something.

"Is that somehow related to the people with the sun tattoos?"

Randolph instantly narrowed his eyes in a silent warning not to pursue that point, but she forged ahead anyway.

"The person who attacked me and the one who kidnapped Kate— they're all members of that organization, aren't they? Who are those people? What are they trying to do?"

She stared into Randolph's sky-blue eyes. He seemed troubled and glanced away, but then he sighed, realizing Connie wasn't going to let the point go.

"They belong to Daeg Gallus. It's a massive criminal organization that's existed since the days of the Faris Empire. They've been the nemesis of the Security Force since long before I joined. Sometimes we capture a few of the lower operatives, but never the higher-ups. Murder, kidnapping, human trafficking, arms sales, smuggling drugs—they'll do anything for a price and without allegiance to any one country. Some people even say they were behind the downfall of the Faris Empire."

Connie felt the blood drain from her face. This was a far more troubling answer than she'd expected.

"Everyone who belongs to the organization has a sun tattoo somewhere on their body. And supposedly they have passwords that are used among colleagues and vary by mission."

"Passwords?"

"Yes, things they say to let each other know they belong to the organization. Mostly just meaningless phrases."

Connie tilted her head in confusion—then gasped. "…Kiriki kirikuku."

"What?"

Those were the words that the redheaded boy at the Maurice Home for Orphaned Children said Miss Lily had taught them.

"A spell to show you who the bad guys are…"

"A spell?"

"Maybe that's what it was…"

When Connie explained the situation, Randolph narrowed his eyes.

"Their passwords vary according to the mission they're on," he said, his bass voice echoing in the carriage. "Which means—Daeg Gallus *is doing something* in this kingdom right now."

When they arrived at the Castiel residence, they were ushered into a dizzyingly opulent room. However, Maximilian was nowhere to be seen. It seemed that another guest had arrived unexpectedly, and he was tied up with them. The elderly servant named Roy bowed his head in profound apology as he delivered this news, then announced that his master had a message for Randolph.

"The list of domains from the reign of King Michelinus that you requested is waiting for you in the library, sir."

Randolph glanced at Connie. She nodded, and he stood up. "I'll be back in a moment," he said before following Roy to the library.

Perhaps taking pity on the poor fiancée—albeit a fake one—left all alone, an elderly butler who had been standing by the wall approached her.

The salvias were blooming magnificently in the garden, he said— would she like to see them?

Narrow red lanes wound through the gardens beneath a blue sky. Row upon row of scarlet, teardrop-shaped petals grew along tall stalks, swaying in the breeze.

"*I'm sure we used to have white hydrangeas here. They've changed out the flowers.*"

"Is that so?"

Connie had turned down the butler's offer to accompany her because she wanted to talk with Scarlett freely. The kindly-looking old man was waiting by the entrance to the garden.

"*Claude is my father's butler. He may look kind, but he's a cunning old devil. Watch out for him.*"

"R-really…?"

As they wandered around the garden chatting aimlessly, a child suddenly ran out from one of the side paths. The little girl was wearing a yellow dress, and as she skipped past Connie, she stumbled on a rock and went flying facedown onto the ground. Connie glanced at Scarlett.

"...Do you know her?"

"Never seen her."

Perhaps she was related to Maximilian's other visitor. Connie walked up to her.

"Are you all right?" she asked, squatting down and holding out her hand. The girl grabbed it firmly and looked up at Connie. Although she looked on the verge of tears, she was a beautiful child. Holding on to Connie, she stood with trembling legs like a newborn fawn and then puffed out her chest resolutely.

"...I'm not going to c-cry! Little girls who cry over nothing aren't ladies! And I'm eight years old already...!"

Even as she spoke, however, tears pooled at the bottom of her pale magenta eyes. Connie scratched her cheek. There was definitely a resemblance...but at the same time, no resemblance at all.

Just then, someone called to her from behind.

"Miss Grail, I'm so sorry to have kept you waiting—"

She turned around to see Maximilian Castiel standing in the garden. For some reason, however, he had stopped midsentence and was staring at her with eyes wide open in surprise.

"Lettie?" he mumbled.

Scarlett gasped.

Lettie? Connie was confused for a second, but then she remembered. The reason the name sounded familiar was because it was the alias Scarlett had given her when she snuck into Lily Orlamunde's family home. She remembered Scarlett saying that she was giving Connie her good luck. In hindsight, she realized it was probably Scarlett's own nickname.

Maximilian had looked this way and said the name *Lettie*. Could it be that he was able to see Scarlett?

As she was panicking over this possibility, the little girl at her side stopped sniffling and ran toward Maximilian.

"*Daddy!*" she cried, diving toward him and wrapping her arms around his waist. "I fell down, but I didn't cry! I'm so strong! Look, my eyes aren't even wet—I mean, these aren't tears! I'm just sweating because I was so surprised!"

"Yes, you're a strong girl, Lettie. Have you greeted our guests?"

The girl slapped her hand over her mouth. Then, with an embarrassed look, she bowed her head elegantly and said, "Pleased to meet you. I'm Leticia Castiel."

"…Leti…cia?" Connie echoed. Yes, the nickname fit.

Just like it had fit Scarlett.

She wondered if it could have been a coincidence, then dismissed the thought. Not likely.

When this little girl was born, the scandal of Scarlett Castiel hadn't yet faded. Now, ten years later, names like Violet and Colette that shared the nickname *Lettie* were no longer unusual, but back then even those would have been avoided.

After all, naming a child Scarlett was taboo even now.

Nevertheless, Maximilian had called his daughter Lettie without a second thought. And the girl didn't seem to dislike the name in the least.

"…That's a lovely name."

The name must have been a conscious choice, but Maximilian grimaced slightly at the compliment. However, he quickly put on a blank face and nodded in agreement.

"…I think so, too."

The faintly nostalgic look in his eyes reminded Connie of what Randolph had told her just before she stepped out of the carriage.

Taking her hand to help her down the steps, he had said, as if he'd only just remembered it, that Maximilian Castiel had tried with all his might to stop Scarlett's execution until the very last second.

The library in the Castiel residence was as large as a drawing room, and its walls were covered from floor to ceiling with bookshelves. Glass-fronted cabinets displayed antique volumes, and portraits of the Castiel dukes through the ages hung from the ceiling. There was a comfortable-looking sofa, armchairs, and a cabriole leg table, among other furniture, as if the room had been designed more for social gatherings than for reading and writing.

As Maximilian's message had promised, the person Randolph wanted to see was there.

"What a coincidence, Duke Castiel."

In response to this greeting, a man of around fifty seated on a chaise lounge slowly turned his gaze from the book he was reading. His deep magenta eyes, a sign of the family's close ties to royalty, rested on Randolph.

It was Adolphus Castiel himself, Maximilian's father and the current Duke Castiel.

"You certainly have a roundabout way of doing things," he said, an amused smile creasing his perfectly formed face. "Using my son to meet with me? And even pulling Roy into it as supervisor? I salute your skill."

"I don't know what you're talking about," Randolph answered innocently. Adolphus frowned theatrically.

"You haven't got a scrap of charm to you. And you were such an angel when you were young! You're nothing like your father, that's for sure. That man made everyone want to spoil him."

Bringing up Randolph's deceased father left him equally at a loss for words. He raised his eyebrows slightly and changed the subject.

"Anyway, Duke Castiel."

"What is it?"

©Yu-nagi

"I'd like to know about the Holy Grail of Eris," he said, carefully observing the older man.

"Whatever could that be?" Those magenta eyes did not waver for an instant. "I regret to tell you I've never heard of it. Was that all you came for?"

"…Yes, for the time being."

He was right not to expect much. Suppressing a sigh, he was turning to leave the library when the duke addressed him.

"In the spirit of friendship, let me give you a little advice."

This man who had lost his daughter to the executioner's sword should have been a tragic character, but he spoke to Randolph in a calm, unreadable voice.

"Make sure you have all your cards in hand when you challenge your opponent. That is the secret to a long life."

※

Even at this late date, Kendall Levine was still attempting to keep secret the existence of Seventh Prince Ulysses, who had now vanished.

No matter how many times Randolph and his colleagues asked him about it, he pretended to know nothing. Which was not to say Randolph had any reason to believe he was taking the initiative in resolving the situation.

Nearly two weeks had passed since the abduction. The special visit, intended partly as a training mission for the next generation of diplomats, was originally scheduled to last about a month.

Thinking they must finally be preparing to make a move, Randolph headed to the palace, where he ran into Levine and his subordinates on their way somewhere. They seemed quite haggard.

"Ambassador Levine," he called out.

The balding man came to a quick stop and looked warily toward Randolph.

Randolph repeated the words he had already said to him numerous times.

"Should you have any need for assistance, the Security Force is ready and willing to help."

"I don't know what you're referring to," Levine said, and strode off casually. He was the very definition of unapproachable.

Back at headquarters, Kyle Hughes took a break from shouting instructions at his coworkers to talk to Randolph.

"How was Kendall Levine?"

"Impossible. He has no trust in us whatsoever," Randolph answered, shaking his head.

"Damned hairless geezer…," Kyle grumbled, clicking his tongue coarsely before seeming to remember something. "By the way, I've been tailing that trader called Vado who frequents Elbaite, but it's not easy. I'd like to ask Princess Cecilia about him directly as soon as I can…"

"That will likely be difficult."

"Think so? But you and the prince were schoolboy chums, weren't you? Can't you pull some strings?"

"Even if I did, that woman would probably make up some excuse not to see you."

Kyle's shoulders slumped.

Both her status and her personality made obtaining an interview with Cecilia unlikely—but there were other ways.

"I've got some questions about Viscount Luze, and his wife, too," Randolph said.

"The wife was a noble from Melvina, wasn't she? …Interesting. Now that you mention it, that place has some problems of its own."

Melvina was neither a large country nor a wealthy one, but its southern provinces were home to rich deposits of saltpeter, a key ingredient in gunpowder. This was a crucial source of income for Melvina, but until now, Adelbide hadn't made a policy of importing it. There had never been a need. The kingdom was only a few centuries old and had never been to war aside from its founding years.

Faris, on the other hand, had a history written in blood that stretched back to the days of the empire, and it was a faithful customer of Melvina's saltpeter mines. The two countries had close bonds, and if Faris was planning to go to war, there would surely be signs of it in Melvina.

In that light, the arms dealer from Melvina whom Kyle had driven himself half-crazy arresting a while back was of some interest as well. When those who trade in death begin to move, war is sure to follow; this had been true for all of human history. War had seemed to be such an unlikely possibility to Randolph at the time that the link hadn't even occurred to him. But that may have been imprudent on his part. Had they perhaps overlooked something because they were too accustomed to the current era of peace?

The arms dealer was already in prison, but maybe they ought to question him again. For now, he would send a spy to Melvina to look into the situation. Just as Randolph was thinking this, Kyle shot him a meaningful glance.

"So what's your view on the princess?"

"Calling it a coincidence suits her interests a bit too well," Randolph answered, lowering his voice.

"…True."

Kyle knit his brows. It was obvious he thought this whole affair was going to be a real pain. And indeed, the situation was tricky. This was the crown princess, after all. If they didn't have irrefutable proof, they could be accused of lèse-majesté, which meant they couldn't rush into questioning people.

But the even trickier question was, when had Cecilia switched sides? The situation had escalated to the point that Randolph could no longer believe this was a personal scheme of hers or her father, the viscount's. But if the plot had been laid a decade ago—or even earlier, considering the time needed to prepare—well, that was a terrifying thought. And he could only think of one organization capable of it.

Daeg Gallus. If Cecilia was a member, then the trader likely was, too.

"Have you told Captain Bart about the coins being reminted?"

"Yeah. The captain said he'd pass it on to Commandant Belsford, so before long, we'll probably be hearing what they plan to do about it."

"Time for Duran the Immortal to take the stage, is it?"

Duran Belsford, the fifty-year-old commandant of the Royal Security Force, was famous for staying alive.

For generations, the Belsford family had held the title of margrave, their domain along the border with Faris. This location meant they were subject to frequent attacks from the northern tribes, and the men of the family—constantly on the front lines of conflict—were said to have lives as brief as match flames on a winter's day.

However, the youngest son of the family, Duran Belsford, was blessed with unusual good fortune. He reached adulthood without incident and quickly fled the province to join the Royal Security Force. Having out-witted death countless times in his youth, he managed to survive life in the capital as well. No matter what perilous situations he found himself in, he inevitably returned unharmed and with new achievements under his belt, finally reaching the position of commandant of the entire Royal Security Force. The only time he had truly been at risk was ten years earlier, when a scheme by his mortal enemy, Earl Solms, led to his being imprisoned and sentenced to death. However, just before he was sched-uled to be executed, evidence emerged proving his innocence, and once again he survived.

Thus his nickname, Duran the Immortal. To top it off, he not only was good at his job but also stood up to the strong and protected the weak like some sort of storybook hero.

"By the way, have you told your fiancée the news?" Kyle asked abruptly.

"I asked Miss Lorraine to do it."

They had learned from Kate Lorraine's testimony that the man called José, a member of Dacg Gallus, was after "Lily Orlamunde's key," and that he thought Constance Grail had it.

Randolph had a hunch he knew what the man was talking about. The key was probably what Constance Grail had stolen the first time he met her—that is, the day she'd snuck into the Orlamunde residence. When he met her for the second time, at the Earl John Doe Ball, she told him the only thing she had found was the note about the Holy Grail of Eris. But there must have been a key as well. No doubt keeping quiet about it had been Scarlett's suggestion.

What he still didn't understand was how Daeg Gallus fit in. Why were they searching for Lily Orlamunde's key? And how did they know Constance Grail had taken it?

Perhaps they had known about the key since long before Constance Grail ever touched it.

But knowing it existed didn't mean they knew where it was. They must have been searching for the hiding place all along. If they were constantly monitoring Lily's family home and the orphanage and the other places she frequented, that would explain how Constance had fallen into their trap.

"…You think the key is important to them?"

"More than a year has passed since Lily died. If they're still searching for it, then it must be important. But I don't think they're desperate to have it."

If they had been, Constance Grail would have been dead long before now. Plus, José and his partner—the one who had been looking for the key, and whom Aldous had killed—were at the lowest level of the organization.

"They may not know themselves what the key is, so they don't want to be careless about taking it."

"What do you mean?"

Abruptly, Kyle looked up and smirked at Randolph. "Your dear little Connie is here."

Randolph felt a flash of antipathy toward his colleague. He knew Kyle was a lady's man. But to call someone you'd never even properly talked to by their nickname, wasn't that a little too familiar—

"What?"

"Nothing…"

Making sure his hazy feelings didn't show on his face, Randolph walked over to greet his fiancée.

He hadn't seen her for several days, and along with the familiar hazelnut hair and green eyes, he noticed an obvious expression of panic on her face.

"I, um, I heard, from Kate! About the key, Miss Lily's key…!"

"Ah, I see."

So Kate Lorraine had already told her. He'd asked her friend to do it because he thought she would feel too intimidated if he told her himself.

But Constance still looked as if she might faint at any moment.

"I—I—I have it!" she said in a strained voice.

An awkward silence followed.

Her statement was so self-evident, Randolph couldn't help thinking, *Well, yes, obviously*, even as he stared at her with a blank expression.

※

"Miss Lily's key…?"

Connie blinked, her fork poised in midair. She had brought an insanely delicious apricot tart over to help Kate recuperate, and the two of them were devouring it in the sunny terrace on the south side of the Lorraine residence.

The sun-colored fruit stewed with sugar went perfectly with the fragrant black tea. No sooner had the two of them cleaned their plates, however, than Kate turned serious and brought up the key.

"Yes, that man said he was looking for Lily Orlamunde's key. I didn't really understand, but he seemed to think you had it… Do you know what he was talking about?"

Oh, she knew all about it…

After Connie got home from Kate's house, she went up to her room. She was in a panic.

"I forgot…! I forgot all about it…!"

Her excuse, if she was allowed one, was that so much had happened in the past month.

"I thought as much," Scarlett said with a shrug, as if to imply that she herself had not forgotten.

Connie looked up.

"Wh-why didn't you say anything…?"

"I still don't trust that man! Unlike you," she replied curtly, then looked away in a huff.

But she was the one who had trusted His Excellency enough to ask him for help when Kate was kidnapped!

Connie sat there opening and closing her mouth like a fish in need of air before shouting so loudly the windows nearly shook.

"Scarlett, you're stubborn as a mule!"

※

Connie was sitting in a corner of the strategy room in the Royal Security Force headquarters, her head bowed.

"I'm so sorry…! So very, very sorry…! It's not at all that I didn't trust you, Your Excellency! Well, I *was* afraid of you at first, because you really were like the Grim Reaper, and to tell you the truth, I didn't trust you very much then, but that's not true anymore, and—"

"The more you talk, the deeper you dig your own grave, idiotic girl," Scarlett pointed out icily.

Cold sweat trickled down Connie's cheek. She had no idea what to say or do.

"Shall I take a guess as to why?" Randolph asked in a surprisingly calm voice.

She looked up. His expression was as lacking in emotion as always, but there was something playful in his cerulean eyes.

"You forgot," he finished.

She groaned. He was absolutely right. As she sat slumped in her chair, his large hand reached out toward her.

"You brought the key with you, didn't you? We'll take a look into it here."

"Your Excellency...!"

She grasped his rough hand, clinging to his kindness, and his mouth fell open in surprise. Scarlett planted her hand on her hip in exasperation. *"You idiot! The key, give him the key!"* she scolded.

Connie snatched back her hand and drew the simple, warded key from her handbag. She handed it to him with a smile that she hoped would cover up her embarrassment. Randolph tilted his head awkwardly.

"I was wondering..." Kyle interrupted. He had been watching the entire exchange and looked fed up. "Why do you call him Your Excellency? You two *are* engaged, aren't you?"

Constance and Randolph exchanged bewildered glances. They responded at almost the exact same time.

"Um, because His Excellency...is His Excellency...?"

"I never even noticed."

Kyle covered his face with his hands in response to their flimsy explanations.

"Connie my dear, that's no answer at all, and Randolph, you'd better start noticing some things...! I mean, it's totally unnatural...!"

Although she was somewhat put off by the force of the handsome young man's argument, she had to admit he was right. In which case...

"Shall I call him Earl Ulster?"

"That's just as bad!"

"Th-then, in that case, what about Lord...Ulster...?"

"Even worse! You sound like you barely know him! Connie my dear, you'll be an Ulster, too, before long, and won't that be a little strange?"

She flinched. That meant she had to call him by his first name. But... but...wouldn't that be just like what *real* fiancés did?

"…Ra…"

"Ra?"

"Ra…Ra…Ran…"

Her face was on fire as the word tangled on her tongue.

Randolph was looking at her with a mystified expression. "Rararan?"

"You be quiet," Kyle interjected. Randolph blinked.

Finding a moment of respite in their exchange, Connie steeled her resolve.

"Sir Ra-Randolph…!"

There was a moment of silence, and then the man himself responded, as if nothing were amiss, "What is it?"

Kyle slapped his forehead and looked up at the ceiling.

"Why 'Sir'…?!"

Connie handed over Lily Orlamunde's key without incident and was on her way out of the building when, as she passed the reception desk, she heard light footsteps drawing near.

"Connie!"

She turned around in surprise to see a man with dark brown eyes, blond hair, and an amiable smile on his strikingly handsome face running after her.

"Mr. Hughes?"

"Call me Kyle." He gave her an easygoing smile before dropping the bomb. "I forgot to ask you before, but are you two…fake fiancés?"

Connie stared at him, stunned. Forgetting entirely to cover up her real feelings, she felt the blood drain from her face.

"Your expression says it all!" Kyle said, bursting out laughing. "But don't worry, I can imagine your situation. Let me guess—my eccentric colleague suggested the idea?" Kyle shrugged, still smiling. "Anyhow, that means one day you two will break it off, right?"

"Um…"

"You really are easy to see through," Kyle said, lowering his eyebrows and smiling wryly before continuing in a casual tone, "I have a request for you, Connie my dear."

"A request…?"

"Yes. Oh, it's nothing difficult. You see, sometimes in the course of our work, we hurt people or even take their lives. Often, people resent us. And because of his childhood, Randolph Ulster is the kind of man who takes on a lot of burdens. On top of that, he's so damn serious, and he thinks in unexpected ways. He feels like he doesn't have the same right to happiness as everyone else—like he's under some kind of curse. It's incredibly annoying."

This last spiteful remark was delivered in his characteristic easygoing tone.

"I'd like to see straitlaced old Randolph loosen up for once," he went on. A smile suddenly spread over Kyle's handsome, playboyish face as he looked at Connie. "I can't quite imagine it, but I would like to see him smiling idiotically from ear to ear, and I want someone by his side who isn't afraid of him and his scruples. Someone honest and good."

As she listened to Kyle's soft words, Connie thought of that eternally blank face, and for some reason her chest grew tight.

"I—"

But she wasn't worthy to be that person. She wasn't especially good-looking, she didn't have an outstanding memory, and she wasn't witty. It went without saying that her social standing was far below his, too.

She glanced down, preparing to tell that to Kyle, but before she could say anything, he placed his pointer finger over her lips.

"I'm not the one you should be giving your answer to, am I?" Then he clasped his hands behind his head, looked up at the ceiling, and said cheerfully, "I was so happy the other day when Randolph followed you to Lake Bernadia. For once, I saw him get visibly upset. He's always been good at withstanding pain and suppressing his own emotions, but that doesn't mean he doesn't have them. I'd like to see him cry when he's sad, yell when he's angry, and laugh when he's happy. No one would hold that against him, but he's so damn obstinate—"

Kyle broke off, then smiled wickedly, as if he were about to bring Connie in on some evil scheme.

"And that, my dear Connie, is why I'd like you to go right on twisting him around your little finger, okay?"

※

Amelia Hobbes was standing outside the gate of Saint Nicholas Hospital, clicking her tongue in irritation. Kevin Jennings had been admitted here, but every time she tried to get in to see him, they slammed the door in her face. She'd tried telling them she was a friend, a coworker, and a relative, but nothing worked. It was like they were trying to cut him off from all outside contact.

Amelia folded her arms and was glaring up at the white building when someone called to her from behind.

"Excuse me, Miss Hobbes?"

She turned around to find a man of medium height and build, probably in his mid-thirties, with a vaguely timid look.

"My name is Rufus May. I'm assistant to the vice-comptroller of the treasury."

Amelia silently took the business card he held out and delicately raised one eyebrow.

"By the way, Miss Hobbes, are you here to visit Kevin Jennings? I believe he contacted you quite a few times over the past several months. The truth is, he's been charged with embezzlement. May I ask what he talked to you about?"

"Embezzlement? Kevin? That's hard to believe!"

She couldn't help sounding reproachful in response to this improbable announcement. How could she feel otherwise? She didn't intend to whitewash Kevin Jennings's character, but he was such a stickler for the rules, it had driven her crazy. On top of that, he was a high-strung clean freak. There was no way he would embezzle money someone else had touched, and if he did, he wouldn't know how to use it.

"…The princess must be behind this," Amelia spat out bitterly.

"What do you mean by that?" Rufus asked, sounding taken aback.

"Don't play innocent. Or do—I'll put it all in my article."

After dismissing his guileless attitude, Amelia walked off. She might as well head back to the *Mayflower* offices. Once she did, she'd write up everything that had happened.

"No, really, what do you mean?" the man called after her. "I know this hospital is run by a charitable organization under Princess Cecilia, but—"

Amelia stopped in her tracks. She craned her neck around suspiciously and stared at the man.

"I thought Saint Nicholas Hospital was run by Earl Campbell."

"About a year ago, the earl transferred control to an organization owned by the princess. There were no financial problems, so it wasn't publicized, but we receive that sort of information at the treasury."

When the meaning of his words sank in, Amelia's suspicious expression turned friendlier.

"In that case, I believe you and I need to exchange some information. What did you want to know about Kevin? Depending on what you can give me in return, I may be willing to tell you."

This time Rufus drew his brows together in confusion.

"…Give you in return?"

"Yes. That's how it works," Amelia declared. The conscientious-looking man appeared to give that some thought. Things were looking good. "For example…"

What information did she want to snag from him? Without realizing what she was doing, she lurched forward toward the man, stumbling over her own feet. Her knees bent and she tilted backward. Now she'd done it.

Surprisingly, it was Rufus who caught her and kept her standing. Wrapping an arm around her shoulder, he asked if she was all right. His arm felt strong, and his voice was unexpectedly close. Amelia widened her eyes and let out an unintentional gasp.

How unusual. Rufus May had two dots in the middle of his eye.

Constance Grail

Sixteen-year-old who is beginning to worry about what to call her (fake) fiancé. Was scolded by Scarlett for focusing more on that than on Scarlett's plans for revenge, and so for the time being will stick with "His Excellency."

 Scarlett Castiel

Eternal sixteen-year-old who has returned home for the first time in ten years, only to discover she now has a niece. Loses her shit after she realizes her revenge plot was overshadowed by youthful melodrama.

 Randolph Ulster

Twenty-six-year-old who couldn't care less what his (fake) fiancée calls him. Usually has emotions of steel but did feel slightly hurt after getting carried away and pressing Adolphus for information, only to be stonewalled.

 Kyle Hughes

A severe workaholic, is screaming in joy at the tsunami of tasks that have pounded down on him in recent months. His subordinates, meanwhile, are simply screaming. Unable to stand the sight of a friend undermining his own love life, made up his mind to keep an eye on his unpredictable boss, but has recently realized that "keeping an eye on him" won't cut it.

Leticia Castiel

A little girl as full of herself and foolish as a certain someone. Shares a nickname, Lettie, with her dead aunt. Growing like a beanstalk under her father's adoring eye.

 **Maximilian Castiel**

The next Duke Castiel and a friend of Randolph's. Determined to keep on lovingly calling his daughter Lettie no matter what anyone says. Easily misread because of his cold face and tone, but actually is one of the better-natured Castiels. Secretly worried that he doesn't have more friends.

 Adolphus Castiel

Current Duke Castiel, has deep magenta eyes. Aloof. Claims to know nothing about the Holy Grail of Eris, but is that true…?

 Amelia Hobbes

Unable to suppress her overabundant ambition, her relentless attempts to get into Saint Nicholas Hospital seem to have drawn something ominous. Part journalist, part medium.

 Rufus May

Assistant vice-comptroller of the treasury who approaches Amelia. Average looks. Has two black dots in his eye.

Two women were walking together beneath the blinding sun.

One was petite and slim with translucent white skin and silver hair, a fresh-faced beauty.

The other was a large, tanned woman with glossy golden hair tied back untidily.

She wore light, comfortable men's clothing with lace-up shoes, and on her back she carried a pole-shaped bundle about as long as she was tall, wrapped in dingy cloth.

Abruptly, the blond woman stopped and slowly surveyed her surroundings.

They were on the main road in Alslain, the capital of Adelbide. On either side, elegant jewelry shops and dignified old dress shops were interspersed with fashionable teahouses and sparkling clean restaurants.

Everyone coming and going on the paved street looked happy—not a beggar or a vagrant to be seen.

The smaller woman threw a suspicious glance toward her companion, suddenly stopped in the middle of a busy street, and frowned.

"Is something the matter, San?"

San's sharp, willful face formed an ironic smile. "No, I was just thinking how different this place is from our own declining kingdom. And all this in just a few hundred years since independence? I tip my hat to them. I can see how their neighbors would be envious. Can't you, Eularia?"

The silver-haired woman cast a glance down the lively street and nodded. "Yes. I imagine they are blessed with fertile lands as well, thanks to the abundant water and mineral deposits in this kingdom."

"Coming from a land like ours on the verge of death, we couldn't want anything more. Our brilliant forefathers really messed up," San said before lowering her voice, wary of being overheard. "And what did the old goat Kendall have to say?"

Eularia, too, lowered her voice knowingly.

"He said the little star twinkling in the sky was stolen by the migratory bird who flew in from the west at dawn. From Adelbide, Faris is in the west, and the bird of dawn is Daeg Gallus. Obviously, the little star must be Prince Ulysses."

San clicked her tongue. She'd been expecting to hear that.

"That damn hairless goat let his guard down."

"He's getting on in years, I suppose. I think it's time to demote him from a slightly useful goat to a completely useless one."

Ignoring this comment from Eularia, whose sharp tongue belied her gentle appearance, San sighed softly and scratched her head.

"We've already got our hands full with Allie… She's probably crying all alone as we speak."

"I'm sure she's fine. She's always been strong. I'm more worried about Uly. He may act grown up, but he's still a child."

San lowered her brows.

"You're right," she said, then went on a bit self-mockingly, "Who could've imagined we'd end up with two damsels in distress? I swear, we can't catch a break."

"There was nothing we could have done about Allie," Eularia said soothingly. "You did the best you could at the time. It's not your fault."

San didn't answer, other than to murmur, "We'd better hurry," looking up at the clear blue sky overhead. Then she turned her strong gaze in the direction of her homeland, Faris, far away to the west.

"If we don't, we might be too late."

©Yu-nagi

San

Woman with golden hair. Tends to say incredibly insensitive things with a smile. Most likely intends no harm. Talks trash about Kendall Levine.

 Eularia

Woman with silver hair. Tends to say vicious things with a smile. Most likely intends nothing but harm. Talks trash about Kendall Levine.

Allie

Acquaintance of San and Eularia. Seems to be in a bad fix back in their home country.

©Yu-nagi

For the past several days, Scarlett Castiel had been in a rotten mood. As for the reason...

"I feel like you've been ignoring my revenge lately!"

That was the crux of it.

"Plus, I don't see why you have to go out of your way to meet with Abigail O'Brian!"

Scarlett was cross. The depths of her amethyst eyes were blazing, bringing a new brilliance to her almost unrealistic beauty.

Wasn't it a bit unfair of the goddesses to make her so beautiful even when she was angry?

Connie sighed, looking over the letter Randolph had sent her. Mostly an account of recent developments, with a buried aside mentioning that he would need a little more time to obtain the *present* that she wanted.

In other words, he still hadn't unraveled the mystery of Lily Orlamunde's key.

Connie gulped down her cup of cold tea and turned to Scarlett.

"But you want to talk to Aisha Huxley about what happened ten years ago, don't you? And the Huxleys are viscounts, aren't they? I'm only a lower noble, just like them, and an insignificant girl at that. If I were to go directly, they would be sure to ignore me. But with an introduction from the Duchess Abigail, I don't think they'll be able to weasel out of it."

Scarlett didn't have a sharp answer to that. Instead, she held her head up haughtily and pronounced, *"I was just thinking the same thing myself."*

Aisha Huxley.

Connie had only glimpsed her briefly at Emilia Godwin's ball.

She remembered the gaudy dress encasing her thin form and the dark-red lipstick on her mouth. According to Scarlett, ten years ago she'd been a gloomy, plain young girl. And there was more.

"That girl was one of my followers—a fan, you might say."

Perching lightly on the top of Connie's dresser, Scarlett crossed her legs gracefully. Strangely, while her manners were horrible, her movements were refined, somehow giving her an overall impression of elegance. Yes, the goddesses truly were unfair.

"I think at the time, Aisha thought I was some kind of goddess. I mean, the first time she talked to me, she cried."

Cried? Connie blinked in disbelief.

True, Scarlett's beauty was otherworldly, but…

"I can tell from your face you don't believe me. But she wasn't the only one," Scarlett said, shrugging as if it was trivial. *"Even so, Aisha was extreme. For instance, if I wore a red dress, without fail she would wear a red dress at the next ball. If I wore a blue one, she'd wear a blue one. Even the style would be the same. Her hairdo, too. But she was so gloomy, she never danced with anyone. Always a silent wallflower. She used to stare and stare at me, like she wanted to say something. But if I looked at her, she would look down. Then right away she'd start looking at me again. Honestly, I had no idea what she wanted. Not that I understand her any better now, acting like she's back to normal."*

A chill ran down Connie's spine. Scarlett's tone was casual, but most people would find the behavior she was describing fairly bizarre.

"There was only one time she looked me in the eye and talked to me. I'm sure it was before the Cecilia incident," Scarlett said, as if she'd just remembered.

"What did she say?" Connie blurted out.

Scarlett rested her chin on her folded hands and said with amusement, "'I wish I were you.'"

They both fell silent.

What could she have meant? Was she simply jealous? Jealous of the girl with beauty and status and a perfect fiancé? Or was it a meaningless joke? Connie had no idea.

And was this sudden feeling of bottomless terror simply her imagination?

"...And what did you say back?"

"That's obvious, isn't it?" Scarlett grinned and tilted her head with her habitual elegance. "The world doesn't need two Scarlett Castiels."

Connie sent Abigail O'Brian a letter saying she wanted to ask her advice about something, and Abigail promptly replied by inviting her to the O'Brian residence.

Connie climbed into the carriage with the O'Brian family seal that Abigail had sent and was carried off toward the family's town house in the central part of the city.

A handsome, silver-haired butler led her into a tastefully appointed drawing room, saying that Abigail would be with her shortly. Connie sat down in a comfortable chaise lounge. A cup of black tea and a plate of cookies were set out on the table. But no sooner had Connie reached for the porcelain teacup than someone jumped out from behind the armchair across from her. Connie gaped in surprise.

"You must be the 'charming guest' Abby told me was coming!"

The person speaking to her with sparkling eyes and an excited voice was a young child. She had big eyes with curly lashes and a misty halo of fine, golden hair. She looked as sweet as a storybook fairy.

"...Huh?"

But who could she be? As Connie stared at her, the girl tilted her head in confusion.

"Did I mistake you for someone else? But your eyes are the prettiest green, just like Abby said. You are Miss Constance Grail, aren't you?"

"Um…"

Connie didn't know what to say. Scarlett snorted.

What a rude little child. Doesn't she know she ought to introduce herself before asking so many questions? I'd like to know who her parents are.

She was absolutely merciless, even toward a child. It was a good thing the girl couldn't see her; this could have been traumatizing. Just as Connie was breathing a sigh of relief, however, the girl spoke up.

"Yes, that's very true…! I was just so happy, I couldn't help it…! I'm terribly sorry, I know it wasn't very ladylike of me…"

The little fairy's face was growing sadder by the second, until her shoulders slumped pitifully.

"…Hm?"

"My name is Lucia O'Brian… Will you forgive me?"

"Um, yes, but just now—"

"Oh, I'm so glad! I'd be so grateful if you could keep this a secret from Sebastian. He's been acting just like an evil stepmother lately."

Every house has a fussy old man in it. And as long as you understand your mistake. Be more careful from now on.

"I know! He *is* fussy! And he's always saying, 'Ladies this, ladies that'! I'm getting sick and tired of ladies!"

He sounds exactly like my Claude.

Connie was staring at them with her mouth hanging open.

"J-just wait one second…!"

Her voice came out high-pitched with panic. But how could it not? After all, this girl was acting like…

"Can you see her?!" Connie squawked in a most unladylike voice. At almost the same moment, the door rattled open.

"Lou!"

A tall young man wearing a white button-down shirt and no jacket strode into the room.

"What are you doing in here, you naughty little tomboy? I know Abby told you we were having guests today! You're leaving this instant."

The young man wrapped his arm around her waist and hoisted her over his shoulder like a sack of potatoes. As Constance looked on in shock, the little fairy shrugged her shoulders precociously from her awkward perch, as if to say, "My, my."

"You're hardly one to speak, 'careless Rudy'!"

"What was that?"

The man raised one eyebrow and turned toward Connie with an embarrassed expression.

"...You?" he groaned, taking in the visitor as she stood there, unsure what to do.

It was Aldous Clayton, the *Mayflower* reporter and Abigail's "hound."

Connie nodded awkwardly.

Just as she was wondering what else to say, a familiar, incongruently cheerful voice broke the silence.

"Oh my, what in the world are you two doing?"

Abigail had finally arrived. She surveyed the awkward scene before tilting her head in question.

"Abby!" Lucia cried excitedly, breaking free from Aldous's arms and throwing herself into Abigail's embrace. "Your visitor brought the most beautiful lady with her!"

"The most interesting things always, always happen when I'm not there," Abigail said, pouting slightly from her spot on an indigo sofa across from Connie. The little fairy was perched beside her. Aldous was sitting in a saber-leg armchair, his elbows resting on the arms as he wearily pressed a finger between his eyebrows.

"It seems the rumor about Scarlett Castiel rising from the depths of hell to attend the ball at the Grand Merillian wasn't entirely wrong after all," Abigail went on. "Scarlett, are you listening right now? We only spoke a handful of times, but your execution grieved me deeply."

Lucia's explosive announcement had forced Connie to tell Abigail about meeting Scarlett and everything that had happened since. Even though she left out some of the details, she knew it was a fishy story. Perhaps Lucia was to thank for the fact that both Abigail and Aldous seemed to accept it at face value.

"I'll thank you to limit the joking to your face, which looks like a squashed frog," Scarlett snapped. Although this rude comment didn't reach Abigail's ears, she nevertheless giggled.

"I'm sure she's saying something spiteful right now," she said shrewdly.

Scarlett grimaced, while Abigail glanced down at Lucia with the expression of a dignified elder.

"This is unusual for you, isn't it?"

"Yes. I don't often see them this clearly... She's so pretty, Abby," she answered, whispering the last part so only Abigail could hear it. She was staring at Scarlett with sparkling eyes the color of a clear aquamarine lake.

Apparently, this little girl could see the ghosts of the dead.

"It's not just the dead," Abigail explained. "She also perceives strong emotions visually or aurally. Anger, sorrow, things like that. So even if someone isn't dead, she might pick up their strongest emotions as voices or colors. But I don't think she's ever seen anything, living or dead, as clearly as this. There's some kind of compatibility at play, I believe—although I must admit it's in character for Scarlett Castiel to stand out even beyond the grave."

Scarlett scowled grumpily at these words, which were completely in earnest.

Anyhow, who was this little girl?

Connie was puzzled. She'd introduced herself as an O'Brian, and at first Connie had assumed she must be Abigail's daughter, but she called her "Abby," not "Mother." Also, if she was honest, she had to admit they looked nothing alike. Abigail was an attractive woman, but she was no beauty. In fact, the girl's even features bore more resemblance to those of Aldous Clayton. Having gotten that far, however, Connie shook her head.

What was she thinking?

But Aldous had called the mysterious girl "Lou," as if he knew her well, he acted like he belonged in the O'Brian house, and he was dressed casually. Was he really only an ordinary employee of Abigail's...?

"You know, Connie, your face is showing every thought in your head right now," Scarlett announced with exasperation. Lucia gave her a carefree smile.

"I'm sorry to say that I'm not the fruit of Rudy and Abby's love."

Someone made a choking sound. Connie glanced over and saw Aldous spewing black tea.

"I swear...that little girl has the mouth of a twenty-year-old!"

Sorry, my fault, Connie thought with a grimace. Abigail giggled.

"Yes, it's an easy mistake to make. But Rudy and I don't have that kind of relationship. He's just my little pet. Around the house, I tell everyone he's my favorite lover, but the servants who have been here a long time know he's my hound."

"Then who in the world is that little girl? She can't be the duke's, can she? After all, Theodore O'Brian is a homosexual."

Connie's eyes widened at this sudden revelation from Scarlett.

"S-Scarlett, what are you talking about...?"

"Oh, everyone knows. You didn't?"

How would she know that? She was at a loss for words. A troubled look came over Lucia's face.

"Teddy is kind to men and women alike," she said.

Apparently guessing what they were talking about, Abigail smiled wryly.

"We all call Theodore 'Teddy' at home, so I hope you don't mind. Teddy is not able to be intimate with women. Of course, that doesn't make him a flawed person. Unfortunately, the world doesn't currently see it that way. But I love Teddy as a family member, and he feels the same about me. Doesn't he, Rudy?"

"Don't ask me," he snapped coldly.

"He's embarrassed," Abigail said with another wry smile.

"I'm not embarrassed!" he bit back. No doubt she brushed it off as a friendly tussle with her pet dog, because she smiled angelically and continued talking.

"Teddy and Rudy and I were childhood friends. That was back when I picked up Rudy on the verge of death in the slums—over twenty years ago now. Teddy looks like a bear, but he's a kind and sensitive person. He doesn't much care for the capital, so he stays in the domain painting pictures. And this little girl…"

Abigail glanced down at Lucia, who finished her sentence with a bright smile.

"I'm his niece."

"…His niece?"

"Yes. We took her in several years ago after there was a little incident. She's got O'Brian blood, and Teddy and I treat her as our adopted daughter."

She paused, as if she was trying to decide whether or not to say any more. Lucia looked up at her.

"It's all right, Abby, you can say it."

Abigail caressed her head before turning back to Connie.

"Her father is Nathaniel O'Brian, Teddy's younger brother by just a few years. The Nathaniel I knew was a timid boy who was always trying hard to read the moods of others."

Connie listened quietly as Abigail retraced her memories.

"Still, back then he tried very hard to live up to the expectations of those around him. But after he married and moved to the capital, he changed. Or perhaps he'd always been like that, only we hadn't noticed it.

"In any case, Nathaniel started acting differently. Before we knew it, he was bringing lovers and friends to the guest houses of his mansion and staying up all night raising a ruckus, living a life of dissipation. His wife soon reached the end of her patience and returned to her parents' home. I don't think she divorced him, but it seemed like only a matter of time.

"Soon, he began gambling and came crying home to the domain, unable to pay off his huge debts. But no matter how many times my father-in-law, the Duke of Orlamunde, scolded him, he would fall again into the same pattern. Everyone already knew that Teddy didn't like women, so I'm sure Nathaniel thought one day he would become duke. At the very least, I doubt he imagined he'd be disowned.

"And at the time, Teddy did, in fact, intend to give up his right to the family title. I had no objection. You don't have to be a noble to live, do you? Before I married Teddy, I traveled the world on a trading ship. I wouldn't have minded going back to that lifestyle, but…"

She paused to grin playfully at the notion of a duchess sailing the world when most of her peers had never even walked barefoot.

"Now that I think of it, Abigail was famous for preferring barbaric voyages to balls," Scarlett mused. Connie could definitely imagine Abigail not only enjoying a journey over the sea but maybe even becoming a pirate.

"Because I'd known Nathaniel when he was young and hardworking, despite his timidity, I thought he would eventually get back on the right path. I should have kept a closer eye on him. I didn't learn he had a child by his lover until five years after she was born."

Abigail looked down regretfully. Lucia squeezed her hand.

"It's not your fault, Abby. After all, Nathaniel himself almost forgot that he had a daughter. And when he saw me, he would hit me and kick me without warning."

Now it was Connie who was speechless. Was such inhumanity acceptable in the world?

"…Nathaniel and his crowd were not normal at that time. They were abusing a certain drug. They shut themselves up in the guest house and raved like madmen. Some of them died from overdoses."

"If I'd been there much longer, I would have joined them," Lucia said nonchalantly. Connie didn't know what to say. The angelic little face looked up at her and smiled. "But Abby rescued me."

"It wasn't only me, was it?" Abigail asked her.

"Of course not!" she answered with an enthusiastic nod. "Rudy was the one who beat those worthless bums to within a hair of their lives, and it was Teddy who walked over fire for me by sitting down to talk with the father he hated to death. I'm so proud that the three of you are my family."

After the story was finished, Aldous and the little lady left the drawing room. Apparently, it was time for her etiquette lesson. The butler took their place, carrying in a fresh tray of tea and cookies. It was the same handsome silver-haired gentleman who had shown Connie in.

"She's laughing now, but...," Abigail muttered, watching Lucia's small form scamper off with Aldous. "When I found her in the guesthouse, she truly was in a wretched state. He didn't feed her properly, and he beat her, so what would you expect? For a month after I brought her back here, she wouldn't cry, smile, or even speak. She must have had to shut out all her feelings to survive that cruel life."

The Lucia O'Brian that Connie had met was a precocious child with an adorable smile.

"Almost everyone at Nathaniel's mansion was horribly addicted to drugs. He and his lover were especially bad, and even now they are receiving treatment for the aftereffects at a facility. Later, I learned they were taking an illegal hallucinogen...but I never did find out who their dealer was, despite my best efforts."

Abigail looked down regretfully. When she lifted her head again, Connie thought she glimpsed a faint fire in the depths of her deep blue eyes.

"...Next time, I won't let them get away."

Her voice was sharp with determination.

"The drug that destroyed Nathaniel was Jackal's Paradise. Though it's quite a bit worse than the Jackal's Paradise that was around when I was young."

Just then, Aldous returned from delivering Lucia to her lesson.

"We learned recently that the same drug was being sold on Rosenkreuz Street," he said with the same sharp look on his face. Abigail narrowed her eyes.

"I don't know what they're trying to do, but I do know that spreading that kind of thing around is trouble. Whoever they are, I won't let them swagger into my backyard and do as they please," she declared, then turned to Connie, her expression softening.

"…You've always puzzled me, but everything makes sense if you had Scarlett by your side. She was always like the eye of the storm."

"Whatever could she mean by that?" Scarlett asked, losing her temper. Connie stood up in a panic and tried to calm her by dramatically patting the air with both hands. Abigail burst out laughing.

"It's fitting that you two met at Viscount Hamsworth's ball."

"…Why?"

Connie couldn't see how any of this related to the viscount.

"Don't you see? Why do you think a man as gluttonous as him became a priest? Because of his monumental donations? I can't deny that, but the church has a reason for wanting him as a clergyman."

"A reason?"

"Yes. It seems that Dominic Hamsworth has the favor of the goddesses."

"Favor…?"

Connie remembered him walking into the church smelling like a barrel of wine. He was the personification of depravity. He surrendered to every suggestion the devil whispered in his ear. Her thoughts must have been obvious, because Abigail explained with a smile, "The viscount says he can see things that aren't human, like Lucia does. Doesn't that ring a bell? I'm certain that was why he agreed to file the paperwork to break your engagement to Neil Bronson. After all, that man would bend over backwards to obey an order from Scarlett Castiel."

Connie was more puzzled than ever.

"You see," said Abigail, lowering her voice, "the viscount is a hopeless masochist who loves nothing more than to be abused by queenly women."

That makes sense, Connie thought as she took a sip of her freshly poured tea. The tea was very fragrant, a perfect match for the rich, crumbly cookies. Yes, it all made perfect sense now.

"Oh, the nouveau riche pig? It made me sick the way he would grovel happily no matter what I said to him, so I decided to stay away. Even that seemed to please him, though. Anyhow, it's none of my business," Scarlett declared.

Connie wished it wasn't any of hers, either. She willed her consciousness far away as Abigail gave her a questioning look.

"But was it all just a baseless rumor?" asked Abigail.

"I did meet the viscount several times, but he never did anything to make me think..."

Suddenly she frowned. A handful of faded memories welled up from the back of her mind. The odd direction of the viscount's gaze when they talked at the Earl John Doe Ball. The words he said after she and Randolph had made their vows of commitment.

May the gods protect *you all.*

She had simply assumed he was referring to herself and Randolph, but now she wasn't so sure.

Only Viscount Hamsworth himself could know his true intention. She didn't plan to get anywhere near him in the future, so it seemed the truth would remain forever shrouded in mystery.

"And speaking of balls, do you remember the kerfuffle at Emilia Godwin's residence?"

"You mean between Teresa Jennings and Margot Tudor?"

"Yes. Teresa's husband, Kevin, is currently in rehabilitation, apparently for drug addiction. Probably Jackal's Paradise. They say he'd been spending all his time at the brothels on Rosenkreuz Street, and his behavior was just like the addicts at Nathaniel's mansion."

"That's..."

"I wanted to look into it, but Teresa is dead and her lover, Linus Tudor, has apparently gone back to Faris. I feel like something else is going on. Do you think your fiancé would be willing to look into it for me at headquarters?"

The information would no doubt be useful to Randolph as well. Connie suppressed her eagerness and nodded. Abigail's face brightened.

"Thank you, Connie. Oh yes, and I'll arrange for you to see Aisha Huxley as well. Sebastian?"

"I shall write you the most splendid introduction to Lord Huxley," the butler announced knowingly, bringing his hand to his chest for a bow before jauntily exiting the room.

"Sebastian is very talented," Abigail said with a giggle. "I'm sure the Huxleys will be contacting you very soon."

"Oh!" Connie exclaimed when she saw the look on her face.

"What's the matter?" Abigail asked. Connie shook her head. It wasn't anything important.

Only that she had thought Lucia and Abigail looked nothing alike—

But they had exactly the same sunny smile.

※

The girl was made of air. Nobody paid any attention to her. Even when they looked at her, they acted like they couldn't see her. Which made sense, if she was made of air.

She liked shiny things. She knew that people laughed at her behind her back for being gloomy and dismal. That was why she never told anyone. Shiny things that drew everyone's attention existed in a separate universe from her. Maybe that was the reason she was pulled so strongly to them. Lately, what she liked more than anything was Scarlett Castiel, who had debuted in society just last year.

The debutante ball was a grand affair held only once a year at Moldavite Palace, where the king and queen lived. The girl happened to be the same age as Scarlett, and they were together in the grand hall. Dressed in a fiery red dress, Scarlett was more beautiful than anyone else there. Her overwhelming presence outshined even the king and queen.

From that day on, the girl's eyes were always on Scarlett. She was all the girl saw. Maybe she was obvious about it, but it didn't matter. After all, she was made of air. Nobody noticed her.

Or so she thought.

"You're Aisha Spencer, aren't you? Did you want something?"

It happened after they had been to several balls together. She was staring at Scarlett as usual when their eyes suddenly met. Scarlett's words pierced her like an arrow, and she shrank back.

There were the glossy black waves of her hair and the jewel-like amethyst eyes. The porcelain skin and the moist lips. The supple limbs.

Scarlett Castiel was standing right in front of her, the invisible Aisha.

"You were looking at me, weren't you? You were doing it last time, too, and the time before that. What in the world do you want?"

"U-um, m-my name…"

It was all she could do to stutter a few words. Scarlett frowned slightly. It was enough to make Aisha's heart contract.

"It's Aisha, isn't it? Aisha Spencer."

"H-how did you know…?"

She'd said her name again. The girl's face felt hot. She didn't understand what was happening.

"Because we've already met. At the debutante party at Moldavite Palace."

"You r-remembered…"

That was several months ago. To Aisha, it was a lifetime, but to Scarlett, the time must have passed in a flash. Her heart pounded.

She could hardly breathe. She pressed her hand to her chest.

"Just who do you think I am?"

Scarlett gazed down at her intimidatingly, her chin held high and her jewel-like eyes narrowed. Aisha gasped at Scarlett's haughty beauty. Then she realized something.

She was a goddess.

Scarlett was a goddess——Aisha's goddess.

Her eyes grew blurry. She blinked, and a hot tear rolled down her cheek. She realized she was crying.

※

"So then, let's get everything in order."

Connie was sitting at her bureau, her sleeves pushed up and a feather pen in her hand. Several sheets of paper were on the desk in front of her. She was preparing to write down all the information she had so far.

At the top of the first sheet, she wrote, *Ten years ago.*

"First, there's the attempted assassination of Crown Princess Cecilia ten years ago. The incident with the poisoned water jug at her house. I've heard the rumors—but why did you become a suspect in the first place, Scarlett?"

"Like that scheming woman said, one of my earrings was found next to the water jug at the Luze residence. It was a moonstone teardrop. Cecilia's maid supposedly found it. Pieces of moonstone large enough to make into jewelry are very rare, so she must have thought of me right away. Unfortunately, I had visited the Luze residence a few hours earlier. I went there to get Enrique. We had a date to see a play that day. Even if he was a prince, I wanted him to feel ashamed for jilting me."

Connie had heard the story about her marching into the Luze residence. It was one of the legends about Scarlett Castiel, the wicked vixen. According to the rumors, she pushed past the servants who tried to stop her, barging into the drawing room to slap Cecilia across the face and drag Enrique out by the scruff of his neck.

Judging by the look on Scarlett's face right now, that probably wasn't far from the truth.

Below *Ten years ago*, she wrote, *Cecilia.*

"I've been told that when the Viscount Luze first heard about it, he planned to pretend it never happened. Most likely he didn't want to make enemies of a duke's family. However, it seems that the maid who found the earing loved her mistress very much. Fearing for Cecilia's safety, she went straight to the Security Force with the earring and filed a report."

"…Wait a second. Was the earring really yours?"

Moonstone was a milky mineral with a rainbow sheen. No commoner and very few nobles could afford such a mystically beautiful and rare jewel. Only the highest-ranked nobles would be able to wear something like that on a regular basis.

"No," Scarlett said immediately. *"I did own teardrop moonstone earrings, but at the time of the incident, both of them were in my possession."*

"Did you tell—"

"Of course I did. I told the investigator who came to my house to question me. I think he only came as a formality. At the very least, I don't think I was their prime suspect at that stage. He asked me to show him the earrings, so I thrust them right under his nose. Then he asked if he could take them with him to verify, and I smiled and told him to do as he pleased. After all, everything I wore was made expressly for me by jewelers. Even if the earring the maid found looked like mine, if the investigator had gone to the workshop and asked for the drawings used to design it, he would have known I was telling the truth. That's what I thought."

Custom-made earrings would be slightly different from off-the-shelf ones, and some jewelers put their own stamp on their work. It did seem that if they'd looked into it, they would have learned Scarlett was telling the truth.

So why hadn't her name been cleared?

Scarlett must have guessed Connie's thoughts, because she narrowed her eyes and continued.

"A few days later, they came out with the results of their investigation. They said that one of the earrings I gave them was fake. They accused me of having it made in a hurry when I found out the investigator was coming. In other words, someone switched my earring in the safe at the Security Force headquarters with the one that was dropped at the Luze residence."

Connie stared at her in shock. Her feather pen rolled out of her hand and onto the sheet of paper.

"I was charged with lying to the investigator and obstructing his investigation. After some other developments, they decided to search our mansion, and the king gave them permission to do so. Or rather, if the king hadn't ordered it, no one would have been able to do such a thing at the Castiel house. As you already know, they found a bottle of half-used poison in my room—and arrested me on the spot."

According to the rumors, Cecilia had tried to stop the execution even though she was the victim. When Connie asked Scarlett if that was true, she snorted.

"Sure, on the surface. She did come to see me once when I was locked up alone in my cell. She said it was a pity things had turned out like this. I don't know what her true feelings were, but we're talking about the kind of she-devil who would make a move on another woman's fiancé. And the crown prince, at that. That alone should prove she's rotten to the core."

"Did you think she was the one who set you up?" Connie asked, pulling herself together. "You think she's suspicious?"

"Yes. Until recently, I thought it was all an act she'd orchestrated herself. After all, she benefited more than anyone else from my death."

The daughter of a country viscount had become crown princess. It was like a fairy tale.

"But wait," Connie said, puzzled. "Only until recently?"

"Yes. To tell you the truth, I'm not sure anymore. I mean, the woman doesn't seem satisfied at all."

Connie thought back to their meeting at the Elbaite Detached Palace. From start to finish, Cecilia's smile had been coldly artificial.

"…Then do you think she might not be involved at all?"

"No. At the very least, she's keeping a secret."

"A secret?"

"That redheaded journalist talked about it, remember? How Cecilia Luze was the daughter of a whore and grew up at an orphanage?"

Connie set down her feather pen, crossed her arms, and groaned.

"We can't exactly trust what Amelia Hobbes says…"

"Maybe not, but Kevin Jennings, who seems to have discovered the truth, has been immobilized. And it's a fact that no one had ever seen Viscount Luze's daughter until she showed up at the debutante ball. It's odd when you think about it."

Connie jotted down "prostitute's daughter," "Luze domain," and "Kevin" beneath "Cecilia."

"If that's true," Scarlett went on, *"then the rumors about Cecilia sneaking out to the castle district might have to do with her meeting that boy at the orphanage she was close with. Cici, was it?"*

The girl seems to have pledged her love to a boy at the orphanage. I think the name was Sarsy or Cici, something like that.

That was what Amelia had said.

"But if she had someone like that, why would she marry His Highness...?"

"People often marry without love. She's a noble, after all. I always thought she'd arranged the assassination attempt to become crown princess, but even after ten years, she still seems to hate Enrique, and she doesn't seem obsessed with money or power. I wondered if her family was pulling the strings, but a country viscount wouldn't have that much power. Also, she seems to have cut most of her family ties. So what in the world can that woman be after?"

Connie had no idea. After thinking for a moment, she left a gap on the paper and wrote, *Cici*.

"And it's not just what happened ten years ago," Scarlett went on. *"Something is going on right now, and Cecilia is part of it. On the day the seventh prince of Faris or whoever it was got kidnapped, a trader came to see Cecilia at the palace. The timing is too perfect to be a coincidence."*

She was talking about the trader named Vado. He had apparently been banned from the castle over the miscarriage herbs, but Cecilia had supposedly been close with him for a long time.

"Speaking of which, the young man Kate Lorraine mentioned in her testimony was called Salvador, wasn't he?" Scarlett asked.

Connie wrote down the words "Vado" and "Salvador," and then noticed something. They were similar.

"Both are unusual names. Could that be a coincidence?" Scarlett asked.

"But what—"

"Randolph said the kidnapper and the man named Salvador both belonged to Daeg Gallus. If the trader named Vado and Salvador are one person, then we can probably assume Cecilia has some connection to the organization. And according to Kate Lorraine, the kidnappers had something to do with Jackal's Paradise being sold on Rosenkreuz Street. Ugh. That would mean Cecilia is a truly wicked person. Enrique really has no taste in women."

Jackal's Paradise.

Connie was hearing that phrase a lot lately.

"…The woman who collapsed at the Earl John Doe Ball had it, the dealers were selling it on Rosenkreuz Street, Duke Theodore's brother was addicted to it…and it's all the same hallucinogen," she mused.

"And don't forget Kevin Jennings," Scarlett added.

Connie looked down at the paper. Kevin's name was connected to Cecilia's. Which meant it was possible that Cecilia also had some connection to Jackal's Paradise.

"Does that mean the kidnappings of Ulysses and Kate and the plan to get more people hooked on Jackal's Paradise are all the work of Daeg Gallus…?"

Randolph had said it was a huge organization that he had been tracking for years. She felt like the closer to it she got, the more insidious it appeared.

As she wrote, something occurred to her.

She'd started out talking about what happened ten years ago, but before she knew it, she was writing about the present.

Did that mean the events of a decade ago were connected to what was happening right now?

"We've forgotten something important," Scarlett said with an unusually serious expression. *"You were attacked by Daeg Gallus, too."*

Connie gasped. She was right.

"The man who kidnapped Kate Lorraine was looking for Lily's key, wasn't he?" Scarlett said.

Kiriki kirikuku. A spell to show you who the bad guys are. Who had the boy who told it to her said he'd heard it from?

And what had Lily Orlamunde hidden behind the painting?

"A moment ago, I said that something is going on right now. That wasn't quite right."

Scarlett's voice was terribly quiet.

"Something has been going on in this kingdom for the entire past ten years."

That "something" was probably to blame for Lily's death.

"And it must somehow be related to my execution."

"…Yes."

Connie nodded, looking down at the sheets of paper covered in a jumble of words and lines. She shouldn't have tried something she had no experience with. It didn't seem like looking over her work would lead her much of anywhere. Still, she wanted to add a few more words—Lily Orlamunde's last words.

Destroy the Holy Grail of Eris.

※

"D-don't you think this looks funny on me…?"

Connie was standing in front of a full-length mirror, gazing intently at her reflection. She was wearing a creamy-lemon-colored dress with a white collar and a narrow yellow ribbon around the waist. The design was nice, but she felt like it looked out of place on someone so plain.

Scarlett raised her eyebrows slightly.

"It looks good on you. After all, I'm the one who chose it," she declared flatly.

That thought put Connie at ease.

Randolph had asked her out a few days ago.

Apparently, Kyle had advised him that "men who can't arrange dates send a message that they're incompetent." Connie couldn't help smiling when she received his letter full of sincere apologies.

Still, the point of their outing wasn't to deepen their relationship. It was so he could report the progress he'd made on Abigail's request regarding Kevin Jennings and explain the details of the attempted poisoning ten years ago. It was all business—as was to be expected from a temporary fiancé. That didn't bother Connie.

Nevertheless, the realization flitted across her mind that this was the first time they were going out alone on a "date."

It wasn't a big deal. It didn't mean anything. She wasn't especially excited. Absolutely not.

Still, Randolph was the well-born son of a duke, and was himself an earl. Connie couldn't disgrace him by showing up in a shabby dress. That was her only concern.

She looked at her reflection again. The face that looked back at her was plain and completely lacking in confidence. Her hair was prettily braided and pinned up with an ornament decorated with tiny pearls. She was wearing light makeup, and her lips were the color of ripe fruit.

Her brother Layli had told her she looked pretty, but she still threw an anxious glance back at Scarlett.

"D-don't you think this lipstick is too bright…?"

Scarlett raised her eyebrows again.

"It looks good on you. After all, I'm the one who chose it."

Connie nodded, somewhat reassured, and gave herself a final look. The girl in the mirror was more done up than usual, even somewhat presentable.

But something felt off. She felt somehow silly.

"S-Scarlett," she wailed, looking for help.

Finally at her wit's end over Connie's nonsense, Scarlett scowled.

"Oh, come off it! I wouldn't make a mistake in judgment, would I? All you have to do is hold your head high!"

She was like an earthshaking bolt of lightning in midsummer.

His Excellency the Grim Reaper arrived precisely on time to pick Connie up and take her not to some scenic riverbank or fashionable play or street lined with stylish shops—but instead to the history museum next to the city hall in Saint Mark's Square.

"*Mr. Unpredictable...,*" Scarlett moaned, pressing her temples as if she had a headache.

"B-but I'd fall asleep if we went to a play...!"

"*Dammit, I should have said from the start I didn't want to go to the square.*"

In fact, Randolph had asked her before they got into the carriage if it was all right to go to Saint Mark's Square, even though Scarlett said she had no memory of the execution.

Scarlett had indicated it truly was fine by her, so Connie had told him it wouldn't be a problem.

"*What in the world can he be thinking, taking you to a moldy old place like this for a date? If I were you, I'd turn around and take that carriage home without a single word.*"

"B-but the building is new...! And it doesn't seem moldy...!"

"*That's not what I meant, idiot!*"

The museum had been built only a few years earlier.

On the day of Scarlett's execution, a bolt of lightning had struck city hall and set it on fire. Fortunately, it hadn't destroyed the building, but some documents had burned up. A few of them were quite valuable historical papers. The history museum had been built as part of the recovery effort.

Scarlett had been grumbling about it, but she quieted down just before they went inside. Slowly, she turned around to look out on the square.

She was surveying the site of her own execution.

"*...I really don't feel anything. I can't remember any of it. Was I really executed here?*" she asked.

Scarlett might not remember, but Connie did. Connie had seen the moment ten years ago when Scarlett's head was sliced off. The color of the blood. The smell of it. The human cruelty that made her hair stand on end.

But she hesitated to say any of that to Scarlett. Instead, she nodded vaguely.

Although it was the middle of summer, the inside of the museum was dark and cool. Items of historical value were vulnerable to light and heat, apparently.

Stifling a yawn, Connie pretended to be interested in the rows of old suits of armor, swords, and insect-eaten books.

"Actually, Kyle gave me the idea to come here," Randolph said as if he'd just remembered. "He said I ought to take my fiancée somewhere quiet, natural—where we didn't ordinarily go. I figured this place met all the requirements."

"I finally understand. This man is fatally lacking in good taste," Scarlett declared solemnly. There was an awkward silence.

Perhaps noticing his fiancée's expression, Randolph tilted his head. "Have you been here before?"

Connie lowered her eyebrows in consternation and shook her head. "No. Is this your first time, too?"

"Actually, I've been here once before. The Orlamunde family donated something to the museum. The director gave Lily and me a tour."

For a moment, Connie didn't know what to say. She could hear Scarlett clucking and calling someone an idiot in an exasperated voice.

That was nothing strange, Connie told herself. After all, they'd been married. Lily Orlamunde had been Randolph's wife for real. Married couples did things like that. It was only natural.

All the same, for some reason Connie felt a pang in her heart. A voice whispered in the back of her mind.

So he used to call her Lily.

Her feet grew heavy, as if her shoes had suddenly turned to lead.

"See that book over there? It's one of the holy scriptures Saint Anastasia is said to have received from a messenger of the goddesses. They say that, a few generations ago, the Marquess Orlamunde won it in a black-market auction. The original manuscript is badly damaged, so the museum almost never exposes it to open air. That's it there, in the case. The volume in front of it is a reproduction—what's the matter?"

Having noticed that his fiancée was no longer beside him, Randolph looked around in surprise. Connie, who had stopped walking a few paces back, looked down. She didn't want him to see the expression on her face.

He stared at her for a moment before nodding like he understood.

"We've been walking a lot this morning. You must be hungry. Why don't we get something to eat?"

Outside, the square was sparkling under the brilliant midday sun.

Oddly enough, a fashionable café with an outdoor terrace shared the same building as the history museum. After Connie had ordered a glass of fruit water, Randolph told her he would need a little more time to do the favor Abigail had asked of him.

"The crown princess owns the hospital where Kevin is being treated, and some complicated paperwork is required. Plus, I can't figure out where Linus Tudor went, though I've heard he's back in Faris."

Connie nodded quietly. There did seem to be more than met the eye to the case of Kevin Jennings.

The conversation shifted to the events of ten years ago and the fact that Scarlett's earring had been switched with a replica.

"So she thinks it was someone with access to the safe? Just about any investigator from headquarters can get in there whenever they want. There's a log of when people go in and out, but that could easily be falsified."

"Oh, I see..."

That would make identifying the criminal difficult. Connie was sighing over this fact when her fruit water arrived. Randolph had ordered a cup of tea and a sandwich. Fluffy slices of well-browned bread filled with sliced steak smothered in sauce sent up a mouthwatering aroma. Randolph must have noticed her eyeing it, because he nudged the plate toward her and told her to help herself.

"I checked for records of the earring that Scarlett was supposed to have dropped at the Luze residence…"

Connie took a sip of her fruit water as she listened. It was icy cold and refreshingly tart.

"It seems the fake earring wasn't real moonstone. It was a type of what they call silver-shell. That's rare and expensive itself, but nothing like moonstone. The appearance is similar, but silver-shell is more fragile and harder to work with."

Since Randolph had said she could have his sandwich, she unabashedly dug in. Juicy meat filled her mouth.

"What about the design?" Scarlett asked, evidently having run out of patience with Connie, who was devouring her meal with relish. Connie gulped down the bite in her mouth—and promptly choked on it. Randolph stood up wordlessly and patted her back until she tearfully swallowed a mouthful of fruit water and cleared her throat again.

"Scarlett wanted to know about the design," she said after a deep breath.

"Identical to hers," he replied, handing Connie a napkin. When she gave him a confused look, he pointed to her mouth. Apparently, there was some sauce on it. She hurriedly wiped it away.

"That's where the records ended, but not many people trade in silver-shell. I asked around about who was buying it at the time, and I recognized one of the names the dealer mentioned." Randolph paused and lowered his voice. "Spencer, as in the earl."

Spencer?

Connie recognized that name, but she couldn't remember right away where she'd heard it. As she was racking her brain, Scarlett gasped softly.

"That was Aisha's maiden name. Aisha Spencer. Ten years ago, she was still a Spencer."

Her quiet words echoed like raindrops, sending ripples across a calm pond.

"Scarlett told me Aisha was an admirer of hers…," Connie said timidly.

"She was," Randolph agreed. "And the Spencers own a number of precious metal workshops."

Scarlett folded her arms and drew her brows together in thought.

"…It wouldn't have been strange for Aisha Spencer to make a pair of earrings exactly like mine."

As Scarlett had said earlier, Aisha had a habit of ordering clothes that looked exactly like hers.

"…You said you were going to the Huxley residence to speak with Aisha, didn't you?" Randolph asked.

"Yes."

As Abigail had promised, within a few days of Connie's visit, the Viscount Huxley had sent her an invitation.

"Even if Aisha was involved in the incident ten years ago, it would be hard to prosecute her unless she turned herself in. And there's a possibility she's involved with Daeg Gallus. Please be careful."

Connie nodded meekly.

"…I will be."

※

Aisha was chewing her nails in irritation. She knew it was a bad habit, but she couldn't stop. That's how wretched her mood was.

She had underestimated Constance Grail. As it turned out, she wasn't a mere child; she was a horribly cunning and unfair young woman.

She had used Abigail O'Brian of all people to get close to Aisha's husband. Her husband, who knew nothing, was overjoyed by the opportunity to forge a connection with a duke's household and immediately invited the Grail girl to their residence.

Ever since, Aisha's mood had been steadily worsening.

Her nails were a ragged mess. If they split, it would be a pain to deal with. She took an amber-colored pipe from a drawer. This was another bad habit of hers, but she couldn't resist the urge at the moment.

The round bowl was already packed with the specially ordered leaves. She struck a match with her practiced hand and lit the pipe.

She puffed until it was burning well and then took a long, slow pull. Her unsettled emotions instantly melted away as if they'd never existed. Purple smoke curled into the air and dissipated.

By the time the last puff of smoke was drifting toward the ceiling, she was utterly calm.

Aisha set the pipe on the table and walked over to the window. Since her rooms were on the second floor, she had a good view of the front gate. Presently, a carriage rolled onto the grounds. A girl with hazelnut hair stepped out. The second Aisha laid eyes on her, her chest began to roil again.

The harder she looked at Constance Grail, the more ordinary she looked.

Why did everyone say this girl reminded them of Scarlett?

Emilia Godwin had told her she'd understand when she met her. Emilia was just the same as she'd been ten years ago: shrill, brainless, and obsessed with men.

Constance might have been able to fool silly old Emilia, but she wouldn't fool Aisha. Aisha knew all about Scarlett Castiel, better than anyone else.

With her jewel-like amethyst eyes and her peerless noble, haughty air, she had been Aisha's goddess.

No one could take the place of Scarlett. Aisha had learned that all too well over the past ten years. She had learned her lesson. A ball without Scarlett was like a hearth without fire. Every time Aisha wished she were like Scarlett, a voice answered back.

Just who do you think I am?

Glancing down, Aisha tucked a knife into her dress for self-defense, just in case. A moment later, the maid announced that her guest had arrived.

"Welcome to our home, Miss Grail."

"Thank you for inviting me, Lady Huxley."

Constance Grail's curtsy did remind her of Scarlett's. But it was just a resemblance. She wasn't her.

She lacked that divine presence that made you want to kneel at her feet.

"What a surprise it was to see a messenger from the House of O'Brian arrive at the home of a lower noble. Of course, when I opened the note, I saw it was about the Grail family."

"I'm sorry about that. I simply had to meet with you."

Aisha had intended her comment as a veiled insult, but Constance responded with extreme earnestness. Aisha had been on guard, ready for a hostile response, but now she felt deflated. The words she had prepared hung uselessly in the air. She couldn't imagine the girl had planned it that way, but in the pause, Constance continued talking.

"To get straight to the point, there's something I'd like to ask you."

So here it was.

She didn't need to hear the rest to know. The girl was going to ask about Scarlett. Chatty Emilia Godwin had only needed a few drinks to tell Aisha everything Constance had said to her. Knowing the girl's intent in advance should make her easy to handle. Aisha was confident that she could remain calm no matter what the girl said about that time ten years ago.

But she hadn't predicted what came next.

"What is that smell?"

"What?"

"Is it tobacco? Yes, but there's something else."

Aisha's heart skipped a beat. This couldn't be.

"…What are you talking about?"

"I have a friend with an outstanding sense of smell and memory. It seems *she recognized it* right away when you walked in."

The eyes looking straight at Aisha may have been ordinary, but they were also bold.

"Please tell me, Lady Huxley. Why is it that you smell like Jackal's Paradise?"

She'd been found out.

Gooseflesh spread on her arms. Her legs quivered. But Aisha suppressed her panic and shook her head as if nothing were wrong.

"Whatever could you be talking about?"

"I'm not sure if you mixed it with tobacco or bought it already mixed, but I'm certain it's Jackal's Paradise. Am I wrong?"

"…Jackal's Paradise? Oh, you mean that hallucinogen that was in fashion ten years ago?" she said, clapping her hands as if she'd just understood.

Constance Grail stared at her silently. Cold sweat trickled down Aisha's back. She forced a smile onto her lips and shrugged.

"You must be mistaken. I'm wearing an unusual perfume today. Perhaps that's what you smell."

"Perfume?"

"Yes… It's quite exotic. Even if I told you the name, you wouldn't recognize it. I don't think you can buy it anywhere."

She knew her lie was obvious, but it didn't matter. If only she could get through the present crisis, she could smooth it over later. Constance Grail could doubt her as much as she wanted, but she had no way of proving Aisha was lying.

Constance seemed to have realized Aisha wasn't going to give her a real answer. She looked down, maybe out of frustration. But the next moment, she snorted.

"You're so bad at lying, it's laughable."

The girl's scornful tone brought the blood rushing to Aisha's head.

"You're a very rude girl. I've had enough. Please go home."

She turned her back, pretending she was in a huff. She still had time. If Constance Grail left now, she could go to *them* for help right away.

"Come now. You're acting like a spoiled child, throwing a tantrum because I've discovered your mischief."

The amused voice most definitely belonged to the girl standing before her, and yet its suddenly haughty tone made Aisha uncomfortable. She knew that voice. She couldn't help glancing over her shoulder.

There was the ordinary-looking girl with hazelnut hair and green eyes. But no, something was different.

"Remember this, Aisha Spencer. You're far ruder for trying to fool me."

The girl glaring at her, chin tipped up and eyes slightly narrowed as if she were looking at a worm, was not Constance Grail.

"Just who do you think I am?"

Aisha's eyes widened. She couldn't help wanting to prostrate herself before that overwhelming presence.

"Scarlett...?"

There was no way she could mistake it for anyone else.

After all, Aisha knew her better than anyone.

Ten years ago, Scarlett Castiel had been the center of Aisha's world.

She had high status and rare beauty, but what drew Aisha most powerfully was her fierce personality. If she deemed someone an enemy, be they young or old, man or woman, she ridiculed them, insulted them, and left them in the cold. She was probably the only one in her social circle at the time who could get away with that.

Her engagement to His Highness Enrique was announced when she was twelve years old. Evidently, the two of them, along with Lily Orlamunde, had known each other since they were young. They were what people called "childhood best friends." And considering the standing of the House of Castiel, the engagement was only natural.

True, the relationship between Scarlett and His Highness may not have been the best. As one might guess from his frail appearance, Enrique

©Yu-nagi

was sensitive, serious, and kind. His role was always to bring Scarlett back in line. Needless to say, Scarlett was not one to bow her head in servitude. They often fought fiercely.

But Aisha had been watching them for years, and she had often seen them laughing and chatting together. They weren't starry-eyed lovers, but they were as relaxed around one another as brother and sister. Aisha had always looked up to the two of them. But then…that woman appeared.

Cecilia Luze. Somehow, that country girl who stank of mud had stolen His Highness Enrique's heart. It had happened one day when His Highness snuck out to the castle district. A gang of hoodlums was just about to attack Cecilia when he happened to pass by and rescue her, or so the story went.

It was straight out of some cheap romance novel.

Nevertheless, anyone could see that His Highness was infatuated with Cecilia.

But Aisha didn't think they were the kind of couple everyone said they were. His Highness was born with a serious temperament and good sense. She didn't know what his innermost feelings were, but at the time, he seemed to treat Cecilia as no more than a close friend.

In fact, it was the irresponsible people around them who seemed desperate to turn the relationship into a tragic love story.

The rumor of romance between a prince and a girl of low standing spread like wildfire. Enrique's obvious attraction was partly to blame, but so was Scarlett's behavior. To go so far—it gave the rumors the ring of truth, though she was most likely only acting out of dislike for Cecilia.

The result was that His Highness and Cecilia Luze really did appear to be secret lovers.

The situation made Aisha anxious. If nothing changed, the rumors seemed likely to turn into truth.

She had to do something.

It was then that she remembered something her cousin had said during a visit several days earlier.

Aisha hadn't seen the woman, a relation of her mother's, in a while and was surprised by how slim she had become.

Her cousin pulled a small bottle from the bodice of her dress and whispered that she was taking medicine to lose weight.

"It's a restorative tonic from abroad. Don't you think the results are amazing? Don't tell anyone else, though. All you need is a drop. If you take too much, it will make you sick."

Make you sick.

The words were music to Aisha's ears.

She had heard that Cecilia Luze was born with a weak constitution. If she fell ill, she would probably have to go back to her domain. The Luze domain was on the border with Melvina. That was very far from the capital, so she would hardly ever be able to see His Highness.

Aisha made up an excuse to visit her cousin. As they chatted idly, she decided she would give up on her plan if she didn't come across the medicine.

But then she saw the little bottle sitting among her cousin's neat row of perfumes, as if she had placed it there hoping no one would notice it. Aisha hesitated for only a moment. When her cousin was looking the other way, she slipped it into her purse. Then, pretending she was dizzy, she swept the remaining perfume bottles onto the ground with her arm, smashing them to bits. When her cousin saw her bloodied arm, she screamed and ran to call a servant.

Not long after that, Aisha visited the Luze residence with her mother. Aisha's maternal grandmother was from Melvina, and her mother was close with the Viscountess Luze, who was also from Melvina. Aisha had no idea that Scarlett had visited only hours before and quarreled with Cecilia.

Dressing like Scarlett was a way for the socially awkward Aisha to protect herself in social situations. She had given up on wearing the whole outfit after her mother chastised her, but she couldn't bring herself give up the jewelry. Scarlett had worn the moonstone earrings at a ball a while back. Aisha chose to wear her copy to the Luze residence. The jeweler had told her to be careful with them because they were fragile, but she hadn't noticed that the metal setting had grown loose.

At the Luze residence, as everywhere, Aisha was like air. Nobody seemed to notice when she left the room in the middle of her mother's lively conversation with the viscountess.

There were surprisingly few servants in the mansion. She had heard that the Luze family had left their domain for the first time in many years, so perhaps they weren't accustomed to the ways of the capital. Thanks to that, Aisha escaped notice.

Still, she hesitated as she stood in front of the water jug. Until then, she had thought only of harming Cecilia, but now she realized that her actions might end up harming other people as well.

She paused for only a moment, however.

After all, it wasn't as if they would die.

It was only medicine. Probably not too different from a laxative. Just a little stronger than normal.

That was what Aisha told herself.

She was doing this for Scarlett. This was what Scarlett would have done. If she were Scarlett—

If she did this, she could become Scarlett.

Aisha unscrewed the lid with trembling fingers and poured the contents of the little bottle into the water jug.

"I didn't know it was poison. Cousin Sharon said it was medicine. I did drop my earring, but I never hid the poison bottle in your room. I could never do something like that…!"

Aisha had been so shocked when she heard the substance in the water jug was poison that her heart nearly stopped beating. At the same time, however, she felt confident Scarlett's name would be cleared. After all, Aisha hadn't dropped Scarlett's moonstone earring, but instead a mere piece of silver-shell.

But the earring was declared to be Scarlett's, and a half-used bottle of poison was found in her room. Aisha didn't have a clue what was going on. She still didn't.

Now, too, she had no idea what was happening. The girl standing before her was Constance Grail, but at the same time she wasn't. She was Scarlett. Aisha knew.

Obviously, the flesh-and-blood Scarlett was dead. She had been executed. Executed ten years ago, in Saint Mark's Square.

On that day, all Aisha could do was cower trembling in her house, praying to the goddesses for a miracle.

"It's a lie! I still have the bottle I used that day! If they evaluated it, they would find it was only ordinary medicine for losing weight! It's not my fault! Please, forgive me, Scarlett…," she pleaded in a shaky voice.

"*Forgive you?*" Scarlett muttered, delicately arching one eyebrow and narrowing her eyes as if she were evaluating some inanimate object. "*Then why didn't you confess your crime?*"

Aisha stiffened.

"*It doesn't matter if you used poison or not. You knew I was innocent. I was executed for a crime that you committed.*"

"But I d-did it for you! I'm certain you would have done the same thing if you had the opportunity! So in your place—"

Scarlett interrupted her.

"*I wouldn't do something so shameful if my life depended on it.*"

Aisha gasped.

"*Everything you did ten years ago, you did for yourself,*" Scarlett continued. "*Know your place. Don't use me as an excuse.*"

Aisha stared at her in a daze. She was right.

"*You said you wished you were me, Aisha Spencer. I'll do you the favor of asking you one more time,*" Scarlett said with a smile. "*Just who do you think I am?*"

Her smile was haughty and noble and more beautiful than anything in the world.

She had known the answer long ago. She sensed something inside her crumble.

She had known. That was the truth. She had shut her eyes out of self-interest. She was the reason it all happened. Everything was her fault.

It was Aisha who had killed Scarlett.

Her vision went black. Before she knew it, her hand was on the hilt of the knife she had tucked into her dress.

"No!"

An instant before she plunged the blade into her own heart, somebody came flying at her.

"What can you do once you're dead? Your death won't erase what you did to Scarlett!"

A strong hand grabbed her wrist and forced her to drop the knife.

It wasn't Scarlett anymore.

Startlingly bright green eyes took in the empty shell that was Aisha.

"You must stay alive to atone for what you have done."

※

In response to Connie's words, Aisha bit her lip regretfully and nodded. Then she collapsed to the floor as if the string holding her up had been cut. Apparently, she had fainted.

Connie called a servant, who seemed unsurprised to see her mistress lying on the ground and picked her up with practiced movements. As Connie gazed at Aisha's body, as thin as a dead branch, she wondered if this happened all the time.

Scarlett glared at Aisha with blazing eyes.

Connie was unsure what to do. Should she call the military police or not? She had nothing that would qualify as evidence. Aisha could easily deny her confession, and that would be the end of it. Plus, several mysteries remained. Even if Aisha were detained, somebody else might get to her first, like they had with the earrings.

"…Scarlett, let's go," Connie whispered, leading the way out of the Huxley residence. She had made up her mind.

"Are you all right?"

Randolph was waiting outside the front gate. Connie had told him she was meeting with Aisha today, and she guessed he'd come by to check on her.

For some reason, the moment Connie saw his stern face, she nearly burst into tears. But she managed to hold them back and tell him briefly what had happened.

"…It was Aisha. She poisoned the Luze family water jug. But she didn't know it was poison. And she says she wasn't the one who switched the earrings or put the poison bottle in Scarlett's room."

"I see. Is there anything that could be used as evidence?"

"She said she still has the bottle from back then. I think the one found in Scarlett's room was put there by someone else."

"From ten years ago? It will definitely take time to prove her story." Randolph frowned, narrowing his cerulean eyes.

"Also, I'm not sure whether it's related, but Aisha uses Jackal's Paradise."

"…So she's involved with Daeg Gallus, as I thought. I'll send someone to watch her. We'll know right away if she tries to do anything."

Connie nodded. She had much more to tell him, but she felt too exhausted to continue. Randolph raised his eyebrows slightly and told her he'd take her home. Taking her hand, he helped her into the carriage. He sat down across from her and silently took out the documents he'd brought with him.

The rustling of paper was the only sound. Since Randolph seemed busy, Connie didn't feel bad about staying silent.

In other words—he was probably doing it for her sake.

They arrived at her house without having exchanged a single word. When she looked up at him apologetically, he patted her head as if to say, *Don't worry about it.*

"Once you've had a chance to rest, tell me all the details."

Back in Connie's room, Scarlett spoke up.

"*Why did you stop her?*" she asked in a low voice. "*We'd be better off if she'd died then and there. If we can't put her in jail, we might as well send her straight to hell!*"

Her amethyst eyes were glowing.

"*You're an idiot, Connie! Why did you save her?! She was the one! She was the one who—*"

"Because!" Connie said, forcing herself to fight back. "It would be no joke for her to take her own life because of something you said!"

When Connie witnessed Aisha Huxley attempt to throw away her life without a second's hesitation, she had felt pure fury.

"I would never be able to forgive her—using you as an excuse until her final moment…!"

Scarlett's eyes widened in surprise.

Connie squeezed her hand into a fist and continued.

"Plus, if Aisha died now, we might lose our only clue. In the end, all Aisha put in the water jug was ordinary medicine. But those ornamental fish died. Someone must have switched the tonic for poison."

"*Yes, or…maybe it was poison to start with, and Aisha simply didn't realize,*" Scarlett said, shaking her head sternly. Connie frowned.

"…What do you mean?"

"*What if Aisha's cousin was lying? Maybe it was Jackal's Paradise in that bottle, not a weight-loss tonic. If you take too much of that kind of hallucinogen, I've heard you lose your appetite and you can stay up for days. Anyone would lose weight if they did that for long enough. Aisha herself is skinny as a stick. Take too much of any medicine and it becomes poison. She poured in the whole bottle of something that works with just one drop. That could easily have been a deadly dose.*"

For the first time, Scarlett's face looked as uneasy as a lost child's. She must have been thinking about it ever since they'd left the Huxley residence. She glanced down.

"…Maybe everything that happened ten years ago was the result of mistakes and coincidence," she blurted out. "If that's the case, then I—"

"But even if that's how it began," Connie broke in, "somebody put that poison bottle in your room. Someone switched the earrings. And we still don't know what happened to Lily, or what Daeg Gallus is up to."

Scarlett looked up and blinked in astonishment.

"Your revenge is still far from complete. Listen to me, Scarlett. I…"

Connie remembered the absurd words Scarlett had spoken when they first met.

I saved you, and I won't take no for an answer!

Constance Grail, prepare yourself.

"I…promised to devote my life to making sure you get your revenge!"

Starting on that day, Connie's fate had been transformed.

Scarlett froze at the sight of Connie with her hand on her hip, spewing out words with utter confidence.

"…Occasionally you do say things that make sense," she said, then burst out laughing. "How saucy! Are you sure you're Connie?"

Several days passed before anything happened.

Abigail had summoned Connie to her home, and she and Randolph had gone together. Apparently, it was a matter of great urgency.

Abigail and Aldous Clayton were already waiting in the drawing room.

"Someone contacted the *Mayflower* yesterday," Aldous said. "Apparently, Aisha Huxley confessed her guilt in the execution of Scarlett Castiel." The room went silent. Connie stared at him wide-eyed, Scarlett frowned, and Randolph blinked slowly.

It was Abigail who broke the silence.

"Quite a scoop, isn't it?" she said with a smile.

"What…?" Connie finally managed to say, breaking out of her shock.

Randolph rested his hand on his chin pensively.

"I was sure she'd go to Daeg Gallus for help. This is a surprise indeed."

©Yu-nagi

According to the guard he'd assigned to watch her, for the past several days Aisha Huxley had made no attempt to see anyone outside her own household. He, too, had been concerned about her movements.

Connie remembered the way Aisha had nodded when she spoke about staying alive to make amends.

Was this her answer?

"I guess interacting with Scarlett hit her hard," Connie said. "And maybe she has something to do with Daeg Gallus but isn't actually a member. At the very least, she doesn't seem to have been in contact with them ten years ago."

It was true that Aisha hadn't said the words "Jackal's Paradise" or "Daeg Gallus" when she talked about the assassination attempt on the crown princess. She had no reason to hide the truth in that situation. Aisha wanted Scarlett to forgive her. If someone else was behind her actions, it would have made sense for her to mention them.

"Aisha was an ardent admirer of Scarlett's," Abigail said. "It wouldn't have been surprising if her guilty conscience forced her to come clean eventually. We still don't know if Daeg Gallus was behind it, but even if they weren't, they would have wanted to avoid suspicion that the poison was Jackal's Paradise. It's one of their sources of income, after all. I wonder if they approached Aisha after it happened."

She narrowed her eyes in obvious hatred.

"It would have been easy for them to take advantage of Aisha's wounded mental state. If they got her hooked on drugs, her guilty conscience would fade, and her movements would be easier to monitor. I heard Aisha has had a lover for some years now. Most likely he belongs to the organization, and Aisha is a valued customer and regular buyer of Jackal's Paradise—don't you think that seems likely?"

She glanced at Aldous, and he picked up her thread.

"According to Constance, Aisha poisoned the water, but beyond that, she knew nothing. Which means that even if we captured her, we wouldn't get much information. In fact, the current situation is probably more than we could have wished for. We can make the first move and deal the crooks a blow."

"As they say, the pen is mightier than the sword," Abigail agreed. "And no matter how hard they try to destroy evidence and hide the truth, they can't sew up people's mouths. If an article comes out, people all over the capital will be talking about it. Then the other papers will come out with their own pieces, leading to a movement to reassess what happened ten years ago. You'd be surprised how hard it is to ignore the voice of the people. We'll use that to our advantage."

Connie listened in amazement to their easy back-and-forth.

Of course, that would be an excellent turn of events. If Aisha's testimony led to a reassessment of the events of ten years ago, Scarlett's guilt would surely be overturned.

But—

"What's wrong, Miss Grail?" Randolph asked, noticing her glum expression. Connie hesitated before replying.

"Um, I was just wondering…about Amelia Hobbes."

The redheaded reporter who had railed against Scarlett had inevitably come to mind. She worked for the *Mayflower*, and if she happened to get involved in this story, a perfect opportunity could be flipped on its head.

"Ah, I see," Aldous said with a wry smile.

"Who?" Abigail asked.

"A colleague, more or less," came the irritated answer. "There's nothing to worry about. Last week, I think it was, the editor switched her assignment to restaurants and plays, uncontroversial things like that. She wasn't happy about it, but she had it coming. She's very ambitious and made a lot of trouble. A gag order's been issued for anything related to Aisha, so there's no way she'll find out."

That was a relief to hear. With her worries calmed, happiness welled up in Connie. She looked up, and her eyes met Scarlett's. Scarlett gave her an annoyed look.

All the same, Connie couldn't help smiling.

"At the very least, this should clear the false accusation…!"

Scarlet snorted.

"Ha! That's far from enough to clear my mood," she said in her usual spiteful tone, pursing her lips in a pout. But her eyes were not as harsh as her words. *"After all, I still haven't slapped that woman!"*

Amelia Hobbes stepped into her old office after nearly a week away, having been told she needed to fix some documents connected to her transfer.

"Awfully hectic around here…"

Cigarette smoke filled the room. Desks were piled with article drafts and documents. But there was a nervousness to the atmosphere that puzzled her.

"Fine time to be lolling around when we've got the scoop of the decade to report!" someone wailed theatrically behind her, having overheard her mumbled comment.

Amelia's eyebrows shot up.

"…A scoop?" she couldn't help asking, turning around.

A panicked look overcame the other reporter's face.

"Oh, damn. You changed departments, didn't you? I totally forgot."

He scratched his head and made a move to escape, but Amelia stopped him.

"Hey, don't be so surly. Just because I'm on a different beat, you treat me like a stranger? Weren't we colleagues a week ago? I could see how I might get in your way if I worked for a different paper, but as things stand, my hands are tied. If you've got a scoop, at least let me congratulate you!"

The man hesitated momentarily, then, perhaps feeling guilty, whispered a warning not to tell anyone.

"Actually, we've turned up some new facts about Scarlett Castiel's execution. It looks like the notorious vixen may have been falsely accused. I can't say anything specific, but sometime next week we should be coming out with an exclusive."

Amelia's eyes widened. "That's amazing."

"Isn't it? Hey, where are you going?" the reporter exclaimed as his red-headed colleague hurried out of the room.

She paused, looked around, and said very cheerfully, "I can't let you fellows beat me. I'm going hunting for an even bigger scoop."

"A scoop? But you're the theater reporter…!" the man cried after her, but she was already gone.

Suppressing her impatience, Amelia left the building and headed for the main street. Halfway there she boarded a fiacre.

She got off in front of the grand palace in the center of the city and lined up by the public gate.

"Please say that Amelia Hobbes is here."

"Whom shall I tell?" the trim woman at the desk asked her in a businesslike tone.

Amelia smiled, her grayish-green eyes narrowing.

"Rufus May."

※

That day, the editor-in-chief, Marcella, had instructed Aldous to visit the Huxley residence for an article on Aisha Huxley's confession.

The rain that had started at dawn was coming down heavier now, and he could hear it pounding the street outside. He climbed down from his carriage and planted his feet on the muddy ground. The rain washed his footprints away as soon as he made them.

People called rain the tears of the goddesses. According to a story from the Book of Genesis, it fell to wash away the sins of the world.

If that was true—then whose sins were these tears meant to absolve?

Once Aldous had announced his business, an elderly maid came out to greet him.

"The viscountess is in her room," the woman told him hoarsely, leading him down a long hallway.

The house was dim, though whether it was like that always or only today, he did not know. They climbed the creaky spiral staircase, and the maid paused to look back at Aldous.

"The viscountess's rooms are at the end of the corridor," she said flatly. "I've had all the servants leave so you can speak in private."

She bowed and returned the way they had come. In other words, he was to go on alone from there.

Just as he stepped forward, a valet pushing a cart came out of a room at the end of the hallway. The cart was covered with a white cloth, on top of which were a ceramic cutlery tray and a teapot. He must have been serving tea. The slim young man met Aldous's eyes and nodded quietly. He pulled his cart into a corner and bowed his head, letting Aldous pass.

Aldous passed the valet and knocked on the door before he suddenly realized something was off.

Hadn't the maid just said she'd had all the servants leave?

He spun around, but the hallway was empty. Only the unmanned cart remained.

"Shit!" Aldous spat out. "Aisha!"

He stepped into the room. A bloodied female form lay on the floor. Despite the quantity of blood, she seemed to be semiconscious. He hurriedly lifted her into a sitting position and searched for her wound—then gasped. Her carotid artery had been severed clear through. It was a perfect cut. A bloody dessert knife lay beside her.

As he held her speechlessly, she twitched.

"...Th-they t-took...the bo...ttle."

"Shhh, don't talk. I'm going to stop the bleeding," he said, starting to move.

Her eyes stopped him.

I know I'm done for, they said.

"...It was...Sal...vador, from Daeg...Gallus."

She must be talking about the man disguised as a valet. Aldous looked Aisha in the eye and nodded firmly.

"Ask…my cousin…Sharon…she'll know…something…"

"I understand. Anything else?"

The light was quickly fading from Aisha's eyes.

"I…made…a mistake, but…," she gasped. "Will…Scar…lett forgive… me…?"

Aldous did not know the answer. He hadn't known Scarlett when she was alive, like Abigail had, and he couldn't see her ghost like Lucia.

Nevertheless, he answered without hesitation that she would. The simple, good-natured Constance Grail flashed across his mind. That's what she would have said.

And the rain was still coming down.

The tears of the goddess would wash her sin away.

"I'm gla—"

With that, Aisha Huxley expired, a girlishly innocent smile on her lips.

Aldous gently closed her eyelids. Right away, his mind began to analyze what had just happened.

They'd gotten to her first. That was certain. Later on, he could look into who had leaked the information. The immediate question was whether they'd been after him specifically.

In other words, did they know he was Rudy the bodyguard from the Folkvangr—and did they intend to entrap Abigail O'Brian? He could answer that easily enough. It wasn't likely. Aldous's assignment had been decided that morning. Another reporter had originally been scheduled to interview Aisha, but he'd been late getting to work because of the rain, and Aldous had been selected to go in his place.

In other words, they didn't care who it was. Their goal was for Aisha's murderer to be captured immediately. They wanted the investigation to end quickly, on the assumption that it was an unpremeditated act. They definitely didn't want anyone poking around Aisha's affairs.

The trap was already set. All that remained was to wait for the mouse to step into it. No doubt if Aldous was arrested, abundant evidence related to Aisha's murder would fortuitously appear.

Which left him only one way to outwit them.

Aldous swiftly pushed open the window in one corner of the room. A strong gust blew inside, ruffling his hair. He looked down. Fortunately, a fine old oak tree was growing below the window. If he jumped right, it should break his fall. He made a mental note of the garden's layout.

He heard footsteps running toward the room. No doubt the man named Salvador had called someone. He had prepared well, but on the other hand, it gave Aldous a momentary opportunity. While the servants were gathered on the second floor, he might be able to escape through the back gate.

"Murderer…!" he heard someone scream from outside the wide-open door. Aldous clicked his tongue, stepped onto the window frame, and leapt into the air.

Rain was dripping onto the floor. Patches of the ceiling in the decrepit building had rotted away, letting in the rain. Here and there, floorboards were coming up, and the walls were cracked. But still, the image of the goddess in the arched stained glass window overhead peered down calmly.

They were in a church in the slums.

A woman wearing a deep, dingy hood was sitting on a bench praying fervently when the stooped young man crept silently in. He sat down beside the woman, whose face was pressed against her knees with her fingers laced together, and he spoke in a carefree voice as if he were humming a song:

"Kiriki kirikuku."

The woman sighed softly. "Lie low and stay calm," she answered, slowly raising her face. "I heard the journalist got away."

"So it seems," Salvador said, shrugging as if it had nothing to do with him. Cecilia couldn't help giving him a nasty glare. He ignored her, instead laughing frivolously.

"Anyway," he went on. As usual, she had no idea what was going through his mind. "Seems like you're unclear on my role here. I was assigned to kill that bag of bones, nothing more. Also, Krishna was the one who came up with the plan and the one who assigned the personnel. In other words, I'm not the one who messed up. Krishna is. If you've got a complaint, say it to him. I think he's going by the name Linus—no, Rufus May right now."

Salvador's reddish-gold eyes widened in amusement. Cecilia had heard that Krishna and Salvador didn't get along, and the rumor seemed to be true. Judging by his attitude, he seemed genuinely delighted by Krishna's blunder.

"...All the same," Salvador continued, "I hardly expected to be outdone by a mere journalist. According to Amelia Hobbes, Aldous is a cowardly half-wit with no ambition, but I wonder who he really is."

Cecilia, too, had heard about the plan in advance and had never imagined he would be able to slip away without a trace. There seemed to be more to him than met the eye.

But his identity wasn't what mattered right now.

"The important thing is that you find him and capture him right away. It will be a pain if they end up investigating Aisha's affairs."

"That's why we set things up so he'd be arrested on the spot. I wish we'd never gotten involved to start with. We didn't have anything to do with Scarlett Castiel's execution."

Salvador's position ten years ago had been essentially the same as it was today. Get rid of people who were in the way—that was all. He'd never had a public presence like Cecilia and Krishna. That was probably why he didn't know the details.

It was true that Daeg Gallus had not *predicted* Scarlett Castiel's execution.

But...

"The problem is who gave Aisha that bottle."

They hadn't been completely uninvolved. The substance Aisha had gotten her hands on was a forerunner of Jackal's Paradise, still under development. Simply put, it was a failed attempt. They had intended to make the drug more addictive but had ended up making it more poison-ous by mistake.

"Sharon, was it? Just couldn't keep her mouth shut. We'll have to be sure she's more careful from now on—oh, wait, she's already dead."

Salvador laughed cynically.

He was right—by now, Sharon should have already been taken care of by someone else.

"But don't you think this is going too far? You'll trip yourself up by being so obvious."

"...Ten years ago, we failed because we overlooked a minor coincidence."

That was why she was determined to nip all the buds this time around. Salvador, however, seemed to have a different opinion. As Cecilia took in his vaguely critical expression, doubt rose within her.

"You didn't do it on purpose, did you?"

"Do what?"

"You wouldn't have let Aldous Clayton get away intentionally, would you? You failed to bring down a target once before, I believe."

Salvador widened his eyes and tilted his head.

"Before? Oh, *that*?" he said, as if her meaning had just registered. Then he grimaced like it was funny. "That was your fault, don't you think, Cess? You said she was an ordinary noble brat. An overprotected, hypo-critical little thing with nothing to her beyond kindness. Nothing to worry about."

"That's not—"

"And who was it that got tripped up by the sweet little thing? Who spilled our secrets to her? That alone would be embarrassing enough. But she even managed to hide the critical information. The higher-ups said to get it out of her even if I had to kill her, but she killed herself before I could. What could I do? There were signs she hid the information. But years have passed, and we still don't know where it is. All we know is that a key exists and it provides some sort of clue."

Salvador coughed and looked at Cecilia, his eyes narrowed.

"As it turned out, she was quite the opponent, that Lily Orlamunde."

※

With a crash, the teacup slipped from her fingers and shattered, splashing tea on her feet and surrounding the chair with ceramic shards. Marta, the maid, ran to fetch a broom and dustpan. But Connie didn't move. She couldn't move. She simply stared in shock.

The front page of the morning newspaper was spread out before her. "What in the world...?"

The article said that the *Mayflower* reporter Aldous Clayton had been named a suspect in the killing of Viscountess Aisha Huxley.

※

"With that, I conclude my report on the murder of Aisha Huxley. Considering that no physical evidence has been found, it is premature to name Aldous Clayton a suspect," Randolph said, standing with his back to a door carved with a lion and sword.

He was in a room in the Royal Security Force headquarters. Located on the top floor at the very end of the hall, it was the one and only opulently decorated room in an organization that prioritized practicality. Partly, that was because it was the room where guests were received. There was a sofa near the door for that reason, and on the right and left walls hung the flag of Adelbide and the Security Force insignia.

Beyond the sofa was a desk of pollard oak with a lustrous, intricate grain and a black leather armchair.

Only one man in the entire organization was permitted to sit in that seat, which symbolized the apex of the Security Force.

"Jeorg Gaina said there was a witness."

As he listened to Randolph's report, the man ran his eyes over the documents stacked on his desk, signing and stamping them one after the next.

"As you will see in the testimony, the witness only saw Aldous next to the victim. They did not witness the crime take place."

"I see. But the fact remains that Aldous Clayton fled the scene. How do you explain that?"

"I can't know without asking him. At the present time, he is no more than a key witness. And what would his motivation be, in any case? Of course, locating his whereabouts is a top priority, but I believe we also need to investigate Aisha Huxley's social connections."

"Jeorg Gaina wanted to bring him in for questioning immediately."

"Yes. It's likely he already has the perfect story all worked out," Randolph said with dripping irony. He heard a coughing sound. When he looked up, the man's hand was pressed to his mouth and his shoulders were shaking. But he must not have been able to control himself—or perhaps he hadn't intended to from the start—because he broke out laughing, holding his stomach.

When his laughter died down, the man let out a long sigh.

"I've been thinking for a while now that he's a little weak on the follow-through."

Royal Security Force Commandant Duran Belsford rested his elbows carelessly on the elegant desk and smiled with malice. He had sharp eyes and graying hair swept back from his forehead. Despite his fierce appearance, however, he was a happy drunk and took good care of his subordinates, who affectionately called him Pops.

Wiping away the tears that had collected in the corners of his eyes from the bout of laughter, he said, "Oh yes," as if he'd just remembered something. "I hear you've been looking into the Scarlett Castiel case. You, or I suppose I should say, your fiancée."

Randolph's face twitched, and he narrowed his eyes without responding.

"Listen here, Randolph. I'm your superior. Not just any superior, either—I'm the commandant. That's a mighty important title. So you'd better stop making that scary face at me. I'll have nightmares. Nightmares,

I say! Anyhow, that's the reason they went after Aisha Huxley, isn't it? It's quite a feat to convince someone who managed to keep quiet for ten years, and that's not all the Grail girl's been up to, I hear."

The Duran domain was on the border with Faris, in what Duran called "the damned boonies," and he made no attempt to hide his country accent. He'd been the youngest of five children, left to do as he pleased, and apparently had spent his days playing with commoners instead of learning the manners of a noble.

Starting out by leading local kids in childhood mischief, he had gone straight into a position defending the borders from the northern tribes. And when the army's central command heard about his achievements, they invited him to the capital to join the Royal Security Force. That was thirty years ago.

Although his battlefield had changed from the borderlands to the capital, and his enemy from raiders to criminals, his skills were no less impressive. He was the youngest person to rise to the position of commandant in the history of the organization. His nickname, Duran the Immortal, referred to his many brushes with death, including his false accusation and near execution ten years ago, from which he was once again freed at the very last moment.

Randolph sighed. "I see you are well-informed," he acknowledged. He hadn't gone out of his way to make a secret of any of it, but he was nevertheless impressed by the effectiveness of Duran's network. Suddenly, a question occurred to him.

"You're not looking into the false charges against Scarlett, are you?"

He wondered if Duran knew something. But the older man simply shrugged.

"I'm more concerned with Faris at the moment. The last report said they were preparing for war. If that's the case, it must be us they're after."

This unexpected turn in the conversation threw Randolph off balance.

"We've been building friendly relations with Faris for decades. So long as we don't make a hostile move ourselves, they have no cause to go to war with us. If they were to suddenly invade, I can't imagine our other neighbors would sit by silently and watch it happen."

It was true that disturbing developments were underway in neighboring Faris. Namely, they were preparing for war. That was a fact, but Randolph didn't think they were turning on Adelbide. There may have been sparks aplenty to cause a war a few hundred years ago, but today the two countries were allies. They had a peace treaty. If Faris unilaterally abrogated it, neighboring countries would surely take them to task. Faris would naturally become isolated.

When Randolph said as much to Duran, he dismissed the idea with a snort.

"Cause for war? They can make one up easily enough. Did you know, Randolph, that our kingdom is fairly unpopular?"

"…Unpopular?"

"Adelbide is rich in resources and water. Plenty of people are jealous of how much we've advanced in a mere few hundred years. Faris, in particular, views us as their own former territory. It wouldn't surprise me if they thought taking that territory back was entirely justifiable. All the more so given they're hard up these days."

"But do you genuinely think they plan to go to war with us…?"

Duran smiled wryly at Randolph's puzzlement and nodded.

"I do. But that's not to say I'll let them," he muttered, directing his piercing gaze into the distance. Overwhelmed by the strength of that gaze, Randolph nevertheless recalled something.

Ten years ago, Duran had nearly been executed. But just before it happened, Scarlett was beheaded, and the subsequent protests by a citizens' organization led to the suspension of all executions. Saved by a hair's breadth, Duran used his reprieve to gather evidence of his innocence. Which is to say, if Scarlett hadn't been executed, Duran would no longer be alive.

After thinking that far, Randolph felt a sudden unease. There was something going on there. But before he could figure out what it was, Duran's voice called him back to the present.

"That's the job of those of us lucky enough to be alive," he murmured very quietly.

※

"Blast it, I can't imagine anything more disappointing!"

A clear voice rang through the Folkvangr, home of the most beautiful flowers of Rosenkreuz Street.

"There I was enjoying time off with my boy toy, and some mongrel gets himself added to the most wanted list?! I was so furious, I came straight back!"

The elderly woman looked refined and well-dressed, but her language was shockingly biting. Connie, who was sitting on a plush sofa drinking a cup of tea, couldn't help staring up wide-eyed at the intruder.

"Audrey, if you lose your temper like that, your blood pressure will go up again!" Miriam admonished her lackadaisically, her plentiful bosom swaying. Miriam was the prostitute in highest demand at the Folkvangr, and she was currently sitting beside Connie on the sofa.

Without a glance at Miriam or Connie, the elderly woman pointed at a divan by the wall.

"What's a wanted murderer doing here to start with?!"

The man reclining on the divan, newspaper in hand, was none other than Aldous Clayton.

He gave the woman a sidelong glance.

"Be quiet, you old skinflint," he muttered before returning to his newspaper. The woman's eyebrows shot up in surprise.

"They said you went and killed a viscountess," she said loudly. "I've always known you were a stupid dog! Leaving a trail like that...if you're going to do something, at least do it well!"

"...This time I was framed. You don't see me messing up on the regular."

"Well, your horrible attitude hasn't changed! That's why you screw up, stray!"

"Listen, old lady! I'm telling you, I didn't do it…!" Aldous said, finally hurling his newspaper aside and sitting up to fight back. Needless to say, the woman was not about to take this in silence. The two of them glared at each other furiously, then launched into an exchange of expletives.

Connie was staring at them in terror when Miriam leaned over and whispered into her ear.

"I've heard that in the old days, Audrey was the most popular girl at this establishment. Time is cruel, isn't it?"

"Shut up, Miriam. She can hear you," said Rebekah, snorting. She had just come in with a tray of cookies. Rebekah was another beauty who, though less voluptuous than Miriam, was the more competitive of the two. "Lady Audrey is our teacher."

Connie gave her a puzzled look.

"She teaches us how to bring in the gentlemen," Miriam added with a smile. "Also how to choose our dresses and makeup. And how to talk and behave, and generally act like cultivated ladies. Training the women here is Audrey's job."

Lady Audrey must have heard them whispering, because she finally turned in their direction.

"If you ask me, that tomboy Abigail and little Theodore are both still wet behind the ears. Not to mention, the former Duke O'Brian directly entrusted this establishment's operation to me. It is my duty to guard it."

She paused for a moment to glare at Aldous. Connie stood up, unable to stand the tension.

"I-it's Aldous Clayton, from the *Mayflower*, who they've put on the wanted list, isn't it?" she asked.

There was a moment of silence before a sharp gaze pierced Connie. She forced herself to go on, although she would rather have retreated.

"I don't see what that has to do with Mr. Rudy, the bodyguard at the Folkvangr…"

Audrey raised her eyebrows unhappily. Then she crossed her arms and looked Connie over from head to toe, appraising her.

"…And who are you?"

"C-Constance Grail."

Audrey turned to Miriam and Rebekah with the same stern expression. "Since when do we hire pug-nosed girls?!" she asked.

"I think Connie's adorable!" Miriam pouted. Audrey said no more, apparently befuddled, and stared at the "ugly girl" intently. A bead of sweat ran down Connie's cheek. Finally, Lady Audrey pressed her hand to her forehead like she was battling a headache and dramatically gazed up at the ceiling. Incomprehensible.

Several days before, Abigail had contacted Connie to tell her the Folkvangr was sheltering Aldous.

Fortunately, neither the Security Force nor Daeg Gallus seemed to realize that Aldous Clayton and Rudy from Rosenkreuz Street were the same man. So for the time being, he should be able to safely stay hidden at the brothel.

Right now, Abigail was running around trying to prove Aldous's innocence, and she'd asked Connie to look in on him in her place, as well as to calm things down in time for the *lady's* return.

Connie wasn't sure if she'd succeeded on this last point, but for now, Aldous seemed to have avoided being ejected from the brothel.

One week had passed since Aisha Huxley was killed.

Marcella, the *Mayflower*'s editor-in-chief, had resigned after her reporter was named a suspect in the homicide. For some reason, the employee selected to succeed her was Amelia Hobbes.

"That redhead must have sold her soul to the devil," Scarlett said with a scowl. Connie was in complete agreement.

Lady Audrey was apparently very busy, and she dragged Aldous off by the ear, saying, "Those who don't work, don't eat!" After they were gone, Miriam and Rebecca said they had better get ready for the evening. Before they left, they mentioned that "the Grim Reaper should be here to pick you up soon," so Connie stayed where she was to wait for him.

As Connie sat in a daze, teacup in hand, Scarlett gave her a puzzled look.

"What's wrong?"

Connie hesitated before answering. "…Aisha was killed because of what happened ten years ago, wasn't she?"

"It seems that way."

"And you said that the poison she put in the water jug at the Luze residence might have been Jackal's Paradise, right? If that's the case, then I'm sure Daeg Gallus must have been involved in some way."

"Yes, I think so, too."

But that wasn't all. Even after the incident ten years ago…

"I think they might have been involved in Miss Lily's death, too," Connie said.

There was the phrase "kiriki kirikuku," and what José, the man who kidnapped Kate, had said.

"…Yes."

"So if we can figure out the mystery of the key and the meaning of 'the Holy Grail of Eris'…"

Wouldn't that help them solve the case? Just as Connie was about to say that, however, someone interrupted her.

"About that key—I found the workshop that manufactured it."

She looked over her shoulder.

"Your Excellency…!"

Randolph, who had appeared without her even noticing, nodded and pulled a shiny, dark gray object from his breast pocket.

He held the simple, warded key on his palm—the very key she had just been talking about.

"Unfortunately, this isn't strictly speaking a key."

"…It isn't?"

"It has the shape of a key, but it fits no lock. In other words, it's a fake. According to the person I spoke with at the workshop, the design is commonly used for decorations. But."

Randolph paused to point at the model number engraved on the circular portion at the top.

"He said Lily specifically requested this engraving."

Connie gasped, squinting at the code. It read P10E3.

What if it wasn't a model number but instead a message that Lily Orlamunde had left behind?

"In other words," Randolph said in his low voice, "that is the puzzle we must solve."

Once again, they had reached an impasse in the puzzle of Lily's key. And the key itself wasn't even the mystery that needed solving—it was the engraving.

A day had passed since Randolph met Connie at the Folkvangr to tell her the latest developments. She had stayed up the entire night thinking about it but, of course, hadn't arrived at an answer.

She had some paperwork related to her engagement to do at the church that day, and it was for that reason she had come to Anastasia Street. She was walking along, brooding over the lack of progress, when someone suddenly called out to her.

"Excuse me, miss?"

She turned around. A tall woman with a messy braid the color of sunshine was standing behind her. She had ultramarine eyes and freckled cheeks. Thick eyebrows framed a healthy-looking face. *She must be a tourist*, Connie thought. Over one shoulder, she was carrying a cloth-wrapped bundle about as tall as a person.

"May I ask you directions? I'm a sightseer here."

"Yes, of course."

A woman traveling alone for pleasure was rare. The woman must have recognized the doubt on Connie's face, because she nodded and smiled.

"I do have a traveling companion with me, but I don't see her at the moment. Wherever could she have gone off to?"

She scanned the wide road, scratching her cheek. Unsurprisingly, she failed to find her friend. Her smile became strained.

"Perhaps she went on to our destination ahead of me. Actually, we want to see the famous Grand Merillian. Anyone visiting this kingdom ought to see it at least once, don't you think?"

It was true that the lavish detached palace was one of the capital's most famous attractions. And luckily, it was within walking distance. Connie nodded and pointed down the road.

"If you head down this main street for a little while toward Saint Mark's Square—"

Her explanation was interrupted by a yell from the crowd.

"San!"

A slender, pretty woman with hair like moonlight streaming down her back came running toward them.

"I looked everywhere for you!" the newcomer cried. "I know you're curious, but I've told you a million times not to wander off! You've got an awful sense of direction!"

"What are you talking about? You're the one who's always getting lost, Eularia," the tall woman called San countered, laughing easily. "I was just asking directions."

The woman who had been angrily berating San slumped her shoulders. "Sure, that must be it… I'm the one who's lost… But somehow, I'm always the one who ends up finding you! Anyway, here's the tourism booklet we got at that restaurant! You said we didn't need it, but look here. At the bottom of this page about the palace, there's a letter and number written in Adelbidian, see? And it shows where the palace is on the map at the front of the booklet. The letter is for the column, and the number is for the row."

"Wow, you're so smart, Eularia!" San exclaimed. Eularia narrowed her eyes.

"They have this kind of thing in most large cities, whatever kingdom you're in. You're really too sheltered, you know? I picked up two pamphlets, so you take this one. Let's go. And don't forget to thank that lady."

The slender woman grabbed San's sleeve and pulled so hard, Connie wondered where in her small body she stored all that strength. Judging by her confident steps, she knew exactly where she was going.

As San let herself be dragged off, she turned a childlike grin toward Connie.

"Thank you, kind miss. My name is San. Please allow me to repay you at a later date. Oh, wait, take this. I don't need it—I've got a great sense of direction."

She winked and, with a flowing, natural motion, pushed the pamphlet into Connie's grasp. Eularia spun around and glared at her, but San seemed not to care in the least. She waved happily at Connie.

"What's your name, miss?"

"C-Constance. Constance Grail."

"Grail?"

San blinked, then slowly smiled.

"What a lovely name."

"I wonder what she had in that big bundle," Scarlett said as she watched the two of them disappear into the crowd.

"...Scarlett?"

"What?"

"...Do you remember the code inscribed on Lily's key?"

"What? Oh, yes, of course I do, but—"

Scarlett raised one eyebrow suspiciously, but Connie wasn't paying attention.

"I th-think I just figured it out!" she said shakily, looking up at Scarlett. Scarlett blinked in confusion.

Connie was holding the pamphlet San had just given her. It was one of those tourist guides you could pick up anywhere in the capital. A moment earlier, she had absently flipped it open and felt an odd flash of recognition. The page contained an explanation of the climate and geography of Adelbide. Simple and easy to understand, nothing strange at all. Still, something about it caught her attention. She felt like she'd read it before.

But where?

Sifting through her memories, she suddenly figured it out. It was from the message Lily had left behind.

The phrase about the "Holy Grail of Eris" was scribbled on a scrap of paper. Searching for any clue she could find, Connie had carefully read the printed text as well as the note. That was why she remembered. That same text was on the page she was looking at now.

At the time, she'd thought to herself that it must be from one of those tourism brochures put out by city hall or the like.

That meant that Lily had used a page from this pamphlet. Connie had thought that the scrap of paper had nothing to do with the message, but what if it did?

What if the meaning wasn't only in the words, but also in the paper they were written on?

"If I recall correctly, the engraving was P10E3," Scarlett said. Connie let out a long breath.

P10E3—most likely, P10 referred to page 10. With shaking hands, she flipped open the pamphlet. Page 10 contained a simplified map of the capital, overlaid with a grid of vertical and horizontal lines.

The letter is for the column, and the number is for the row.

Wasn't that what the woman named Eularia had said? The numbers and letters were used to identify locations on the map. E was the column, and 3 was the row. They pointed to…

"Saint Mark's Square."

The place where Scarlett was executed.

Was it deliberate or a coincidence? Either way, it was a step forward. But the area identified was larger than she'd expected. The square also contained the city hall. Connie bit her lip, wondering what to do next.

"The history museum," Scarlett whispered.

"What?"

"You went there the other day with Randolph, didn't you? He said they had received a donation from the Orlamunde family. The place is under constant guard. That must be the hiding place, don't you think?"

Footsteps echoed through the deserted museum. There was no sign of the guards, leaving Connie and Randolph alone in the building.

When Connie told Randolph about her latest discovery, he brought her to the museum right away and asked for the director. When he appeared, Randolph announced that someone may have planted a suspicious object in the museum and had the director remove everyone from the building.

"I couldn't very well tell him we were going to damage the Orlamunde family's holy scripture," Randolph explained, shrugging off his white lie as he lifted up the ring of keys the director had loaned him. Scarlett nodded emphatically.

"Wise move. If he knew the truth, he'd faint from shock. Anyway, Lily really did plant a suspicious object here," she joked. By then, they had arrived at the donation in question. There, in the glass case, was the old, yellowed book and, in front of it, the new copy.

"If she was going to hide something," said Scarlett, *"I think it would be in the original, not the replica."*

"B-but isn't this a valuable historical relic…?" Connie asked.

It was one of the scriptures Saint Anastasia was said to have received from a messenger of the goddesses. Several generations back, the then-Duke of Orlamunde was said to have exhausted all means to obtain it, finally winning it in a black-market auction.

Scarlett nodded knowingly. *"That's exactly why she would put it here. Who would dare touch such a precious object?"*

"What an outrageous thing to do…"

"She was an outrageous woman."

Connie felt like she'd had a similar conversation with Scarlett in the past. It had been a mere few months earlier, but it felt like a lifetime ago. Or was she imagining things?

"I'm opening it," Randolph said, inserting a key into a lock on the glass case.

The smell of dust and mold assaulted Connie's nose.

Randolph carefully picked up the ancient scripture.

"...As far as I can see, there's nothing unusual here."

"Of course not," Scarlett said. *"After all, there's always a chance someone might pick up the book. She wouldn't hide it anywhere obvious. What would Lily do... How about the back cover?"*

"Scarlett is saying to check the back cover," Connie told Randolph. He carefully checked the back of the book, but there didn't seem to be anything there. He shook his head, then opened the volume and ran his finger over the inside.

One of his eyebrows shot up.

"...There's a slight indentation. I wonder if it's a sign that the paper was replaced...," he muttered, pulling a knife from his breast pocket. Connie flinched in surprise. Without a moment's pause, he ran the blade over the paper as smoothly as if he were cutting open a letter. Apparently, Lily Orlamunde wasn't the only person who allotted scant value to historical treasures.

"Found it," he announced, pulling out a white envelope.

※

Two women who looked like tourists stood chatting in front of a fountain in the Grand Merillian courtyard.

"The bald old goat certainly is late. He's a bit young to go senile, isn't he?"

"I imagine moving an old body like that must take time."

To the casual observer, they created a peaceful scene, though their topic of conversation was far from tranquil.

Presently, the man they were waiting for arrived.

"Hey there, Grandpa. You've lost some more hair, I see."

San smiled, raising one hand in a casual greeting.

"...I've had a lot to worry about," he answered sourly. "All the more so now that I hear Princess Alexandra has been locked up."

Kendall Levine, the ambassador from Faris, squinted slightly, then gave San a probing look. She smiled wryly.

"True, true. We've got to get Allie out of there fast."

Normally, San would have dropped whatever she was doing to save the imprisoned woman.

"But first, we have to fix the Ulysses situation."

Circumstances, however, had made that difficult.

"It seems the war hawks led by Fourth Prince Theophilis would like to claim that Adelbide struck first by harming the seventh prince. They need an excuse for seizing all this fertile land. Although it seems that when they tried that ten years ago, Adelbide managed to pull one over on them."

San glared up at Kendall Levine.

"If we don't find the boy—there will be war."

※

Randolph handed Connie the envelope he'd pulled from the holy scripture. Aside from the fact that it was not addressed to anyone, it looked completely ordinary. Connie looked up at Randolph. Her eyes met his sky-blue ones, and he nodded firmly.

Well, here goes. She took a deep breath and opened the envelope. Several sheets of stationery were inside. Her fingers were cold with nervousness as she plucked them out. Her heart was pounding. Her mouth was horribly dry.

"Eight years ago..."

She began to read the words on the paper. If she recalled correctly, it was two years ago that Lily Orlamunde had died.

Eight years ago, a top-secret mission was undertaken in Adelbide.
Daeg Gallus was in charge of the operation. Using their huge criminal

organization boasting members all across the continent, they secretly infiltrated Adelbide and began distributing the hallucinogen Jackal's Paradise. Their aim was not to raise capital but rather to undermine the strength of the kingdom.

But they were not the masterminds of this plan.

The entity that hired Daeg Gallus and pulled the strings from the shadows was none other than our ally, Faris.

In other words, the Holy Grail of Eris was...

...the name of a military strategy concocted by Faris to invade Adelbide.

Constance Grail

Sixteen-year-old who is starting to realize she can't be a dreamy maiden forever. Has recently made so many new friends, she honestly doesn't know who's who at times. ←**new!**

 Scarlett Castiel

Eternal sixteen-year-old currently shaking with anger. Literally five seconds from losing her shit because, after taking more than four hundred pages to find them, the target of her revenge left the stage immediately. ←**new!**

 Randolph Ulster

Twenty-six-year-old who just managed to take his fiancée on a date to a history museum that neither of them was actually interested in. Afterward, caught hell from a friend for it, but honestly still doesn't see what the problem was. His subordinates have started to call him "His Unfortunate Excellency" behind his back. ←**new!**

 Abigail O'Brian

A duchess who proves that appearances can be deceptive. Has a backstory like the heroine of a girl's manga, including taking a trip around the world on a ship in her teens. Has a history with Jackal's Paradise.

 Lucia O'Brian

Precocious little girl who can see Scarlett. Had a hard life from the second she was born, which has made her more mature than other kids her age.

 Aldous Clayton

Surprisingly serious despite having an atrocious mouth and attitude. Secretly feels bad for accidentally stepping into a trap and causing everyone a lot of problems.

Lady Audrey

Once a legendary prostitute called the crown jewel of Rosenkreuz Street, now an old skinflint who strikes fear into the hearts of everyone she knows. Big shots who were trained by Audrey when young are incapable of disobeying her even now.

 Aisha Huxley

The person who actually poisoned the water jug at the Luze residence. Further enrages Scarlett by leaving the stage as soon as it is revealed that she is the rightful target of her revenge.

©Yu-nagi

I still dream about it sometimes.

The sweltering heat. The jeers of the crowd. The feeling of death approaching.

But the glint in her amethyst eyes was the same as it always was.

Every time I remember it, I can't help but wonder.

Why was she able to smile like that at such a time?

※

I always hated to lose.

Fortunately, I was blessed with better-than-average looks and talent from a young age. I was called a child prodigy more than once. Of course, I realize now that some of the praise was mere brownnosing to the daughter of Marquess Orlamunde. But at the time, I was ignorant of the ways of the world. I believed without a shadow of a doubt that I was someone special, chosen by the goddesses.

But all of that was demolished the winter I turned five years old.

"Look, Lily! There's the young lady from the House of Castiel!"

That morning, the maids had spent hours dressing me so that my father could bring me with him to a lavish mansion. I remember being overwhelmed by the gorgeous decorations inside, so sumptuous even the Orlamunde residence paled in comparison.

That day, a birthday celebration was being held for Duke Castiel's only daughter. Amid applause and cheers, the duke led the young girl leisurely down the spiral staircase. With only one look, I was charmed.

What a beautiful child she was.

Her wavy hair was like the night sky against her translucent white skin. Her amethyst eyes sparkled like stars. And her smile—such a grown-up smile. All of it was breathtakingly beautiful.

She'd beaten me.

In that moment, I tasted defeat for the first time in my life. No matter how expensive the jewels I wore or how stunning the clothes, I would never be more beautiful than her.

I remember how frustrating that realization was.

"Pleased to meet you. My name is Lily Orlamunde."

When I think back on it now, I believe I did hold at least some antipathy in my heart as I greeted her. So as not to be taken lightly, I tried to be more polite than usual. I thought that the more perfect my manners, the worse the other girl would look in comparison to me.

The girl's response, however, was extremely cold.

"What a horrid face you have," she said, glancing in my direction.

"...That's a rude thing to say," I said, trying not to show how upset I was. But the other girl only shrugged like she didn't care.

"It's true," she said, spinning on her heels. The blood rushed to my face.

"Please wait!" I shouted at her. "Just now, I told you my name. It's proper that you tell me your name, too!" The girl stopped walking and looked over her shoulder at me. Smiling, she curtsied elegantly. I felt like she'd just thrown cold water over my head. It was an impeccable lady's curtsy.

"It's Scarlett. Scarlett Castiel. But I must say that you were the first one to be rude."

I glared at her, my brows drawn together. What could she be talking about?

"Those eyes of yours. Haven't you ever looked in a mirror? Your eyes are so cold and awful. Just like Aunt Meaghan's. Everyone hates her, you know, because she's so mean."

"What...?"

"You were thinking mean things about me, too, weren't you? I think that's rude."

I was speechless. She was right. I had been jealous of her beauty and wanted to shame her.

"That sort of behavior in a lady is fourth-rate."

"Fourth-rate?"

"My mother always says that," answered Scarlett, proudly puffing out her chest.

That was my first encounter with Scarlett Castiel.

One day several years later, I heard that Scarlett's mother, Aliénore, had died. It seemed she had always been weak and had spent most of the time since her daughter was born confined to her bed. Aliénore was from the Republic of Soldita, across the ocean. They said she was a beauty, with black hair and amethyst eyes.

"Your face is as horrid as ever, Lily Orlamunde. Did you want something?"

But even though she had just lost her mother, Scarlett acted exactly the same as always.

"Of course not. You just happened to be in front of me. Don't you think you're a bit overly self-conscious?"

I couldn't help responding spitefully. She snorted, as she always did.

Though I didn't realize it at the time, when I think back on it now, Aliénore was something of a curiosity. Soon after the duke's former wife, Veronica, gave birth to their eldest child, Maximilian, she eloped with her lover. Several years later, she and the duke were officially divorced by the church, meaning he was free to marry again.

The problem was, Aliénore wasn't a noble.

It would be one thing to keep her in his mansion as a lover, but for a duke to make such a woman his proper wife was unthinkable.

For that reason, people assumed there must be some kind of secret about her—that she was a noble's illegitimate child, or of an esteemed lineage from some fallen country, or something similar.

At the time, I knew nothing of those circumstances, and I had never experienced the death of a person close to me. When I heard that Scarlett's mother had died, it felt unreal, as if it had happened in some far-off kingdom.

Scarlett must have sensed my bewilderment, because she sighed affectedly.

"How depressing to think I'm going to be seeing you every day from now on," she said.

It was early summer. We had left our respective domains and come to verdant Greenfields, one of the domains under the direct control of the royal family.

That summer, the king had invited the Orlamunde and Castiel families to the royal summer retreat as a reward for our devotion. It was no mere coincidence that both families had brought their daughters with them—we had been chosen as playmates for the first prince, who was recovering from an illness. Acknowledging our service was only a pretense.

His Highness Enrique hid behind his nurse when he met us. Though he was a year older than us, he looked much younger. I was taller than most children my age to start with, but he was even shorter than Scarlett. His skin was a sickly white, and he was very thin. He looked as if he would snap in two if you pushed him.

Before we arrived at Greenfields, my father had reminded me many times that I mustn't play roughly around the prince because he was weak. That was probably one reason we were chosen for his playmates, rather than boys his own age.

But what were we to do if he showed no interest in playing with us? When his nurse tried to coax him out, Enrique only shook his head and retreated farther behind her. Then he stared down at the floor.

I was unsure what to do and unable to speak to him, when a flash of shiny black hair shot out before me.

"Hello. I'm Scarlett. Scarlett Castiel."

It was strange—although Scarlett's voice was by no means loud, it always carried so well.

"By the way, can't you talk?"

Enrique's eyes widened at her high-handed tone. He took another step backward, as if he was afraid. Then, for the first time, he spoke. His voice was so soft, it was almost inaudible.

"...Y-you're very rude. D-don't you know who I am?"

Scarlett's eyebrows shot up, and she smiled boldly.

"What a foolish boy you are," she said. "If you don't introduce yourself, how do you expect people to know who you are?"

I was very anxious. This was a member of the royal family—the first prince at that.

"S-Scarlett!" I scolded softly. But Scarlett's answer was bold.

"What? I introduced myself properly. I'm not the one being rude."

Everyone could hear her. The look on Enrique's face changed to one of astonishment.

"...I'm Enrique."

Scarlett smiled with satisfaction. "So you can talk! I've heard you're a recluse. I've only just gotten here, but I already know this place better than you do. Follow me. I'll show you something good."

She took the prince's hand and headed off. I froze in fear, but neither his nurse nor the guards standing several paces back said a word. I understand now that Scarlett had her own unique role to play.

At the time, I think, His Highness was rejecting the outside world.

Greenfields Castle sat atop a hill overlooking the whole domain. Scarlett strode out of the building with guards trailing behind, looked all around, and headed toward a castle wall with a lookout tower. She did not run. She walked quickly, but with each step, she planted her feet firmly on the ground. At first, Enrique was confused, but soon his eyes lit up and his cheeks flushed.

Before long, we reached the stone tower. At the top of the steep staircase inside, we emerged to an expansive view.

"Look."

Scarlett pointed to a hillside sloping gently down toward the village. It was covered completely in olive trees, whose white flowers fluttered in the breeze. Far away, the boundary between sky and land blurred into an indigo haze.

Clouds trailed across the sunny blue sky.

A refreshing breeze was ruffling our hair and clothes.

"...How beautiful," Enrique mumbled.

"Isn't it?" Scarlett answered with a carefree smile. "It's such a waste to stay inside the castle all the time. Just look how wide the world is."

Enrique squinted in the sun and gazed out over the endless landscape.

I watched the two of them from a slight distance. After a moment, Scarlett noticed and met my gaze. She rolled her amethyst eyes as she placed her pointer finger over her mouth and smiled casually.

"My mother always used to say that."

After that day, Enrique slowly began to change. He turned his gaze toward the outside world. To be honest, Scarlett usually had to drag him out and lead him around by the nose. Nevertheless, lean muscles developed on his stick-thin body, and the color started returning to his bluish-white skin.

"Oh no," Enrique mumbled in a daze as his tart tumbled to the ground.

On days when the weather was good, teatime was held in the courtyard. A parasol was set up over the table, and bite-size tarts and cookies were arranged on each plate.

There were cookies like snowballs that crumbled in your mouth and golden-brown madeleines shaped like seashells. Spicy orange carrot cake and tarts overflowing with bilberries from the nearby forest, which Enrique liked best of all. He always saved them for last to savor slowly.

This time, he had dropped his on the ground.

"...My tart..."

"How clumsy of you," Scarlett said callously. Tears filled Enrique's magenta eyes. I would have given him my tart, but I'd already eaten it.

"I suppose I have no choice."

A jewel-like piece of red tart appeared on Enrique's plate.

"I gave you half."

"B-but it'd be rude of me..."

"Be quiet. I will allow it."

However many times I think back on those words, I feel like pulling my own hair and asking her just who she thought she was. But at moments like that, Scarlett carried herself with absolute confidence, and if you were with her, you somehow thought she was right. It was very annoying.

"And just how long do you intend to embarrass me? If a lady says she's allowing it, then you ought to stop worrying about it and do it in a hurry!"

A solemn bell chimed from inside the castle grounds. It was the bell on the watchtower at the top of the hill.

"...We're too late," the boy said sorrowfully when the bell had stopped ringing. Until a moment earlier, he had been rushing ahead with unusual restlessness, but now he was plodding along as if he had lost heart. I looked at him, wondering what was wrong, and saw his beautiful magenta eyes slowly fill with tears.

He had been a crybaby ever since I met him. Scarlett was the cause of ninety percent of his tears, but today was different.

He held in his hand an assignment the tutor had given him the day before. He was to turn it in before the afternoon prayer bell rang. The reading room where he was supposed to bring it was just in front of us.

"It's fine," I said, smiling at the dejected boy.

Just then, the hook-nosed tutor appeared from around a corner in the hallway, and Enrique looked down, forlorn. "It's not fine…"

"True, if we did nothing. But I'll buy you some time," I said.

Fortunately, the tutor hadn't yet entered the room. We had plenty of options. The important thing was that he didn't notice.

I glanced at Scarlett, still smiling. She raised her eyebrows crossly, as if she'd just realized what I was thinking.

"I'll tell you now, I'm not helping you. It's too much trouble."

"What, you don't have the guts to do it?"

"…What did you say?" Scarlett had a short fuse, and I could see her growing more outraged by the second. Of course, I didn't care. I knew her too well for that.

I placed my hand dramatically on my forehead and swooned.

"L-Lily?!" Enrique cried.

At the same moment, I heard someone clicking their tongue in disgust—Scarlett.

She sighed with profound distaste, then in a loud voice said, "Someone, please help us! Lily has fainted!"

The servants who were nearby gathered round in a flurry.

"Miss Lily?!"

"Quick, fetch a doctor!"

In a flash, I was surrounded by grown-ups. Surveying the scene through barely open eyes, I spotted the tutor. His attention was focused on me. I turned my head slightly. I saw Scarlett grab Enrique's hand, taking advantage of the chaos.

"Scarlett! What are you doing?"

"Stop daydreaming and come with me! You need to turn in your assignment, don't you? He's distracted right now, so you can still make it."

"B-but, Lily…"

"Lily's the one who wants you to do it! Urgh! Why do I always get pulled into these annoying schemes…?!"

Enrique turned in surprise to look at me. My eyes met his magenta ones. When I saw they were no longer teary, I winked at him playfully.

Several weeks after our arrival in Greenfields, the reclusive prince had turned into a curious, happy boy.

He was getting stronger, and while he used to often skip his lessons with the tutors, he now had them every day. Scarlett and I were allowed to attend, too, while we waited for them to finish.

On this day, his teacher was the middle-aged man with the hooked nose from before. At the end of class, there was to be an oral quiz, and if we passed, we would be allowed to play outside.

However, Enrique seemed to be having trouble answering.

"At this rate, you'll never catch up with your clever younger brother. You already have to make up for the time you missed." The tutor sighed. Enrique's face clouded over, and I became angry. The tutor didn't need to speak to him like that. True, the Second Prince, Johann, was said to be intelligent, but the sickly Enrique had spent half a year in bed. Although he'd revived a bit lately, comparing the brothers wasn't fair.

"If you're talking about the traders' city that thrived in the reign of King Endielle, then the answer is the Markland, to the west of the City of Alslain. Although I hear it no longer exists," a nonchalant voice announced.

"What?"

We all turned in the direction of the speaker, caught off guard.

"I believe that's the end of today's lesson. Let's go, Enrique."

But the speaker, already used to being the center of attention, ignored our stares and stood up as if her business here was done.

"Wh-where in the world did you learn that?" the tutor asked her.

Scarlett gazed coolly at him. "You told us yourself just yesterday."

"...Th-then tell me this. What is the name of the bell tower that was constructed in the capital during the reign of King Endielle to allow for surveillance of Markland?"

"Saint Mark's Bell Tower in Saint Mark's Square. You said that yesterday, too."

The hook-nosed tutor widened his eyes and stepped closer to Scarlett, his fists trembling.

"Outstanding! You have an outstanding mind! You ought to have a tutor yourself! I would be happy to—"

"Oh, stop blathering. It's rude. Step aside."

Scarlett pressed her hands over her ears and scowled theatrically. Then she looked down at the prince, who was still sitting, and tilted her head.

"What's wrong?"

He looked down, a dark expression on his face.

"...going."

"What?" Scarlett drew her brows together.

Enrique jerked his head up. His eyes were moist. "I'm not going! I hate you, Scarlett!" he shouted, then flew from the room. The guards hurried after him.

I'm sure it was simply a temper tantrum. But he hadn't run in so long that it brought on a fit, and he was once again confined to bed rest.

We returned to the capital without exchanging another word with him.

※

Several years passed. Before I knew it, Scarlett had been executed, and Enrique had married a viscount's daughter below his rank. Life is always unpredictable.

And no matter how piously one lives one's life, in the end, we are no match for fate.

In which case, why not live as we please?

I couldn't help feeling that way.

And so, for the time being, I stopped caring what the rest of noble society thought of me. I didn't need their approval. I had no regrets. I would never get what I wanted by staying in that world.

Fortunately, by *pretending* to be wounded by the execution of my friend at such an impressionable age, I managed to avoid the prison of marriage and instead satisfied myself with charitable work. Until.

"...An arranged marriage. I see."

After some years of this, my parents finally ran out of patience and began loading me down with a mountain of résumés from potential suitors.

One day, after I had grown bored of feeding the fire with such garbage, I came across a familiar name. The moment I saw it, I realized it was my chance.

The name was Randolph Ulster, the Grim Reaper.

"I'm sorry, but I have no intention of marrying anyone at the moment."

A meeting was arranged right away. But no sooner had my mother announced that she would "leave the rest to you young folks" than he rejected me. According to him, his father had proposed the marriage without his consent. I'm sure he wanted me to decline the proposal. I thought I knew what kind of person Randolph was, but he had even less delicacy than I had expected. Most girls would probably have burst into tears or flown into a rage.

But I simply smiled.

"I know that," I said. "That's why I invited you here. I have something of a proposal for you."

Randolph knit his brows suspiciously.

"To tell you the truth, I have no interest in marrying, either. But if I go on like this, people will be lecturing me for the rest of my life. For my own sanity, I'd like to avoid that. So I had an idea. What about a marriage of convenience?"

"A marriage...of convenience?"

"Yes. Our lives would remain exactly the same as before we married. Of course, you and I would have to live together. The condition would be that neither of us interfered in the other party's life. You would be able to devote yourself to work as much as you like, and I would be allowed to do as I please as well. In other words, we would be strangers who pledged our commitment to each other in a church. That would allow us to avoid all sorts of annoyances. Quite appealing, isn't it?"

His cerulean eyes narrowed as if he were considering the proposition. Theoretically, it ought to suit him as well as it did me.

"...You would be all right with that?" he asked.

"I'm the one who should ask you that. I'll tell you this from the outset: I don't want children. I want to give my life over to the activities I'm involved in now. If you want an heir, I'll ask you to produce one elsewhere. Do you still accept the idea?"

The young man nodded.

"What a coincidence. I feel the same way."

This was even better than I'd imagined. I thrust out my hand in high spirits.

"I look forward to our collaboration—my dear accomplice."

In the end, there could have been no one as suitable as Randolph Ulster. For one thing, he hardly ever came home. This was important because I wanted to prioritize time for myself. Plus, he wasn't the sort to complain about a woman being active in the public sphere. To the contrary, he respected my position as his partner.

Our relationship began on paper, but the outcome wasn't bad. He was like a roommate I only saw from time to time.

"It's been quite a while, Lily! I've been longing to see you!"

Cecilia, who had leapt from viscount's daughter to crown princess, greeted me with apparent joy sparkling in her rose-colored eyes. A consummate actress, as always.

"And I am glad to see you in good health, Your Highness," I said. We both giggled.

Cecilia was a smart woman. She never let you guess what she was really thinking. And she hadn't for the past eight years.

I handed her the petition I'd received from a nun who was my acquaintance. It had to do with the education of children at the orphanage.

I explained the circumstances, then took my leave. On my way down the long passage, I passed a dark-skinned trader. When I looked at him, he gave me a sunny smile typical of someone from the south, then continued to Cecilia's rooms. I assumed he was one of her favored traders.

I had left the palace and was walking through the courtyard when someone called my name. I turned around. It was a frail, handsome young man—Enrique, the first prince.

"...It's been a while," he said.

"Eight years, Your Highness," I said wryly. His placid face tensed. It was clear whom he was thinking of. Something prickly settled into my own heart.

How unpleasant and bothersome and gloomy. Even after eight years, her memory hadn't had the courtesy to fade.

I sighed, irritated by memories flooding back as vividly as if they'd happened the day before. Enrique's shoulders twitched, but he lowered his head and pretended not to notice.

"Well, I must be going. I have some pressing business to see to," I said.

"Lily...are you...angry?"

Angry about what? I thought but didn't say it.

"Why, of course not," I said instead, smiling. "I should apologize. I couldn't help lashing out at you, but I shouldn't have behaved in such a fourth-rate way."

"Fourth-rate...?"

I smiled bitterly at the familiar phrase.

"Just something a wicked girl I once knew liked to say."

Several days passed.

I had stopped by the Maurice Orphanage to borrow a nun's habit. I needed it for a visit I planned to make to a slum in preparation for a new charitable project. If I went out in my noblewoman's clothing, I could expect to be stripped of all I had, but if I dressed as a nun, people generally left me alone. Of course, I always carried a gun to protect myself.

Vagrants and beggars lay like corpses on the foul-smelling streets, and young children sold flowers on the busier byways.

I seared those images into my mind. I wanted to give the children in this district the education they deserved.

In which case, my home base would have to be the church.

I found the local house of worship, which looked like no more than a dilapidated shed. There were holes in the walls, and parts of the ceiling were caving in. I sighed and made up my mind to begin by collecting donations for its repair.

At that moment, I glimpsed the profile of a woman wearing a deep hood.

"…Cecilia?" I mumbled before I could stop myself. She looked exactly like the crown princess I had seen only days before.

Almost without thinking, I followed her. Fortunately, she didn't notice me as she walked into the church. She walked without a moment's hesitation toward the altar and addressed a man sitting on a bench there.

"Kiriki kirikuku."

What strange words she spoke. The man raised his head and quietly said something in return. The woman nodded and pushed back her hood.

She had pale golden hair and rose-colored eyes. It was Princess Cecilia after all.

"Good news," I heard the man say. "Very soon, the Holy Grail of Eris will be revived."

"It's too late. Do you know how many years I've been waiting?"

"It can't be helped. We can't make the same mistake twice. Not us—and not Faris. You understand that, I'm sure."

Cecilia clicked her tongue in annoyance.

"And how are things in the Luze domain?" the man asked.

"The viscount is already severely addicted. As long as he gets his Jackal's Paradise, he'll do anything he's told. One of our people holds the real power there. We've been having them stockpile regular shipments of explosives smuggled from Melvina in the guest house. We can launch the rebellion whenever we want."

"I'm delighted to hear it," the man said with a low laugh.

Cecilia pulled her hood back up over her head. The meeting seemed about to end, so I hurriedly left the church.

What just happened?

Explosives? Rebellion? I placed my hand over my pounding heart and whispered in a shaking voice, "The Holy Grail of Eris…?"

Eris was the Goddess of Discord. The Holy Grail brought blessings to the kingdom. Both terms had originated in the old Faris Empire.

Cecilia had used the word "rebellion."

Discord that brought blessings to the kingdom. In other words—were they talking about a planned invasion by Faris?

A light rain was falling. In a corner of a dingy alley, a man was sprawled on the open ground, unbothered.

I stood wordlessly in front of him and dropped a few coins into his palm.

"You know the earl who went bankrupt the other day? It was the same drug again," he said.

"You mean Earl Burnes?"

"Aye. Couldn't pay his gambling debts, I hear, but it seems he was hooked on more than betting. No doubt he became a slave to it and ruined himself."

"…Where was he getting the Paradise?"

From that day forward, I began to secretly gather information. Appearances to the contrary, the man before me was a skilled informer.

As I investigated Faris, I realized a strange drug had become all the rage among nobles lately. Jackal's Paradise. It was illegal now, but in the past, it was an indispensable amusement for those who enjoyed the nightlife, just like alcohol and tobacco.

But now it was different.

"A gambling house. Place called The Goat's Ankle. To think it'd get this bad. That drug is a poison that ruins people."

A poison that ruins people—the words brought flooding back a dark memory I had long suppressed.

※

It happened a few years after the summer we spent at Greenfields.

Enrique had grown from a sickly boy into a fine young man.

But his relationship with Scarlett remained uneasy. Of course, the two had various opportunities to meet over the years. Each time, Enrique seemed to want to say something to Scarlett, but she must have been unable to forgive him for saying he hated her, because she always made a point of ignoring him.

I was fed up with how childish they were both acting.

Their relationship changed only after the engagement was announced. Forced to meet whether they liked it or not, the ice gradually began to melt.

To be honest, I didn't foresee that Cecilia Luze would be a problem. Of course, I poked at her playfully to keep her in check, but it didn't occur to me to actively try to crush her.

Who is it that said love is like a fever? True, Cecilia may have been Enrique's first love, but I'm sure that love would have cooled with time. As the successor to the throne, he needed influence. In that sense, Scarlett had the perfect lineage. I saw no need to get worked up over a mere viscount's daughter.

But within no time at all, I found out Scarlett had been imprisoned.

"...Poison, you say?"

When I first heard the story, it struck me as so ridiculous, I couldn't even laugh. Scarlett Castiel tried to poison Cecilia? The same Scarlett who acted the second a thought occurred to her? Impossible!

But evidence and testimonies kept cropping up, and eventually they said she had dropped her earring at the Luze residence.

To top it all off, her own fiancé denounced her at the Grand Merillian.

"Your Highness!"

I marched into the Moldavite Palace knowing full well I might be ignored. I lifted the hem of my skirt in a perfunctory curtsy and continued, without waiting for the crown prince to respond.

"What in the world is going on? Do you honestly think Scarlett would stoop so low?" I demanded. Enrique's face tensed.

"…No, I don't."

"Then why?"

"I heard that a moonstone earring was found at the Luze residence."

I held my breath.

"I went to see it so I could clear her name," he went on. "I, of all people, would surely be able to tell the difference. After all, I gave those earrings to her myself shortly after our engagement."

Enrique's lips trembled slightly.

"It was the real thing. I felt betrayed, like she was no longer the Scarlett I knew. I called her to the Grand Merillian and broke our engagement on the spot. I brought Cecilia, the victim of the crime, along with me, but I never said she and I were getting engaged. That's only a rumor. Afterwards, they searched the Castiel residence and discovered the poison bottle in Scarlett's room." He paused. "…But I never thought she would be executed. I didn't want that."

I could never want that, his eyes all but told me. He looked on the verge of crying.

I sighed softly. But there was no undoing what had been done.

"Can't you do anything about it?" I asked.

"It's impossible. My father—His Highness—has made a decision."

"But why…?"

It simply did not make sense. True, there was material evidence. But no one who knew Scarlett Castiel would believe she had planned an assassination. It was much easier to imagine she had been framed. Plus, it was odd that the king would involve himself in a failed assassination attempt on a mere viscount's daughter.

And what was Duke Castiel doing in the face of his own daughter's execution?

Was he unable to act—or simply unwilling?

"I'm a fool," Enrique said in a strained voice. "I'm the one who let this happen...Lily."

Hearing my name, I looked up and met the prince's bright magenta eyes. Purple was the royal color. The eyes of the Castiel family were purple, too—proof of a lineage rich in royal blood. But as I looked at Enrique's eyes, I realized that Scarlett's were not tinged with red like his were. Instead, they were a shade of amethyst exactly between red and blue.

"Scarlett's execution is certain—which is why I hope you will forgive me for marrying Cecilia."

I don't believe those words came from a man who wanted to be with the woman he loved. His expression was too grief-stricken for that.

But I could not bring myself to answer his request.

Because the girl who once told him, *I will allow it*, with that confident smile of hers, was no longer with us.

※

"...You beat me."

The man sitting across from me threw the cards in his hand onto the table.

"Damn it, I've lost again. You're pretty good at this, young lady."

I wasn't particularly good at gambling. I was good at numbers and statistics, which was why I limited myself to card games.

I was in the gambling hall my informant had told me about. The Goat's Ankle was, at first glance, just like any other restaurant for the masses. However, in its basement was a gambling hall awash with greed.

It wasn't only cash the gamblers wagered for.

"Was it Paradise you wanted to know about? The bird brings it."

"The bird?"

"The bird that signals a new day. I can say no more."

His words led me to the criminal organization Daeg Gallus. I considered discussing it with Randolph, but I knew that people from the organization were already in the Security Force. I didn't suspect that straitlaced man of being one of them, but the fact remained that I didn't know him well enough yet to trust him.

It was around the same time that I began to sense someone watching me. But whenever I turned around, no one was there.

One day several weeks later, I noticed a dark-skinned, sunny-looking young man out of the corner of my eye.

Cecilia's trader.

The hair on my arms stood on end. Perhaps I had been too obvious in my attempts to gather information.

I don't remember how I got home that day. I was exhausted in both body and mind. For once, Randolph came home early.

The moment he saw me lying on the sofa, he furrowed his brows.

"You look pale," he said, sounding less like a worried husband and more like a senior employee scolding his subordinate for failing to take care of her health. I frowned and sat up.

"I haven't been getting enough sleep. My new project is at an impasse."

"I see. Can I help you with anything?"

"…Why?"

For some reason, I felt defensive. He had never involved himself in my business before. Why now?

"A colleague told me married couples are supposed to support one another. He's always been a nosy one."

His unexpected response took the wind from my sails. I blinked. Normally I would have laughed it off, but at that moment, his proposal struck me as appealing. A little devil whispered in my ear: *Just pretend you never heard about that silly old plot. Then you can return to your peaceful, satisfying old life…*

Suddenly, a vision of my future with Randolph flashed before my eyes. He was a workaholic without the least bit of delicacy, but I had already come to realize that underneath all that was a serious, kind man. Living out our lives as partners who supported one another wouldn't be so bad.

Not bad, but…

Not the path I was meant to take.

※

"Miss Lily!"

George came running from the far side of the sparkling fountain, gasping for breath.

"Look, look! I can write my name!"

He handed me a crumpled scrap of paper. I flattened it out. The letters of his name were written across it, lines unsteady like wriggling worms.

"Hey, no fair, I did too!"

"Me too!"

"And me!"

Mira, Mark, and Carol, four-year-olds like George, had soon surrounded me. They were all grinning with pride in their newfound ability to write their names.

If war breaks out—

These children with no families of their own would be the first victims.

I bit my lip at the thought. I was boxed in on every side. In the end, I was no more than a helpless young girl. I was no match for the hulking enemy I had so carelessly offended.

"…Tony," I said, calling over the redheaded boy who was keeping watch over the others from a slight distance. With a solemn expression, I told him the password I'd heard the man use with Cecilia, so that at the very least, the children might be able to avoid danger.

Tony gave me a puzzled look. "Kiriki kirikuku? What's that?"

"It's a spell to show you who the bad guys are… If something happens to me in the future, I want you to say this spell to anyone who comes asking about me."

"A spell…"

"Yes. If they react even a little, that means they are a very bad person, and I want you to take everyone with you and run away. You can do that, right, Tony?"

Of all the children at the orphanage, Tony had the strongest sense of responsibility and was the most reliable. I thought he would handle my request quite well, but he stared at me in silence with a troubled expression.

"What's the matter?"

"…You have to come with us, Miss Lily," he said, on the verge of tears. "I wouldn't like it if you weren't with us."

I gulped.

"What do you mean about something happening to you?" he went on. "Do you mean something bad? I'll do anything to keep the bad things away from you! Don't worry. I'm a kid, but I'm strong…!"

What should I do?

How could I protect these innocent children from a horrible future?

That very instant, I made up my mind.

I would place my final bet.

※

"Oh, Miss Lily! You seem to have dropped something."

As I walked down the street, an acquaintance who happened to be passing by stopped me.

"Oh dear, how could I have been so careless!" I said, making a great show of hurriedly picking up the object I had dropped.

"…Is that a key?" the woman asked, peering with interest into my hand.

Someone was still following me. The other day I had allowed myself to become panicked, but upon reflection, I realized it was already clear they did not plan to attack me immediately.

Which meant I could use the situation to my own advantage.

"Yes, but please don't tell anyone about it. It's a secret."

That was why I was acting in a way I was sure would draw their attention. I was sending a message that I knew about their plans. That I had information—that I had a *trump card*. That's what I wanted them to think.

"I've hidden something very important," I said, flashing the fake key at her. I knew someone must be watching.

The key to ensuring a plot succeeds is to finish before anyone realizes what you're up to. That's what Scarlett told me.

I had sent a letter to Cecilia asking to speak with her about charitable education and had received an appointment with surprising speed. Was it coincidence, or wasn't it?

Several days later, I was walking down a hallway in the Elbaite Palace heading to my audience with the princess when I bumped into Enrique.

I stepped aside and looked down, but he told me to raise my head.

"You're on your way to meet Cecilia, aren't you? I've been hearing good things about you lately. My father was praising—"

"Your Highness," I interrupted, at the risk of sounding disrespectful. "Do you remember when you asked me to forgive you for marrying Cecilia?"

His face tensed slightly.

That was the day I had learned that Scarlett, imprisoned for a crime she did not commit, had no chance of escaping execution.

That day I had been unable to answer his question, which had sounded more like a plea.

But now, for some reason, I found the words spilling effortlessly from my mouth, just as they had when the three of us had played and laughed together.

"What in the world have you been doing these eight years? It's downright fourth-rate."

He must not have been expecting those words, because his magenta eyes widened in surprise. Then he grimaced as if deeply hurt.

"...You're right. As things stand, I cannot expect forgiveness."

I couldn't help snorting in laughter at his pitiful, unkingly attitude.

"I'm the wrong person to ask in the first place," I replied. "Only one person in the world can forgive you."

That young girl who was haughtier, fiercer, and more beautiful than anyone else.

Enrique's eyelids trembled. *Still a crybaby*, I thought, remembering the old days.

"You haven't given up yet, have you, Your Highness?"

He must have had some goal in marrying Cecilia. Unfortunately, he seemed not to have achieved it yet.

He nodded, biting his lip.

"In that case," I said, like I had once long ago, "I will buy you some time."

※

"Which is to say, I believe that the advancement of Adelbide itself hinges on educating the children of the slums," I said, wrapping up my argument for the future of charitable education.

Cecilia clapped her hands enthusiastically. "I knew I could expect something marvelous from you, Lily! It's a wonderful idea!"

"Thank you very much. Actually, I have already been to the slum several times to get a sense of the situation. I think the church on Leda Street will require some repairs."

Cecilia looked at me, expressionless.

"Speaking of which," I went on, "I saw Your Highness the other day."

"Do you mean to suggest that I would go to a place like that?"

"I never said where I saw you," I replied with a smile, tilting my head slowly. "But that reminds me, have you ever heard of the Holy Grail of Eris?"

Silence descended. I stood and curtsied gracefully. "If you have, I suggest that you reconsider your plans. You can't make the same mistake twice now, can you?"

I had thought and thought about what to do, trying to find another way.

But in the end, I realized it was an impossible task for a sheltered noble's daughter.

Accepting defeat, however, was out of the question.

Lily Orlamunde has always hated losing.

I left the palace and climbed into a fiacre by the side of the road. I told the driver to take me not to the Ulster residence but instead to the Orlamunde mansion.

The cheap carriage rattled down the street. It had been a long time since I'd ridden in a carriage without a family crest.

The last time, in fact, was immediately after Scarlett was sentenced to death.

On that day, too, I had boarded a carriage hoping to avoid prying eyes and taken it to the prison where she was locked up.

Executions were vulgar public carnivals at which the victim was paraded before a mocking, jeering mob.

I couldn't stand the thought of haughty, beautiful Scarlett meeting such an end.

And so I immediately secured what I thought she needed.

It would work quickly, ensuring death with as little suffering as possible. At the very least, her dignity would be preserved. But—

※

"No thank you."

Her voice was terribly nonchalant and cold.

Even dressed in a dull gray shift, Scarlett was as beautiful as ever.

"Just who in the world do you think I am?" she asked, snorting disdainfully. She was acting exactly as she always did. "You think I'm going to turn my back and flee? You must be joking."

I stood there gaping at her.

"A public execution, is it? What could be better? I'll have the last laugh, and then I'll rub their noses in it."

At that moment, Scarlett Castiel was as beautiful as she was the day I met her.

She had beaten me again.

※

Inside the swaying carriage, I ripped a page from the tourism pamphlet I had brought with me and wrote a note on the paper. Then I slipped it into an envelope holding the fake key and sealed it shut. I tossed the rest of the pamphlet out the carriage window.

When I arrived at my family home, I went immediately to the chapel. Fortunately, nobody questioned me.

I had done everything I needed to do. I had had the key engraved with the code and left all the information I could gather at the museum. And I had told the children at the orphanage what they needed to do if it came to that.

Most likely, Daeg Gallus would come for me very soon. That was only natural. I had set it up that way myself. I had hinted at the existence of the key to those around me and said I'd hidden something more important than life itself.

I had lit the fuse myself, of my own will.

Not to brag, but before this, I had never done anything violent. I was not confident that I could withstand torture or the like.

In other words, once I had placed this bet, my only choice was to act before they did.

Cecilia had said at the church that they could not afford to make any

©Yu-nagi

more mistakes. I would use that against them. As long as they didn't know what cards I held, they would be temporarily immobilized.

The envelope rustled in my hand.

I was not holding despair. I was holding hope. My only hope.

Destroy the Holy Grail of Eris.

That was more than I could do.

But I was buying time with my own death. I trusted that someone else would carry on from there. If I didn't believe that, I wouldn't have been able to do it.

Surely someone would search behind the painting, tear open the holy scripture, and risk their own life to save our kingdom.

Someone with Scarlett Castiel's haughty disdain for the sacred but also with the goodness to spare no effort for the common good—

I burst out laughing. It would be a miracle if a person like that existed!

Still, I thought. *Still, nobody knows the future.* I used my finger to trace the bottle of poison I had hidden in the bodice of my dress. It was the same poison I had tried to give Scarlett on the eve of her execution. I had never dreamed that one day I would need it for myself.

Slowly, I raised my head. The sublime painting of the goddesses looked back at me. The three sisters who presided over human destiny. I met their gaze as I pulled the painting from the wall and attached the envelope to the back.

The henchmen who had been trailing me did not appear.

I had won my bet.

I'll have the last laugh, and then I'll rub their noses in it.

Once again, I heard that familiar voice. Haughty, insolent, but somehow magnetic. I remembered the way Scarlett smiled before the mob on the day of her execution. Just as she had promised, she kept her smile until the moment of her death, never losing hope.

Why was she able to smile like that?

I didn't know, but it saved me. Because there was nothing Scarlett could do that I couldn't.

After all, Lily Orlamunde always hated to lose.

I flashed a proud smile at the Fates gazing leisurely down at me, and I drank the poison.

©Yu-nagi

Lily Orlamunde

Deceased daughter of a marquess, hated to lose. So irritated by her childhood nemesis, she could never help lashing out at the girl, but in truth was a little jealous of her. Of course, she would never humiliate herself by admitting that. Used Scarlett's execution as an excuse to distance herself from society in hopes of becoming an independent woman. Momentarily thought she and Randolph might come to trust each other in time, then remembered how weird he was and decided that would never happen. Lost to only one person in her entire life.

 Scarlett Castiel

Walking disaster who stomps on people's hearts with her bare feet. Also an indiscriminate machine for inflicting trauma. During her life, never had what she would call a friend, but may have considered the first prince a kind of underling. Incidentally, later made the hook-nosed tutor cry. Never considered her a friend but acknowledged Lily's presence at her side. Would never humiliate herself by admitting that. Smiled at her last moment, though no one knows why.

 **Enrique Adelbide**

Prince and childhood crybaby. Although ninety percent of his tears were caused by a certain younger girl, he admired her strength and, before he knew it, was trailing after her like a duckling. Incidentally, Lily Orlamunde thought he was just a hopeless masochist. Lost faith in Scarlett after the attempted poisoning of Cecilia Luze, ultimately sending her to her death. As a result, everyone thinks it was his fault, but no one has been able to say it for the past ten years. ←**new!**

Abigail O'Brian sighed.

Her enemy seemed bent on wrapping up the Aisha incident as quickly as possible.

Randolph had been kind enough to raise the issue of inadequate evidence, but Aldous Clayton nevertheless remained the prime suspect. Out of an abundance of caution, Rudy from the Folkvangr had vanished for the time being.

Fortunately, neither the Security Force nor Daeg Gallus had shown any sign of realizing that the two men were one and the same.

The real Aldous Clayton had died ages ago. Abigail had never even met him. She had used his identity so that Rudy could be active in public.

Rosenkreuz Street was the capital's prime entertainment district. Its residents and visitors had many connections with the underworld. Abigail had made use of those connections and doubted her actions could be traced, but it would be annoying if someone looked into it. Even if they didn't have evidence, her name might come up in the investigation. Of course, it wouldn't be enough to land her in jail, and she herself couldn't care less, but if the case ended up causing trouble for her, Rudy might become reckless.

She had wanted to find out the truth about Aisha's death before that happened, but...

She sighed again at her lack of progress. The chandelier above her head glittered dazzlingly. Rhythmic music was playing in the drawing room, and people were chatting amicably.

This evening, she had been invited to a party hosted by a marchioness she knew. Although she had hardly slept the past few nights, she couldn't very well skip the event. An evening party was the perfect place to gather information, and anyhow, she wanted to avoid any misguided inferences that might be drawn from her absence.

"Good evening, Abigail."

Unsurprisingly, Abigail had soon grown dizzy as she circulated among the crowd and had escaped to rest on the pretense of getting a drink. That was when a tasteful voice greeted her from behind. Tasteful, perhaps, but cold and not at all to Abigail's taste.

She knew without looking who it was.

"Good evening, Debbie," she answered, turning around with a smile.

Deborah Darkian frowned slightly. She was famous for hating her nickname. All the more so when the person addressing her was Abigail, with whom she was constantly quarreling.

Needless to say, Abigail had done it deliberately.

Of course, the only reason Deborah would have approached Abigail in the first place was to harass her. Abigail felt entitled to at least a little preemptive revenge.

Predictably, Deborah curled her blood-red lips. "I hear your boy is nowhere to be found these days."

Just as she'd thought. Abigail silently cursed her.

"Whatever could you be talking about? I only have one child, my adorable little girl." Hiding her irritation, Abigail tilted her head. She was fine. Although her sharp-eyed conversation partner annoyed her, she felt relieved.

Deborah didn't seem to have any idea that Aldous Clayton was the same person as Rudy. She was simply trying to find out if the latter's disappearance could lead to Abigail's downfall. She was trying to shake her up because she didn't actually know anything.

If she had known, she probably would have kept quiet and waited to catch Abigail off guard.

"Oh, don't insult me by pretending innocence. I'm talking about your hound, who's not adorable in the least."

Nevertheless, Abigail couldn't let her guard down. Deborah Darkian was a cunning, cruel woman.

"Has the boy gone and done something bad?"

Sharon Spencer's funeral was a solemn affair.

Sharon, Aisha's cousin, had divorced several years prior, and at the time of her death, she was living with her parents.

The cause of death was suicide—by poison, apparently. Rumor had it she was an alcoholic and recently had grown mentally unstable, even deranged. Although she left no suicide note, she regularly took tranquilizers, so no one suspected foul play in her death.

Strangely enough, she had died on the same day as Aisha Huxley.

A chill ran down Connie's back as she thought it over.

Ask Sharon. She'll know something.

According to Aldous Clayton, those were Aisha's last words.

Sharon Spencer was Aisha's cousin. The very same cousin from whom she had obtained the bottle of poison she tried to use on Cecilia.

Which meant this probably wasn't a suicide.

Connie had decided to attend Sharon's funeral to gather information.

After making an offering of flowers at the church, she had headed with the other guests to the Spencer family cemetery for the burial. Sharon's father stood beside her gravestone and cried as he spoke about her life.

Connie hung toward the back of the crowd and scanned the guests for anyone who looked suspicious. As she was doing so, someone addressed her with surprise.

"Connie?"

She turned around.

"Mylene?"

It was her gossip-loving, slightly insensitive friend.

"Who would ever have imagined that Sharon would die so soon?" Mylene whispered to Connie as the crowd sang a hymn.

"Did you know her?" Connie whispered back.

"My sister-in-law was friends with her. She's due this month, so she asked me to come in her place. I met her a few times myself, too. What about you?"

"M-me? Um, I'm here for someone else, too… Uh, anyway, do you know anything about her?" Connie asked, caught off guard. Mylene brightened.

"I heard some really juicy stuff from my sister-in-law. Want to hear it?"

This was better than Connie could have hoped for. She nodded enthusiastically.

"It was back when Sharon was engaged…so it must have been about ten years ago. Apparently she was seeing someone other than her fiancé. I heard she was always a plain, serious person. The idea of her two-timing is unbelievable in itself, but that wasn't the half of it. Can you guess who she was seeing?"

Ten years ago. That was just around the time of the attempted poisoning. Connie looked up at Mylene, who glanced around and lowered her voice.

"Simon Darkian."

Who? Connie was secretly puzzled, but Scarlett immediately drew her brows together.

"…Simon? Isn't that Deborah's husband?" she asked.

Connie gasped. Deborah. Deborah Darkian. The woman who had summoned Connie to the Starlight Room in the Grand Merillian on the pretense of an "investigation" and then brutally harassed her.

"If I remember correctly," Scarlett mused, "it was Simon who married into

Deborah's family. Having to please that woman all the time, it's no wonder he wanted an escape."

Connie's face tensed at the unexpected mention of Deborah.

Mylene grinned. "I see you're familiar with Deborah Darkian. She isn't the kind of woman you want to make an enemy of. Personally, though, I love all the gossip."

Connie was trying to think of something to say when she heard a familiar sneer.

"Well, well, if it isn't Constance Grail. Have you come to cause more mayhem?"

Connie moaned as the nightmarish figure of a woman with curly red hair appeared before her.

"...Don't tell me Amelia Hobbes is here."

But Mylene, a longtime fan of the reporter's work, must not have heard her, because she tilted her head and whispered, "Who's that?"

"How striking that two women in the Spencer family should die on the same day. They must have had horrible karma."

Mylene frowned. This woman had shown up out of nowhere, and now she was mocking the dead.

"I don't know who you are, but I think that's an awfully rude thing to say."

Amelia's smoky-gray eyes widened in momentary surprise. She quickly regained her poise, however, and jutted out her chin.

"I am Amelia Hobbes, editor of the news department at the *Mayflower*. And you must be a friend of Constance Grail, the troublemaker."

"What?" Mylene asked, raising her eyebrows in suspicion.

"Oh, you needn't say a word. I'll just write an article if anything happens. Please go right ahead and raise a ruckus. And what are you up to today? Pretending you're Scarlett again?"

As usual, Connie ignored Amelia's provocation, but Mylene did not.

"It doesn't seem right for a journalist to be throwing around speculations when they're supposed to be following the facts," she said in a chilling tone.

"Any greenhorn can follow the facts. The important thing is how you expose them. I'll tell you right now, I take risks in my work. Although an ignorant child like you wouldn't know anything about that," Amelia shot back.

While Mylene was still reeling from all that, Amelia announced that she had an interview to do and marched off.

Only when she was gone did Mylene recover. "What just happened?! Who does that pompous redhead think she is?! I'd like to pull those curls right out of her scalp!"

"I understand completely, Mylene...!" Connie said, grabbing her friend's hand with tearful eyes. Mylene was finally on her side.

"It's unbelievable! I never imagined Amelia Hobbes was such a horrible person...!" Instead of calming down, Mylene seemed to be getting angrier by the second. "I feel like slapping myself for looking up to someone like that! Right now, straight across the face!"

"I don't think you should do that," Connie said, unconsciously pulling back her hand.

Mylene Reese's eyes were brimming with determination.

"I've made up my mind, Connie!" she announced boldly. "I'm going to get a job at the *Mayflower*! And I'm going to make sure that idiotic redhead never holds a pen again!"

That same day, the arrival of an unexpected guest had thrown the Folkvangr into a quiet furor.

Normally, Audrey would have borne the brunt of the attack, but unfortunately she was out at the time. Instead, the guest was greeted by Miriam—whose pretty face and friendly personality made her popular—and thus the highest-ranking despite her youth.

She smiled sweetly at the uninvited visitor. "Welcome, Lady Deborah."

The guest who gracefully took a seat in the inner room Miriam had led her to was none other than Abigail O'Brian's sworn enemy, Deborah Darkian.

"So the hound is out again today?" she asked imposingly, glancing around the room.

Miriam did not reply. She simply stayed calm and continued to smile, her lips sealed.

Deborah raised her eyebrows as if she found the girl's attitude displeasing.

"I feel sorry for you," she said with a mocking smile.

This was not Deborah's first visit to the Folkvangr. Now and then, she would stop by to make a few vile comments and harass the prostitutes. If Abigail, Audrey, or Rudy was there, they would chase her off, but on this day, they all happened to be out. It was up to Miriam to protect the others.

But Deborah was very skilled at worming her way into the most vulnerable part of people's hearts.

"I believe his name is Rudy or something like that, yes? And you're in love with him? Oh, it's obvious from watching you. He's a good man, too. But that kind of love doesn't pay off. A hound is only loyal to its master. Don't you think Abigail is hateful? And cunning? Toying around with a boy like that when she's married. Very unfaithful, wouldn't you say?"

She directed her mocking gaze at Miriam, waiting for a reply. Miriam smiled.

"But didn't you know? Hounds aren't the only ones who swear loyalty to their masters," she said.

Deborah must not have been expecting this, because she blinked in confusion.

"And today, since our dog is on a walk, won't you play with me instead, *Debbie*?"

Deborah scowled at this intentional use of her nickname.

Serves you right, Miriam thought. True, she was interested in Rudy, just like Deborah said. Not as a family member, either—in a romantic way.

All the same, ever since the day she'd reached out her hand like a ray of sunshine, Abigail had been the center of Miriam's universe. She wouldn't dream of betraying her.

Deborah narrowed her ashen eyes and rested her chin in her palm in apparent boredom.

"…Call my driver, would you? The thrill has worn off."

You're just a whore.
Deborah glared at the girl as she walked off.
The nerve! You were no more than an uneducated hussy when you came here, and now you're baring your fangs at Deborah Darkian?!
She suppressed her rising outrage. She knew from experience that it was not advantageous to show one's irritation.

Abigail was hiding something. She had looked exhausted when they met at the party. Without a doubt, she was in some sort of trouble.

And just around the same time, her lover, the security guard at her brothel, had vanished. It was only natural to think the two must be connected. If only she could find out how…then she might be able to drag that detestable woman through the mud.

Just then, a servant announced that her carriage was ready. She stood up. A slender girl with almond eyes accompanied her out of the room.

"What's your name?" she asked.

"…My name is Rebekah."

She spoke nicely, without accent or dialect. Watching her, Deborah realized she walked and moved with an elegance that seemed like more than a veneer of refinement.

"…Were you by chance born to a noble family?" Deborah asked.

The girl paused for a second. "…I was born into a low noble family, no different from commoners."

Deborah couldn't help smiling at her embarrassed expression. "That must have been very difficult for you. And perhaps it still is?"

Rebekah's eyes widened slightly, and Deborah seized the opportunity.

"If you're a noble, that means you and Abigail are of the same standing, doesn't it?"

"My family can hardly be compared to a duchess's…"

"No, nobles are nobles. You must resent her."

"...It's not Abigail's fault that I ended up like this." Rebekah had sounded hesitant before, but now her denial was firm.

She had made a mistake. It seemed that Abigail was more popular than Deborah had realized.

Then what about the boy?

"How's *Rudy*?"

Rebekah looked at her warily. Deborah could hardly keep herself from smiling.

This girl was much more transparent than Miriam.

"If he is in some sort of trouble, I may be able to help him. My husband is a very important man."

The girl's fiercely determined eyes wavered with uncertainty.

"And to follow up my earlier point," Deborah said ever so gently, as if she were speaking to a small child, "even if you don't hold a grudge against Abigail, I'm sure you've felt jealous of her, haven't you? After all, she has beside her..."

Rebekah reached her breaking point and looked down. But Deborah would not let her escape.

"Haven't you ever wished he was gazing into your eyes? Not Abigail's, but yours?" Deborah giggled, then whispered devilishly to the girl's still-downturned face. "I'm sure he'd thank you for it. He'd notice you."

Rebekah slowly looked up. Her eyes were glossy, almost feverish.

"You'll tell me what happened, won't you? After all, you, and you alone, can save him."

※

Several days had passed since Connie attended Sharon Spencer's funeral and learned about her illicit affair with Simon Darkian.

Randolph had stopped by for a visit, and the first thing out of his mouth was this: Abigail was going to be questioned as a key witness in the murder of Aisha Huxley.

"Whaa…?!" Connie exclaimed incoherently, leaping from the sofa where she'd been sitting.

"By now, the detectives are probably on their way to her house to arrest her."

"But why…?"

This unexpected twist had the blood draining from Connie's face.

"Someone talked. The detectives found out that the *Mayflower*'s Aldous Clayton was going by a false name, and that in fact he was Rudy, the security guard from the Folkvangr. It was Abigail who registered the false name and hired him. Plus, it's well-known that the security guard at the Folkvangr is Abigail's lover, so people have started saying that she must have been the one who planned Aisha's murder."

"But Lady Abigail has no connection at all to Aisha!"

Abigail had no reason to kill her. They had probably never even crossed paths.

"A week before Aisha was killed, Abigail sent a letter to Viscount Huxley. The viscount testified that Aisha had been acting strangely ever since the letter arrived. The Security Force thinks that may lead to a motive for the crime. It's a complete misinterpretation of the facts, but it will most likely take time to correct. I was removed from the investigation because Abigail and I are related, however distantly."

Connie caught her breath. The letter to Viscount Huxley…Abigail had written that for her.

"It's my fault."

"No it's not. It's the fault of the people trying to entrap her," Randolph said, swiftly dismissing her worry. "But the situation being what it is, you may end up being questioned, too."

Connie shook her head. That didn't matter. She felt her knees buckle.

Randolph assured her that, at this point, there was no evidence to prove Abigail had committed a crime. But His Excellency must know— evidence could always be fabricated.

What if someone simply cooked up a plausible motive?

Then what would happen to Abigail?

※

The O'Brians' townhouse was quiet enough to hear a pin drop. The younger servants had been dismissed. The only ones left were those who had been around since before Abigail's marriage. They had already been told what was happening. They must have been very worried about their mistress, because they had all given up their tasks to gather in the drawing room.

"They're here," Abigail muttered as a horse whinnied in the distance. She stood up, her expression stern, and spoke to a servant standing nearby. "Send a fast horse to the O'Brian domain."

The man nodded.

"You must keep Teddy there. When he finds out what's happened to me, he will probably want to leave immediately, but this is no time for us to go down together. If he resists, tie him up with rope. The church has power in the domain, so Deborah will have a hard time interfering there. Take Lucia and leave right away. After that, do everything as we've arranged. The necessary documents are in the third safe. Leave the business end of things to Walter Robinson. I know I can count on Wal."

Abigail paused.

"In the off chance that anything happens to me—" She looked each of the servants in the eye before continuing in a strong voice. "All of you must escape immediately to the domain."

This was not a plea. It was an order from their mistress.

"Don't worry. Whatever happens, we won't let them touch Rosenkreuz Street or the O'Brian domain," Abigail promised with a smile. She was grateful to Randolph for warning her in advance, at risk to his own safety. They hadn't had much time, but at least they had been able to make arrangements to protect those two places.

Most likely, Deborah was behind this. Abigail had heard about her visit to the Folkvangr several days ago. And Deborah was very good at manipulating people.

"Did you hear me? That applies to you, too, Sebastian."

She had just noticed that the white-haired butler was preparing tea in a corner of the room as if nothing were amiss.

"Oh, did you say something?" he asked placidly. "My hearing isn't so good these days, you know."

Abigail blinked at him in confusion. He didn't look upset in the least.

Abigail had known Sebastian since she first married—no, even longer. He'd been there when she, Teddy, and Rudy were children, playing together to their hearts' content.

Every time she joined in pranks with the two young men, Sebastian used to scold her for being unladylike. Just like he did with Lucia now.

"And my legs aren't what they used to be. I'm afraid I won't be able to leave the mansion for the time being. But if you'll just allow me to say one thing," he said, his eyes crinkling gently. "You, too, are a member of our beloved O'Brian family."

This was the cue for all the other servants to bow their heads. Abigail couldn't help her breath catching.

"If I may say something else—a lady never gives up. We will all be waiting for your safe return, right here."

Abigail felt something hot rising in her chest.

"...You're hopeless," she finally managed to say, knowing full well her voice was shaking pitifully.

※

The dry sound of a palm hitting a cheek filled the room.

Connie shrank back at the mercilessness of it. The slender form swayed before her eyes, stunned by the force of the blow.

Meanwhile, the woman who had just delivered the strike stood with her shoulders slowly heaving, as if she was trying to suppress her fury.

Shortly before this, after hearing that Abigail had been arrested by the Security Force, Connie and Randolph had decided to head to the Folkvangr in hopes of coming up with a plan to help her. When they arrived at the brothel, however, they had stumbled into a warzone unfolding in the drawing room.

"Where did that come from?" Rebekah yelled, glaring at her attacker as she pressed her red cheek.

"Where did that come from, you ask?" came the icy reply. "I should be asking you that question. What the hell did you do?"

Rebekah flinched slightly under the piercing gaze of her companion, who was usually all smiles.

"Wh-why are you so mad? You really are a fool, Miriam. Abby is a duchess. They won't punish her for something like this. It's obvious they'll let her go right away—"

She got no further before Miriam's eyes ignited with anger, and she shook the air with an explosive shout.

"Have you forgotten how easily they executed a duchess's daughter ten years ago?! Aisha Huxley was killed for trying to say that Scarlett Castiel was innocent! Don't you understand what that means?!"

Rebekah's eyes widened.

"You're the fool, Rebekah! Who cares if you've got noble blood? Who cares if you can read? Your so-called beautiful lineage and refined litera-ture didn't save us! Abby did! Abby was the one who rescued us from that hell! Abby…!"

Tears spilled from Miriam's eyes.

"What will we do if she dies…?!" she wailed.

At that point, Rebekah finally seemed to realize what she had done. The blood drained from her face, and the atmosphere in the room grew leaden.

Just then, the door banged open, and Aldous Clayton walked in.

"…What happened to Abigail?"

He must have overheard part of their conversation, because his voice was tense. It was likely he had not yet learned of her arrest. But while he was bound to find out eventually, no one in the room was up to the task of telling him. Abigail had been arrested in the process of trying to help Aldous. Connie, too, found herself unable to tell him the truth.

Nevertheless, after looking around the room—Miriam sobbing, Rebekah pale and downcast, Connie tense—he seemed to guess what had happened.

He drew in a small breath, then spun on his heels and was about to rush out of the room when Connie let out a cry and Randolph grabbed hold of his shoulder.

"Where are you planning to go?"

"To turn myself in."

"…Why?" Randolph asked, groaning as if his head hurt. Instead of answering, Aldous shook off the hand on his shoulder.

"Wait, Aldous Clayton!"

Without replying or hesitating, Aldous spun and swung out his right arm. Connie gasped at the sound of it cutting through the air, but Randolph remained impassive. He simply leaned back slightly and dodged. Aldous swore and immediately followed up with a swing from the left.

This time, Randolph didn't dodge. Diffusing the blow by stepping backward, he caught Aldous's arm with one hand and then lunged toward him, sweeping his foot at Aldous's legs. As Aldous stumbled, Randolph looped behind him, twisted both his hands over his head, and brought him to his knees.

"Let go! I'll kill you!" Aldous shouted, giving Randolph a murderous glare.

Randolph sighed. "Cool down," he said. But his captive showed no sign of playing nice. Twisting lithely from his kneeling position, and with his arms still in Randolph's grasp, Aldous unleashed a roundhouse kick.

Connie ran up to the two in a panic. "P-please, calm down, Mr. Aldous!"

"Get back, Miss Grail!" Randolph shouted.

Connie froze momentarily under his sharp gaze, but she took a deep breath and returned his with her own.

©Yu-nagi

"I will not!" she protested, stepping around so she was in front of the thrashing Aldous. "Listen to me, Mr. Aldous!"

However fiery he might be, he was apparently unwilling to keep struggling in front of Connie. Nevertheless, he gave her a restless, irritated stare.

She understood his sentiment. But...

"If you go now, you'll be playing straight into Deborah's hands! Why do you think Lady Abby went without a fight?! It was for your sake, and for everyone else here! If you ignore that and rush out only to be caught, you won't be helping her at all!"

Aldous had no response to that.

"Then what do you suggest I do...?!" he croaked, devastated.

"We're trying to figure that out!" Connie shouted, projecting her voice. "Right now! All together! We don't have a second to spare! How can you waste time by fighting?!"

She must have looked desperate as she hovered over him, because he blinked in confusion, then mumbled guiltily, "I'm sorry."

Sensing that the gloomy mood had lightened somewhat, Connie let the tension drain from her shoulders. Just then, she heard a commotion coming from the hallway.

"No, stay out!"

A large man with the rough-hewn face of a pirate barged past the prostitutes guarding the door. The man surveyed the room with narrowed eyes, his shoulders squared imposingly.

"*Walter Robinson?*" Scarlett asked in surprise, jogging Connie's memory.

Walter Robinson, king of the shipping business. Yes—the man standing in front of them was one of the top merchants in the capital. Neil Bronson had introduced them.

When Walter noticed Aldous Clayton there, hands held behind his back, his terrible face contorted even more. He strode right toward him. Before Connie or anyone else could stop him, he had punched Aldous in the face.

The prostitutes screamed.

"Damn it, man!" he growled. "How did you let this happen under your watch? Why—why is *Abby* gone…!"

Connie blinked in shock, staring back and forth between Aldous and the intruder.

True, when she met Walter Robinson, he'd told her that Abigail was one of his best customers, but…

"I didn't let Abby leave my ship just so she could end up like this!"

What was he talking about?

Aldous pressed a bag of ice to his cheek, grimaced slightly, and spat out a bloody lump of phlegm.

"Shit, that hurts. Someone as strong as you should hold back a little," he moaned.

Walter glanced at his victim, then sat down innocently on the sofa.

When she was still a teenager, Abigail O'Brian, he explained, once took a trip around the world by ship. Connie had heard the story from Abigail herself. As it happened, the owner of the ship was Walter Robinson, who was at the time a newly minted merchant.

Walter and Abigail were more than merchant and customer—they were old friends.

"Back then, my ship was so small, it could hold only a few passengers. The notion of a nobleman's daughter hitching a ride on a ship like that sounds like a bad joke, doesn't it? But she paid me well, so I let her come and turned a blind eye to her mangy hound, too. I was planning to kick her off the second she complained. As it turned out, she didn't shed a tear. To the contrary, before I knew it, she was bossing me around about how to do business and jumping in on my negotiations with foreign countries. Her quick wit saved me more than once. She was my goddess, and I even proposed to her."

"Of course, she didn't take you seriously," Aldous cut in.

"Shut up, brat," Walter spat back, turning on him with a monstrous expression. Then he sighed and wiped the scowl from his face. "Anyway, I understand the situation. It's worse than I expected. On top of that, we have no plan to turn it around."

He was absolutely right. Since no one could contradict him, quiet filled the room. Walter's strong voice again broke the silence.

"I'm going to break her out of jail and send her off on a ship. As soon as we're at sea, everything will be set. All I have to do is take her to some kingdom that has no diplomatic relations with Adelbide."

Randolph frowned. "…There are too many risks. I can't agree to it."

"Are you saying I should sit by and watch in silence while she's sentenced? You must be kidding. If we use force, we'll have a good chance of winning… Of course, she'll never be able to return to Adelbide."

"What would you do with your company?"

"Not to brag, but I've got a lot of good people. They'll be able to get by without me. Abby's the only reason I settled down in this kingdom to start with. I would happily give up my last penny to save her."

Aldous nodded in agreement. As Walter's plan seemed about to move forward, Connie spoke up on reflex.

"Wh-what about little Lucia?" she blurted out. "And Duke Theodore…!"

"They can join her once things calm down."

"But…"

That wouldn't be a real solution. As Connie hesitated over what to say, Walter lowered his eyebrows in concern.

"I don't think this is an ideal plan myself. I know what you're thinking. But tell me—do you have any other ideas?"

"Um…"

"I thought so. I'm not trying to pick on you, but please don't interrupt."

Connie sighed, slumping against the wall as the others went ahead with their planning.

"Oh, don't make that depressing face," Scarlett said, looking down at her with crossed arms.

"…But I don't think Abby wants to be broken out of jail," Connie said.

Knowing Abigail, she wouldn't want others to put themselves at risk for her sake. On the other hand, Connie understood very well the urge Walter and the others felt to rescue her.

More than anything, Connie was angry at herself for being so helpless. As she bit her lip in frustration, Scarlett shrugged.

"Leave those hotheaded men to themselves. We have our own way of doing things, don't we?" she said.

"But how…?"

If they had no idea who had really killed Aisha, how were they supposed to find evidence to prove Aldous's and Abby's innocence?

"Now, now, just who do you think I am?" came the lighthearted voice from above.

Connie jerked her head up. "You have an idea?!"

"Before I tell you, don't you have something to say to me?" she asked, curling her lips triumphantly.

"Help me, Scarlett…!" Connie pleaded.

Connie couldn't be sure if it was because her words were unexpected, or because she looked so idiotically desperate saying them, but Scarlett widened her amethyst eyes in surprise. Then she broke into a smile.

"Oh well, it can't be helped. I suppose I will assist you," she announced. "Since Abigail is a noble, her sentence will be determined in the Starlight Room of the Grand Merillian. And since there currently is no definite evidence against her, it wouldn't surprise me if some people realize how weak the case is for her as the mastermind. There's a chance she'll be acquitted. To avoid that possibility, her enemies are sure to install someone they can manipulate as judge."

"Then we'd better find the real culprit, and fast—" Connie said in a panic.

"Idiot," Scarlett interrupted. "The reason you never get anywhere is because you're so hung up on truth and evidence and all that silly honesty nonsense. Weren't they the ones who behaved rudely to start with?"

"…Huh?"

"Listen. Any judge they select is bound to be a shady character. So…all we need to do is find the judge's weakness and threaten him into delivering an innocent verdict."

Connie was speechless for a second.

"Threaten him?" she echoed.

Was she imagining things, or had the conversation just turned a little unsavory?

"Yes. A rude greeting for rude people. It's the correct thing for a lady to do," Scarlett said, puffing her chest out before smiling proudly, as if to ask, *What do you think about that?*

Several days passed before they learned the schedule and the name of the judge presiding over Abigail's trial.

Randolph slipped away from work to stop by the Grail residence, dressed in his military uniform and accompanied by Kyle Hughes, which was unusual.

"The judge is Kalvin Campbell, the earl. Members of the Campbell family have been active in judicial circles for generations," Randolph explained. "Their domain is not particularly productive, but they run a number of orphanages and hospitals which seem to bring in a fair amount of money. The family has two sons and one daughter."

"Excuse me," Kyle said, raising his hand. "Additional facts. The bloke divorced and remarried a girl his daughter's age. If that weren't off-putting enough, rumor has it he won't leave the maids alone and has so many bastard kids, he can't count them on one hand. He may be smart, but he's a typical decadent noble who likes his nightlife and his women."

Scarlett nodded knowingly.

"Sounds like there are plenty of skeletons in his closet. That makes our job easy."

Connie gave her a questioning look. She sighed.

"What I mean is, so long as we set an appealing trap, that idiot Kalvin Campbell

is *bound to stumble straight into it,*" Scarlett said, as if she were giving a lesson to a dull student.

She smiled, obviously pleased with her evil scheme.

"And I know just the trap to set."

"You want me to host the Earl John Doe Ball?" Viscount Hamsworth asked, his round belly shaking in disbelief. "No matter how much money I make, I've never been more than a guest, so I assumed the privilege was reserved for high nobles."

Hamsworth's eyes glittered with excitement as he sat in the neighborhood church.

He was right. Only high-ranking nobles with a long lineage—Deborah Darkian topping the list—were allowed to oversee the questionable gatherings. For this occasion, Randolph was allowing Connie to use his family connection to Duke Richelieu. Incidentally, when Connie brought the idea up with His Excellency the Grim Reaper, he had let out a long sigh and said, "Please don't do anything reckless."

"I assume this comes with a price?" asked the viscount, who appeared very excited about the chance to host. He was practically panting as he leaned toward Connie. She leaned away from him.

"I'd like you to invite K-Kalvin Campbell," she said.

He blinked. "Really, is that all?"

He seemed surprised.

"Hey you, if Kalvin doesn't show up, we'll do more than slap you across the face," Scarlett said, fixing an icy gaze on the viscount.

Hamsworth showed no reaction.

Abigail had said the viscount could see spirits, like Lucia, but as far as Connie could see, he showed no sign of it today.

It must be a rumor after all.

"Knowing the viscount, all I have to say is that if I invite some pretty girls, he'll come running. But just to be sure, why don't I line up some high-class prostitutes and throw a wild party? People will be less suspicious if I do something newsworthy. No one's ever invited prostitutes to the Earl John Doe Ball before, so I'll have bragging rights. By the way, do you know any elegant goddesses up to the task of entertaining nobles?"

Scarlett sighed with exasperation.

"The only thing you've ever excelled at is thinking up low-class party ideas," she said.

Not to say he heard her words, but the viscount curled his lips in profound amusement.

"A party?"

As soon as Connie had related her conversation with the viscount to Miriam, the latter made up her mind.

"I'll go." She didn't seem at all hesitant. "You want me to snag the man named Campbell, right?" she asked, looking very serious.

If Miriam, the flower of the Folkvangr, was part of the plan, then the ball was sure to be every bit as newsworthy as Hamsworth hoped. Earl Campbell, the rumored playboy, was sure to show an interest as well.

Connie gave a firm nod. But Rebekah must have been listening in on their conversation, because she broke in sharply.

"...You're taking off work without asking? That's against our contract. Audrey will charge you an arm and a leg for that. She might even suspend you," she said sternly.

Connie was surprised to hear that, but Miriam didn't bat an eyelash.

"You don't need to tell me that," she said coolly. "And what of it?"

Today, however, Rebekah did not flinch.

"I'll go," she said, fixing a repentant gaze on Miriam. "...I know what I did was stupid. You might not believe me at this point, but I never meant to get Abby in trouble. I was just acting like a foolish, selfish child. Give me a chance to make it up. I'll do whatever it takes to save Abby."

But despite her desperate plea, Miriam seemed unmoved.

"You don't have what it takes. After all, you've never once outearned me."

Rebekah bit her lip.

"So...," Miriam continued, a little more gently. "What if we went together?"

Rebekah's almond eyes widened. Miriam shook her head, frowning.

"I'm going to be honest. I still haven't forgiven you for what you did. But I must admit—I'll be in trouble if Campbell turns out to like flat-chested women," she announced with resignation, sticking out her bountiful chest.

It was the day of the Earl John Doe Ball. Among the more sharp-eared, the event was already a topic of conversation. Viscount Hamsworth informed Connie with great pleasure that Kalvin Campbell was, of course, included on the guest list.

When she arrived at the Folkvangr to pick up Miriam and Rebekah, she found a line of beautiful prostitutes waiting for her inside.

"What's going on?" she asked, confused. One of the women, slightly older than the others, stepped forward.

"We heard about the situation. Please do your best for Abby."

She lowered her head. The other women followed her lead.

"Oh, um, please, you don't have to bow to me...!" Connie said, trying to stop them.

They shook their heads in unison.

"We appreciate what you're doing. And we're sorry. We'd all very much like to go, but we can't leave the Folkvangr empty. We're sure Miriam and Rebekah will do a wonderful job. Go now. Before Audrey finds out what you're up to."

Rebekah and Miriam, both wearing broad-brimmed hats, stepped forward and stood one on each side of Connie.

"Good luck!" "We're counting on you!" "I hope it goes well!" the other women called after them as they prepared to depart.

Just then, a hoarse voice called out from the entryway.

"Who is doing what?"

The excitement abruptly subsided to a hush.

Audrey narrowed her eyes and strode briskly inside. She gazed around at the group of prostitutes. When she reached the elaborately dressed pair beside Connie, she raised her eyebrows slightly.

"You mean to tell me that Miriam and Rebekah are the only flowers to be offered up at this *funeral?* If that is the best we can do, I'm afraid the good name of the Folkvangr will suffer."

Miriam couldn't let that go unanswered. "Abby isn't dead yet. I think you're a bit young to be going senile, old lady!"

"Miriam. You may look like you wouldn't hurt a fly, but you're as willful as ever. Just like I was in my younger days. Laura, pull down the shutters."

Laura was the woman who had spoken to Connie first. She glanced suspiciously at Audrey.

"Don't you get it? I'm closing the establishment."

The women exchanged confused glances. Audrey pulled a letter from her bosom.

"Do you know what this is? I whipped this old body into shape and rode all the way out to the country to fetch this from Theodo—I mean, Duke O'Brian. It's a bond that states until Abigail returns, I am the rightful owner of this brothel. And that means what I say goes, and no backtalk."

She gazed slowly around the room.

"Your job today is to cultivate some new customers. You will be working at the old Montrose residence. I hear there will be a grand party there tonight. So hurry up and get dressed. All of you!"

The old Montrose residence—the longtime site of the Earl John Doe Ball.

In other words, she was telling the entire staff to take part in the ball to rescue Abigail.

There was a moment of silence, then a chorus of delighted voices.

Miriam and Rebekah stood in shock while the other women swung into action with sparkling eyes.

"Audrey, may I use the powdered pearl makeup?" "What about the coral lipstick?" "I want to wear the moonlight silk dress!"

Although her arms were crossed sternly, the older woman generously approved all their requests.

"Tonight is special. Use whatever you want," she said. Then she added, loudly enough for Connie to hear, "Honestly, I couldn't care less what happens to that tomboy Abigail. But making a move on that busybody is the same as picking a fight with me. I'm a mild, merciful, generous woman, but if someone slaps me, I'm not going to turn the other cheek." She snorted disdainfully. "Listen up, my beautiful girls. You are a chaste and prudent lot, so I would like to give you a bit of advice."

The manager of the Folkvangr fixed her employees with the same stern expression she used to scold rowdy customers causing trouble in the pleasure district.

"If those idiots want a fight, they deserve no mercy. I want you to use all your wiles and charms to strip them of everything they have. Don't leave them a single breadcrumb."

Kalvin Campbell felt his agitation rising.

A particularly ugly, nouveau riche viscount was hosting the Earl John Doe Ball and had invited prostitutes from the Folkvangr.

This sensational story had made the rounds of society in a flash.

Despite the event's fast-approaching date, everyone who was anyone had probed their connections, trying to secure an invitation. All of them were captives to vulgar entertainment—no matter how much they furrowed their brows and put on a prim and proper face.

Kalvin was no different. He had called the barber specially for the event, put on a custom-made mask, and applied cologne liberally. He might be past forty, but he felt confident in his good looks.

For some reason, though, the gorgeously blooming flowers gracing the hall of the old Montrose residence seemed interested in every man except Kalvin.

It was immediately obvious which ones were the prostitutes. They were not guests but rather entertainment arranged by the viscount. For that reason, they did not wear masks. Their beautiful faces were on full display.

Kalvin glared bitterly at the other men, so satisfied with themselves. He hadn't arrived late. He had had plenty of opportunity to lavish attention on the flowers. But they had not chosen him. This hurt his pride severely.

Suddenly, a buzz ran through the room. A lady with the alluring body of an enchantress and the innocent face of an angel had arrived.

It was Miriam—greatest treasure of the Folkvangr, the Rose Fairy.

She was both bewitching and delicate, and Kalvin felt himself stumbling toward her like a bee to honey.

"Lady," he said.

Miriam turned to him and smiled as joyfully as if she were greeting an old lover. Despite his age, his heart fluttered at her favorable response. He took a step forward. Just then, a plump arm encircled her waist, followed by a boorish announcement.

"Excuse me. This is my date."

The man's mask was virtually meaningless. It was Hamsworth, host of the evening's festivities.

Kalvin hesitated. He might be poorer than Hamsworth, but he was certainly of higher standing. Normally, even if he was talking to a priest, he would have had an easy time making the man apologize for his rudeness. But this was the Earl John Doe Ball. Here, showing off one's social standing was the real discourtesy, and it would make him the object of ridicule.

He'd lost out to a man who was clearly uglier and of lower standing than him, and he could hear the sounds of mocking laughter from the other guests. Kalvin ground his teeth and silently retreated.

It was humiliating. Frustrating, vexing, and humiliating.

He could hardly bear to look at the ballroom. He tossed back drinks recklessly.

As he was standing around in irritation, he felt someone bump into him. He clicked his tongue loudly.

It was a woman with black hair. She flinched.

"I-I'm so sorry."

The face that looked up at him in fear wore no mask. In other words, she was a prostitute. And not a bad-looking one at that. Tears gathered in her eyes as a hint of distress overcame her features.

Kalvin felt his anger melting away. He took the woman's hand and spoke to her in a soothing voice.

"Oh dear, this will not do. Your face is like a beautiful moon hidden behind dark clouds. It can't only be because we bumped into each other, can it? Has something sad happened?"

The black-haired beauty shook her head.

"This is not the right place for such a story…"

"Perhaps I can become the wind that blows away the clouds." He drew his brows together in a show of deep concern.

The woman hesitated, then spoke. "You may know that my employer has been detained."

She must be talking about Abigail O'Brian. He didn't just know her; he was the one who would determine her fate.

That was right. But unfortunately, that verdict had already been decided. Poor Abigail O'Brian would never see the light of day again.

"My name is Rebekah. I was raised in a lower noble family, but we fell on hard times and I took up this line of work. When I think about becoming destitute again, I feel so afraid, I simply can't stand it."

"Perhaps I can do something to help you." Rebekah's face jerked up.

Kalvin gave a satisfied nod. "I have money, if that's what you need. I can't think of anything better to spend it on than a beautiful woman like you."

He was proposing monetary support—in other words, to become her patron.

The woman before him was not as alluring as Miriam, but she was still more than worthy of his admiration.

Just as he was thinking of how pleased she must be by his proposal, she sighed as if she had lost hope completely.

"The truth is, Viscount Hamsworth made exactly the same offer."

"What?"

The insult he had received from Hamsworth earlier flitted across his mind. After that, there was no way he could stand by in this situation.

"How much did he offer?"

The figure Rebekah named for a month of support would allow a commoner to live a life of ease and enjoyment for an entire year.

Noveau riche pig, Kalvin thought, clicking his tongue in irritation.

"...I'll double it," he said decisively.

Rebekah's eyes widened.

"What's wrong?" he asked.

She seemed to be thinking about something. Then she furrowed her brows and leaned in close to him. "...I couldn't possibly accept such a generous offer from someone I've never even met," she whispered into his ear.

Ah, so she was asking him to reveal his identity. She seemed awfully prudent for a whore.

"I'm Kalvin. Kalvin Campbell."

"The earl?"

She gasped theatrically. He surmised that she was shocked to discover his position was higher than Hamsworth's. Kalvin's pent-up anger subsided. Yet for some reason, the woman still appeared glum.

"But I've heard that the lord of the Campbell domain is very *frugal*, as are his subjects. I wouldn't wish to burden you. Perhaps the viscount's offer is more..."

He had assumed she would jump at his offer once she knew he was a high-ranked noble, but it seemed she had quite the education, as expected of the capital's most high-class brothel. Her pointed mention of the "frugal" nature of the Campbell domain, which was indeed far from wealthy, suggested that she knew all about his financial situation.

Having evidently given up on Kalvin, Rebekah said she really must be going, then she straightened up and turned away. The room beyond her was filled with men either chatting happily or dancing cheek to cheek with the prostitutes.

Out of the corner of his eye, Kalvin glimpsed Miriam and the pig smiling warmly at one another.

Blood rushed to Kalvin's head. His pride would not allow him to lose out to Hamsworth a second time.

"I—I have the money! I really do!"

Rebekah stopped and slowly turned back toward him. Tilting her head and narrowing her almond eyes, she asked, "…And how is that?"

The colorfully dressed women spun around and around the entrance hall.

Who would guess the delicate creatures were in reality carnivorous flowers waiting to devour their prey?

Wearing her jet-black mask, Connie gazed down on the scene from the second-floor balcony. It seemed that Rebekah had already skillfully nabbed the earl.

Just as she was letting out a sigh of relief, however, Scarlett tilted her head in confusion.

"What's Kimberly Smith doing here?"

Her slender white finger was pointing to the balcony directly across from them. Connie glanced up casually, then made a sound like a strangled goose.

Although the woman's face was covered, her plump form was swathed in a pink dress and a pink mask. Connie knew only one person with such an utterly incomprehensible fashion sense. She must be the lady's committee representative of that citizen's group—the Violet Association, if she remembered right. She had once subjected Connie to quite a tongue-lashing.

"What in the world could a person who hates nobles so much be doing at this party? ...Although, she does seem to be enjoying herself," Scarlett noted.

Criticizing the privileged class in public while skimming the cream off their lifestyle in private. *I suppose such people do exist*, Connie thought. Whatever she was up to, Connie didn't want to cross her path.

Turning in the opposite direction, she spotted two women coming toward her from the other side of the hallway.

One was tall with a large build and blond hair, while the other—who seemed to be warning her companion about something—was slender with silver hair and eyes.

Connie found that particular combination of features very familiar. Although they were wearing masks, she was certain they were the tourists she had met on the main street, San and Eularia.

But what were they doing here...?

San must have felt Connie's eyes on her, because just as she was about to pass by, she stopped and turned toward her, then tilted her head in thought.

After a moment, she seemed to realize that the girl in the black mask was the same young woman who had given them directions several days earlier.

"What a coincidence!" San said cheerfully, removing her mask. "We heard there was a suspicious ball going on tonight, and to tell you the truth, I'm wild about suspicious things these days."

Well, that's unsettling. Connie's cheek twitched as she took a step back.

"But enough about that," the woman went on. "Thank you for your kindness the other day! It was a huge help. The Holy Grail girl, wasn't it?"

"What?"

Did she just say the *Holy Grail?*

Eularia sighed in exasperation. "San, you really are hopeless. You must mean Miss Grail." She turned to Connie. "I'm sorry. The name Grail seems to have reminded her of the Old Farish story about the Holy Grail."

"Exactly! It's not a very common name over there," San said with an easygoing smile.

Connie blinked. "Are you from Faris?"

"We are," San answered, placing her hand on her chest and bowing politely. Then, with a flowing gesture, she took Connie's hand.

"Um?" Connie said, confused.

Ignoring her, San kissed her fingertips.

"Umm?"

"May I have this dance, my lady?"

"…Ummm?"

San grinned, satisfied with Connie's flustered reaction. She seemed like the playful type.

After Connie politely turned down the invitation, San stepped back so readily, Connie almost felt disappointed. The visitors from Faris then turned and took their leave.

Scarlett watched pair walk off, her arms crossed.

"…*There's more to them than meets the eye, I think. No ordinary tourist would be able to attend this party. Who in the world could have invited them? And judging by their behavior, I'm certain they're nobles.*"

Connie nodded in agreement. The two women moved and spoke with impressive refinement. That was certainly true of the delicate Eularia, but even San, who at first glance seemed rougher—and did indeed behave a little sloppily—spoke and moved with great elegance.

If it was true that they had come from Faris, then they were probably Farish nobles.

Faris. Connie unconsciously frowned. According to Lily's letter, the aim of the Holy Grail of Eris was the invasion of Adelbide by Faris.

Did that make those women their enemies? Or—

"Miss Connie?"

Connie turned around in surprise. A familiar figure was standing beside her, her hand resting gently on her cheek.

"Laura!"

Partly because of her age, Laura was treated a bit like an older sister or spokeswoman by the other prostitutes.

She flipped her hair alluringly to one side and flashed a gorgeous smile. "Rebekah has the information," she whispered.

The "information" Laura related was somewhat unexpected.

"...Black money?"

"Yes. You said Campbell had debts, didn't you?"

Connie nodded. One of Kalvin Campbell's favorite pastimes was gambling, and he was being hounded to repay his resulting debts. She had gotten this information from Randolph and passed it on to the prostitutes before they arrived at the ball.

The Campbell domain wasn't rich to start with, and the earl, at his wit's end, had begun to sell off hospitals and orphanages long owned by his family to help pay what he owed.

"But he claimed to have money to give Rebekah. When she pressed him on it, he said he'd been filching money from one of the institutions he oversees."

"Dear me," Scarlett broke in with a smile. *"His lips are so loose, they seem liable to fall right off his face. I'll bet he's got a few screws loose upstairs, too."*

Connie was skeptical.

"But wouldn't he be found out right away...?"

Everyone had to report their income to the government. A sudden increase would surely raise questions about its source.

When she said as much to Laura, the older woman smiled casually.

"Oh, but you can launder it. For example, you could inflate your invoices here and there, or fabricate some business with a company that doesn't exist. But it seems Campbell wasn't able to do anything that audacious. He simply made use of an existing citizens' group."

"A citizens' group...?"

"Yes. Have you ever heard of the Violet Association? Apparently, a friend of his does the accounting for their youth committee. He transferred loads of money under the heading of 'Donations.' A clear-cut crime, isn't it?"

"The Violet Association…"

Connie thought of the woman in pink, Kimberly Smith.

Scarlett snorted.

"It's time we had a little talk with that woman, Connie."

The blindingly bright mass of pink glared at Connie.

"And who are you?"

Both her dress and the mask covering the upper portion of her face were the same revolting shade.

She was quite a contrast to Connie in her jet mask and high-necked mourning dress. Connie hesitated for a moment.

"I am the viscount's daughter, C.," she finally said with a curtsy. Kimberly narrowed her eyes.

"Well, well," she said, having most likely recognized her from the hint. "Did you need something?"

Although her smile was welcoming, the eyes behind her mask were a different story. They were filled instead with a cold, probing light.

Wanting to avoid a long conversation, Connie decided to get straight to the point.

"What is your relationship to Kalvin Campbell?"

"The earl? He is a marvelous man, despite being a noble. He approves of our activities."

"And who's the one enjoying herself so much at the nobles' party?" Scarlett asked, sounding fed up.

Excellent point, Connie thought to herself. Her face must have revealed her thoughts, because Kimberly added sheepishly, "…The earl said this would be a good opportunity for me to learn more about the behavior of nobles and brought me as his guest. He's so thoughtful about things like that."

Connie couldn't help frowning.

"Is he also thoughtful about donations?" she asked.

"No need to glower at me," Kimberly said, looking confused. "Donating money isn't a crime, is it?"

"Not as long as the money was obtained legally."

"…What are you talking about?"

"I heard someone is cooking the books."

Kimberly's suspicious expression betrayed no hint of recognition. "Cooking the books?"

She looked genuinely puzzled. Connie blinked. According to Laura, Kalvin Campbell's friend was on the youth committee. Kimberly had said she represented the ladies' committee, so maybe she really didn't have anything to do with this.

"…Did the earl say that?"

Kimberly's expression had hardened noticeably. She glanced toward the entrance hall.

"I do believe…the purpose of tonight's ball is to save Abigail O'Brian."

Connie froze.

Perhaps because she was so obviously upset, Kimberly laughed, her stout body shaking all over with mirth. "I never dreamed there was a rat in our midst. The blunder may have been in the youth committee, but it's still a disgrace. The nerve of that man, using a poor citizens' organization to hide his crimes! I've been taken for a fool."

"Huh?" Connie interjected, confused. She was met with more laughter before the woman continued.

"But you did come up with an interesting plan. Instead of playing fair and relying on the weight of the law, you've chosen to fight fire with fire. Quite a scheme for someone so sincere! Don't worry, that's a compliment. After all, your approach is much faster and surer than arranging a jailbreak."

Having grown suddenly loquacious, Kimberly stepped deliberately toward Connie and whispered in her ear.

"You meant to free Abigail by threatening him, didn't you?"

Connie gulped, but her interrogator continued.

"Not a bad plan at all, I must admit. But I don't think you're quite up to the task. Kalvin is an idiotic fool, but he's very good at wicked deeds. We all have our strengths and weaknesses. And you, from what I can tell, seem to be awful at wickedness," she announced with a laugh.

It seemed she wasn't the bad-tempered middle-aged housewife Connie had taken her for after all.

"As they say, dressmaking should be left to the tailors. I happen to be an expert in this kind of thing, and I have an inkling who the traitor is. I'll settle things for you. We can't allow the O'Brians to be overthrown now. And certainly not to the Darkians' advantage. Not after ten years of chipping away at their strength. It's a nice opportunity for *us* as well."

Connie stared at her, mouth agape.

"You don't believe me? Then I'll give you a hint," she whispered in a singsong voice. "What color are violets?"

Connie stood staring at a violet sprouting by the side of the road. Its magenta petals fluttered in the breeze.

In Adelbide, these flowers were also called "purples." Their color was affected by geography, and so the shade varied slightly from kingdom to kingdom, but here they were all magenta. They were the first thing that came to mind at the mention of purple. A brilliant reddish hue, somewhat different from the amethyst of Scarlett's eyes.

And it was also a symbol of royalty.

What color are violets?

What could she have meant?

No matter how much Connie pondered the question, she couldn't come up with an answer. But the fierce look in Kimberly's eyes had been enough to convince her to leave Kalvin Campbell in her hands. Scarlett did not oppose this, though from time to time she seemed to be contemplating something.

Incidentally, the violets in neighboring Faris had a bluer hue more in line with their name. That shade of purple had been the color of the royal family in the days of the Faris Empire, and in that land where bloodlines were intensely valued, violet eyes (or something very close) were said to be indispensable for succeeding to the throne even today.

Connie sighed. She felt like she would start shaking if she didn't keep distracting herself with unrelated trains of thought.

Several hours had already passed since Abigail's trial began. Randolph was attending the proceedings in the Starlight Room of the Grand Merillian. He had promised to stop by the house afterward, but she had been too nervous to stand around doing nothing and finally left in a rush for the palace. Now she was standing in front of the building, waiting for the verdict to be delivered.

"I wonder if it'll turn out all right," she said to Scarlett.

"That depends on Kimberly Smith."

"I wonder...!"

Connie was growing more and more worried. What if Kimberly had been putting on an act? What if she was in on the earl's scheme?

If Abigail was found guilty, they would be forced to implement the jailbreak Walter and Aldous had cooked up. According to the women at the brothel, the two men were moving steadily ahead with preparations.

"Oh, she'll be fine," Scarlett said, unable to watch Connie torment herself any longer. *"After all, I think that woman..."*

But before she could finish her thought, an unexpected voice called Connie's name.

"Miss Grail?"

It was Randolph.

Connie instantly took off running. "Your Excellency!" She rushed to the front gate and grabbed both of his hands. "Wh-what happened? What was the verdict?!"

Randolph Ulster's habitual blank face showed no change in response to his fiancée's desperate pleas.

"Abigail was acquitted due to lack of evidence. Although the judge looked as if he'd received a death sentence."

Connie took in the words slowly.

Acquitted due to lack of evidence.

In other words—

"I'm so glad!!!!"

Abigail was free. Connie let out a long sigh of relief, and tears blurred her vision. The tension drained from every corner of her body. She felt as if she was going to crumble to the ground then and there.

Just as she was about to topple over, however, a strong arm encircled her waist and pulled her close.

"Are you all right?"

He was so close.

Unexpectedly, she found herself in a kind of embrace. Her body tensed. He was so close. So very close. She was so close to his body. That manly face of his was right there when she looked up.

The cerulean eyes staring down at her made her feel jittery. As she might expect for a military man, every bit of him was muscular. It was like he was embracing her—no, he was just helping her keep her balance. A Good Samaritan's clutch was completely different from a lover's caress. *Get a grip, Constance Grail!*

She felt her face growing hot.

Randolph gave her a puzzled look.

"Your face is flushed. Do you have a fever—"

His angular finger stretched toward her face.

"Oh no, noo!" she shrieked. "No, I'm fine!"

Later, a very suitable suspect was apprehended, and the night after admitting to Aisha's murder, he committed suicide. Aldous Clayton's name was cleared, and Marcella, once again the editor of the *Mayflower*, was given back the position she had previously resigned from.

And Amelia Hobbes, who had started the whole ruckus, was fired.

©Yu-nagi

According to Aldous, knowledge of the incident had spread throughout the industry, and it was unlikely anyone would publish an article by her ever again.

"Well, she made her bed and now she's lying in it," Scarlett said when she heard the news, a frighteningly beautiful smile gracing her lips.

※

They think I'll just give up?

A sour smell assaulted Amelia's nose. She was waiting doggedly for her prey outside the ramshackle little church. *Me, give up?* After being turned away by several other papers, she finally realized that her former employer must have a hand in it and flew into a rage. She would not let this be the end of her. She would stage a comeback. And to do that, she needed a scandal so big, everyone would pounce on it.

Presently, a woman emerged from the church, her hood pulled low over her eyes. Amelia leapt in front of her path.

"Crown Princess Cecilia!"

The woman slowly raised her head, exposing an even-featured face. Contrary to Amelia's expectation, however, her expression was scornful.

"The crown princess? Who's that? You've got the wrong woman, I reckon."

Amelia flinched at her tone, which contained no trace of refinement. To start with, Amelia was a commoner, and she had no idea what Cecilia looked like. She had seen her only occasionally and from a great distance at public ceremonies. Doubt boiled up within her. Maybe this really was someone else?

But the woman's eyes were rose-colored, just like the crown princess's. Amelia decided to risk it.

"…You're not really a viscount's daughter, are you? You're the child of a prostitute."

The woman did not seem shaken in the least.

"Most of us around here are the children of whores or criminals," she said with a cackle.

"I went to the Luze domain," Amelia continued. "Unfortunately, I heard the orphanage where you grew up was lost in a fire. Most of the orphans burned to death, they said. Only two of them were unaccounted for. You—and a boy called Cici."

The woman abruptly stopped laughing.

"I heard you were as close as lovers... Where is he now?"

The woman's emotionless eyes fixed on Amelia. A chill ran down her back.

"...Cici is dead," the woman spat out.

Amelia looked up in surprise. "So it is you...!"

As she stepped toward the crown princess, a knife flashed dully at her throat.

"Do you want to die, too?"

Her voice was chillingly calm. Amelia was too terrified to speak.

The tip of the knife pushed into her skin. She felt sharp pain and the trickle of something warm. Her heart pounded. The blood drained from her face, and she broke out in a cold sweat. Trembling, Amelia shook her head again and again. The knife edged backward. She was safe. She sank to the ground.

Cecilia looked down on Amelia and smiled as gently as the Holy Mother.

"Then pack up your things and leave the kingdom by tonight. If you don't—I'll dye that pathetic hair of yours a brighter shade of red."

※

Lucia came flying into Abigail's arms, her eyes red and puffy.

"I wasn't worried about you, not even the tiniest bit!" she cried.

But her voice hiccupped here and there, and her small shoulders shook as if she were holding back sobs. Abigail hugged Lucia close, her expression somewhere between tears and laughter. The maids watching the scene dabbed their eyes.

The elderly butler was there, too, standing beside the pair with a gentle smile on his lips.

©Yu-nagi

Watching this heartwarming scene, Connie felt herself on the verge of tears, too.

It had taken several days for Abigail to complete the various forms required to be released after the trial. Connie had gone to pick her up and had been invited inside once they arrived at the O'Brian residence. Everyone seemed to have been eagerly anticipating their mistress's return home.

No sooner had Abigail stepped down from the carriage than the little princess came running headlong into her arms. Her brave front aside, it was clear she had been unbearably worried.

Connie joined Abigail and Lucia for tea and then took her leave. She thought the family probably wanted to enjoy some time alone, today more than ever.

As she was getting ready to leave, Aldous approached her.

"Sorry," he said bluntly. As Connie blinked in confusion, Abigail burst out laughing.

"You don't sound very repentant," she said.

"Shut up. You shouldn't have been arrested to start with. Caused us a hell of a lot of trouble, I'll say. Next time you'd better split before they catch you so you don't slow us down."

"Yes, I do suppose it was all my fault. So please stop sulking."

"I'm not sulking."

"Once again, unrepentant."

The three of them walked to the front door, chatting casually. But when they opened it, they discovered two people waiting outside. The smile vanished from Aldous's face as he stepped protectively in front of Connie and Abigail.

"Greetings, Holy Grail girl."

Ignoring the bloodthirsty look in Aldous's eyes, the blond woman whom Connie had met only a few days ago greeted her with a relaxed wave. Today she was dressed casually and carried the same long, cloth-wrapped bundle she had the first time they'd met.

"Her name is Miss Grail, San! Are you doing that on purpose?" her slender, silver-haired companion corrected her. She looked like she had a headache.

"Friends of yours?" Abigail asked Connie, who tensed.

"They're tourists from Faris, supposedly. We've only met by chance twice, so I wouldn't call them friends, exactly…"

"By chance?" Abigail echoed, sounding puzzled, but quickly put on a perfect smile and turned to the women. "Then this must be the third *chance* meeting, I suppose? Did you have some business with my young friend here?"

Connie couldn't tell if San was intentionally ignoring the air of intimidation in that question or if she had simply missed it, but the woman smiled brightly back at Abigail as she replied.

"No, I stopped by because I was impressed by the rescue operation. I see Miss Grail's friend is a worrywart, so I'll be straightforward," she said, taking a step forward. "About Daeg Gallus, that is."

The moment she said those words, Aldous pulled a pistol from his breast pocket. At the same time, Connie felt a gust of wind and heard something cutting through the air.

"The men of Adelbide certainly are quick on the draw," San said with a low chuckle as she held the blade of a large, old-fashioned sword to Abigail's neck.

Connie wondered where in the world the weapon had come from— then noticed that the bundle on her back was gone. So this was what it had held.

"Not as fast as women from Faris," Aldous muttered, his gun still pointed straight at San.

"I wonder which would come first, the bullet in my head or this blade in your mistress's throat?"

"Should we test it and see?" Aldous asked with a cynical grimace. The tension grew.

What should I do?

Connie held her breath. Someone sighed—no, two people.

"Rudy, stop it."

"San, your jokes really do go too far."

"Can't help it," she said with a smile, lowering her sword.

Seeing that, Aldous reluctantly lowered his gun. Eularia bowed her head apologetically.

"I'm very sorry for my companion's excessive rudeness. The truth is, we are here to ask your help."

Aldous clicked his tongue in irritation. "Is that how you act when you want our cooperation?" he sneered.

"Rudy!"

"No, he's right. San is just…a very free spirit."

"A fine compliment," San interjected with a loud laugh. "But it's true that I can't exactly depend on weaklings."

"San, you don't need to say anything else. By which I mean, please be quiet now or we'll never get anywhere."

Pierced by an icy stare from Eularia, even the bold San nodded meekly and fell silent.

"We are supporters of Faris's third princess," Eularia said. Abigail frowned as if she was trying to remember something.

"The third princess…would that be Alexandra?" she asked after a moment. "If I recall correctly, she has been imprisoned by the opposing faction, no? But why have you abandoned your leader to come here?"

"Because it is the wish of the princess herself. She was close with Sir Ulysses, so we swiftly received news of his kidnapping."

"Kidnapping?" Abigail asked, her eyes widening in surprise. Connie gasped. So much had happened that she'd forgotten all about the fate of the young prince.

"Yes. Of course, if circumstances allowed, we would like nothing more than to devote ourselves to freeing the princess. But that cannot be. Do you know anything about Faris's financial situation?"

"A trader and acquaintance of mine told me the kingdom is barely surviving."

"That is true. King Hendrick collapsed at a truly unfortunate time," Eularia said with a tired sigh. She appeared to have no strong respect for or attachment to the king.

"Anyhow…the princess opposes the war," she concluded.

"Got tired of explaining?" San muttered.

The statement did lack context. Connie and even Abigail were left feeling confused.

"…Wait. What do you mean?"

"Right now, the people holding the reins while the king is on his sickbed are in favor of starting a war. Now do you understand? The king's other children have all been won over, and preparations for war are underway in our homeland. And their target is Adelbide."

Abigail's face darkened.

"…I thought there was a peace treaty between our two kingdoms. If Faris ignores that treaty and starts a war, wouldn't that give our neighbors an excuse to interfere?" she asked.

"Yes, if the invasion were unprovoked. That is why they are creating a justification."

"Exactly," San interrupted in a casual tone. "That's why they've taken Ulysses. It seems the hawks intend to expose his kidnapping, then advance on Adelbide in retaliation. It was fortunate that he wasn't an official member of the delegation. Our people are parading a double around back home so as many people as possible will see him. It's no more than a diversion, of course. I don't know how long the situation will last, but for now, both sides are watching the other. My guess is we have until the delegation returns home. That's in less than a month."

San lowered her head, her face serious. "Daeg Gallus is behind the kidnapping. Both of us want to crush them. So will you consider helping us find Ulysses?" she asked.

Connie considered the situation. The women did not seem to be lying. Ulysses really had been kidnapped, and Lily Orlamunde's letter had said that the Holy Grail of Eris referred to Faris's operation to invade Adelbide. Everything lined up.

Connie hated the idea of war. She wanted to help them if she could. But one person could only do so much.

"I think we ought to ask the Security Force to help...," she suggested timidly.

Eularia shook her head. "They may already be infiltrated by the organization. That's why Kendall Levine came to us for help without saying anything publicly. We've heard there are Daeg Gallus operatives at the highest levels of Adelbide's government."

"I-I'm getting dizzy..."

Connie had thought the criminal group was only involved in selling drugs, but it seemed she had been wrong.

"This plan has been in the works for over a decade, after all," said San. "It's hugely important. In fact, our chancellor tried to start a war with Adelbide back then, too. Although they were forced to give it up at the last moment."

Abigail, who had been listening with arms crossed, broke in.

"...Why did the attempt ten years ago fail?"

She was probably hoping to find a clue as to their next move.

"You don't know?" San asked, looking puzzled for once.

What had brought down Daeg Gallus's scheme and plunged Faris into a decade of hardship?

Sunlight glinting off her blond hair, San continued as if the answer were the most obvious thing in the world.

"Why, the execution of Scarlett Castiel, of course."

※

Unfortunately, the master of the house was not at home. The butler who answered the door informed Randolph that he would be back soon and led him into the drawing room.

He wasn't sure how long he waited. He was the one who had decided to come in the first place. And yet, in his heart of hearts, he wouldn't have minded if the master never arrived.

Because if Randolph's line of thought was right—then the truth was unbearably cruel and sad.

"Have you come with all your cards in hand this time?"

Perhaps that was why the taunting voice rattled him so much.

Randolph let out the breath he had been holding and slowly raised his face. The man standing before him had lost none of his beauty to age. Adolphus Castiel. A key figure in the kingdom, with the magenta eyes of royalty.

Everyone associated the Grails with sincerity, but truth be told, Randolph knew of no more *sincere* a man than Adolphus.

Not as a person, but rather in his loyalty to the kingdom.

As far as Randolph knew, he had never lived his life as the individual man Adolphus. He lived it as a Castiel who had sworn his loyalty to Adelbide.

The principle behind his actions was always the same: service to the kingdom.

"…Scarlett's mother was Aliénore Shibola, am I right?" Randolph asked.

From his place on the sofa, Adolphus smiled warmly in affirmation. "According to my research, the originator of the Shibola line was Cornelia Faris. What's more, Aliénore was a direct descendant of Cornelia," Randolph went on.

Randolph didn't know why Adolphus married Aliénore. But at the very least, the man before him had known where she came from—the origin of Crownless Aliénore. Randolph was also certain it had been the will of the king. Because every move Adolphus Castiel made was for the sake of the kingdom.

"Lily's letter didn't include the details, but I think the Holy Grail of Eris—"

Adolphus slowly narrowed his eyes. Their strong red tint was characteristic of Adelbide's royal family.

But Scarlett's eyes were amethyst, a perfect blend of red and blue.

In contrast, the eyes of Faris's current royal family were a bluish purple. Eyes the shade of Scarlett's held a different meaning.

They were the symbol of the lost Starry Crown.

"The true aim of the Holy Grail of Eris was to enthrone Scarlett Castiel, who carried the blood of Faris's old imperial family. With her as their new queen, Adelbide would become a vassal state of Faris in both name and fact."

The blood that ran in Scarlett's veins was, for Faris, the Starry Crown itself.

"Those bloodline-obsessed Farish nobles must have been trying to revive the colonial arrangement from back in the days of empire," Randolph said.

Adolphus remained silent. He listened to Randolph with no sign of anxiety or agitation.

"In the beginning, Cecilia Luze's role was simply to become Enrique's lover and manipulate him from the shadows. I doubt she set out to become crown princess. To start with, no ordinary duke's daughter—and a Castiel, one of the four great noble families, at that—would have paid attention to a mere viscount's daughter. But contrary to Cecilia's expectations, Scarlett dragged her into the public eye. They must have panicked. I'm sure they wanted to avoid drawing attention to Cecilia. Not to say they intended to have Scarlett executed. If she died, their grand plan would come to a grinding halt. The original Holy Grail of Eris could not work without Scarlett. Or rather, Scarlett herself *was* the plan."

When she was executed, Faris was forced to retreat and rework its strategy—a process that took ten years.

"Adelbide would have been caught completely off guard. And it was Adelbide that was saved by Scarlett's death, wasn't it?"

Adelbide had not engaged in war with any country since it won its independence against Faris and became a kingdom of its own. Of course, there had been minor skirmishes along the borders, but ten years ago, the military was likely quite weak. It would have had no chance of winning a war. If the kingdom's elites had learned of the plan, what would they have done?

If Randolph had been in their shoes, he would have sought a way to avoid war.

And as he was poring over the records from that time, something strange had caught his attention. The primary piece of evidence in the attempted assassination of Cecilia Luze was a poison bottle found in Scarlett's room. There was no sign that anyone had broken into her family residence to plant it there. That was taken as proof of her guilt, but Randolph knew she had been framed.

Which left only one explanation.

"Breaking into a duke's mansion is an entirely different thing from breaking into the safe at headquarters. To sneak in and plant a bottle of poison in the duke's daughter's room without leaving a shred of evidence? There's only one person in the world who could have pulled that off."

Aisha's twisted mix of love and hatred was the trigger.

But when Randolph looked closely, he realized sparks were smoldering everywhere.

The Faris plot. The shadowy work of Daeg Gallus. Scarlett's own actions, too, were not without fault.

A jumble of trivial events became entangled by chance, forming a thread that looked very much like fate.

Was it a thread of destruction, or of salvation? Randolph didn't know. But he did know that this kingdom had survived as a result.

And who had cut the thread of Scarlett Castiel's life just like the Goddess Atropos?

Randolph fixed the man sitting before him with a steady, unclouded gaze.

"Am I wrong, Duke Castiel?"

Constance Grail

Sixteen-year-old who's not sure if she's helping or hurting the situation. The events of ten years ago are becoming so huge and disturbing, she's running out of heartburn medicine. Honestly hasn't heard anything about a war.

 Scarlett Castiel

Couldn't care less about what happens to Aldous or Abby, but her good-for-nothing accomplice was all upset about it, so she decided to lend a hand. Not that she would ever admit that. Honestly couldn't care less about war.

 Randolph Ulster

After the first-date incident, adds to his reputation for being tone-deaf by ignoring the two main characters and arriving at the truth about the events of ten years ago on his own. ←**new!**

 Aldous Clayton

Abby's unrepentant dog. Secretly wagging his tail that his owner has returned home unharmed. Has been getting into fistfights with that despicable master of sea trade since the day they met.

Walter Robinson

Purehearted master of the seas who has been devoted to Abigail for over ten years. Got rich and settled in Adelbide all for her sake, but she has no inkling of his feelings. Still gets into a fistfight with that despicable mongrel Aldous once in every three times they meet.

 Abigail O'Brian

Duchess who got out of jail free. Her relationships are so complicated, if she were to take one wrong step, she could go from afternoon soap to Dante's *Inferno*. Only her clumsiness when it comes to romance has allowed her to miraculously keep things aboveboard.

Kimberly Smith

Made a loaded comment about violets, but most likely the main character didn't get the point.

 San

Woman with a large build and golden hair, from Faris. Seems insensitive. Supporter of Princess Alexandra and searching for Ulysses. Being lectured by Eularia is her pet peeve.

 Eularia

Slender woman with silver hair, from Faris. Seems high-strung. Supporter of Princess Alexandra and searching for Ulysses. San's lack of tact is her pet peeve.

 Amelia Hobbes

Tried to get the better of the crown princess as a ploy to revitalize her career, only to discover her opponent was not a cute squirrel but instead a starving wolverine. Ran away, tail between her legs.

 Adolphus Castiel

Just what kind of dad is this guy?

©Yu-nagi

Bizarrely enough, we were born on the same day.

We looked quite similar when we were young. People would often tell us we were like twins as we grew up because of the color of our eyes. Of course, that was mere flattery. From his looks to his brains to his magnetism, he was my superior in every way. I believe the gods accidentally switched our souls in the womb. And every time I would tell him that, self-deprecatingly, he would smile as if to say I was a hopeless case.

"Although I must admit I surprise even myself with my excellence," he would say.

He was so handsome, even other boys would turn their heads, with the same magenta eyes as me.

"But even so, I wish to serve you," he went on. "Be confident in yourself, Ern. You are fit to be king."

"…What's that supposed to mean?" I asked. Needless to say, my furrowed brow and scowl were intended to hide my embarrassment, while he smiled as if he saw through everything.

He was always there, just a little ahead on the path I needed to take, pulling me forward like a big brother helping along his underachieving sibling.

Adolphus Castiel.

It's been many years since I called him Dolphy.

*   *   *

"I heard Veronica eloped."

The duchess had run off with her lover just after giving birth to her first child.

I heard the outlandish rumor the day it happened.

It was only because I felt sorry for the newborn Maximilian that I took a scolding tone with Adolphus. He had arrived at the castle the following day appearing the same as always. He looked at me as if it were no big deal. I felt the energy drain from my shoulders.

"...Why did you forgive her?"

There was no chance he hadn't known her plans.

But Adolphus just shrugged. "The only thing between us was a responsibility to carry on the family line. She did her duty, so I don't see the problem."

You don't see the problem?! I thought. Not only had baby Maximilian been abandoned by his mother, but this was indisputably a scandal for the Castiel family. Adolphus put on a brave front, but he surely knew that.

"John's a good fellow. I'm sure Veronica will be happy with him," he added casually.

I sulked in silence. Although Adolphus always kept his cool, I knew he was not a heartless man. Veronica had never had the inner strength demanded of a duchess. Which meant this was probably Adolphus's version of kindness. Although his methods were so roundabout, neither she nor the average onlooker would ever realize that.

As I continued to frown in silence, Adolphus burst out laughing.

"...What?"

"Nothing, just that you're as easy to read as ever."

"Sorry, I've always been bad at hiding my feelings."

"I meant it as a compliment."

"How's that?!" I snapped. A smile creased his stunningly handsome face.

"See? You've lightened my mood. That's not any easy thing to do."

Adolphus beamed at me, as if to say I ought to be proud of myself, but my scowl only deepened.

Several years passed. When Adolphus's divorce from Veronica was officially sanctioned by the church, I called him to the palace.

"…Remarry?"

The handsome divorcé, who still attracted swarms of women each time he went out in society, looked at me with suspicion. I nodded confidently and continued.

"Don't you think Max needs a mother?"

"He has Claude, so I'm not too worried. Claude's more motherly than most mothers."

Claude was the butler who had been watching over the Castiel family since Adolphus's father was duke. He'd taught Adolphus himself how to behave.

I was at a momentary loss for words, but I quickly coughed.

"…Little children need warm, soft arms to hold them, not a bony old man."

I knew it was a lousy argument, but as usual, Adolphus smiled. That smile charmed both women and men.

"I understand the cover story. Now what's your real motivation?"

"…What are you talking about?"

"Do you think you can hide from me, Ern?"

"…I have nothing to hide."

"Let me give you a piece of friendly criticism. Your ability to conceal your feelings hasn't improved at all these past ten years."

I looked up at the ceiling and raised both hands in surrender.

"People from Soldita came to me in tears. They want me to take in a girl directly descended from Cornelia Faris."

The rumor that the last empress had sought refuge in the Republic of Soldita was true.

Ever since, her bloodline had been quietly protected there. But several years ago, Faris had started to interfere. Given that country's obsession with bloodlines, the motive was probably to infuse the declining royal family with old imperial stock.

The visitors from Soldita had said they wanted to prevent that from happening. That confused me, but they said the problem was the man Cornelia Faris had married. Several years after fleeing, she had married the nephew of the then-sovereign. If one of their descendants became the monarch of Faris, there would be unrest in Soldita at the very least. They wanted to avoid unnecessary turmoil.

The conditions they offered Adelbide weren't bad. But it wouldn't do to bring such a troublesome bloodline into an incompetent noble family.

There was only one person I could truly trust in a situation like this.

"…What else can I do? No one other than you is fit for the job," I told Adolphus guiltily.

He smiled wryly, as if to say, like he always did, that I was a hopeless case.

Several months passed. When I finally saw the bride who had traveled all the way from a faraway land across the sea, I couldn't believe my eyes.

Her glossy black hair was like a reflection of the night sky, and her eyes were an amethyst shade not seen in either Adelbide or Faris. Hers was the beauty of a fleeting dream.

"She's lovely, isn't she?" I said to Adolphus. But his reaction was cold. He took one glance and looked away, unmoved.

"She's a child."

That was all.

I unconsciously pressed my hand to my forehead. True, she was young, but likely less than a decade his junior.

"…You have nothing more to say? This woman will be your wife."

"On paper. My job is to shelter the child, correct?"

"Shelter? She's not a dog or a cat…"

"She might as well be one. Anyhow, don't worry. I'm good at this sort of thing."

He shrugged and turned to take the hand of his beautiful bride.

"…What happened to your face?"

When Adolphus Castiel returned to the capital after a long sojourn in his domain, his cheek was plastered with a large bandage. A shame for someone so handsome. He answered with a single phrase, dejected.

"A cat."

"I didn't know you had a—" I started to say, then smiled. "A cat, eh?"

"…Yes."

"A black one?"

"…No comment."

No doubt the cat had amethyst eyes. I didn't know what had happened, but it seemed interesting. I knew if I pushed him for details, he would only grow more sullen, so I decided to hold back and wait.

The seasons passed, and before I knew it, the bride from across the sea was with child.

I shot the father a questioning look, only to receive a scowl in return.

"She's a force of nature," he moaned.

I didn't say anything. But apparently my ability to hide my thoughts was as poor as ever.

"I told you, she's a force of nature!"

It was rare for the ever-calm Adolphus to become so agitated. I laughed out loud for the first time in what felt like years.

"By the way, I heard Sarah safely delivered her second child. It's a boy," I said, wiping my eyes.

This mention of an old mutual friend changed the grumpy look on Adolphus's face to a smile. "A boy, is it? Owen looks like Sarah, so I hope this one takes after Lew."

I smiled wryly at the predictable response. "You've always liked Lewain, haven't you?"

Ever since we were boys, Adolphus had had a soft spot for Lewain Richelieu. The feeling wasn't mutual, though, and Lew had grown weary of Adolphus's constant meddling.

Adolphus really was awful at showing his affection.

"Naturally. He's so adorable."

"I don't see what's so adorable about that huge man."

"His unpredictability."

"I see."

True enough, Lewain did have a habit of saying and doing unexpected things. Still, it was hard to call his looks adorable. I gave him a puzzled look.

"*Simon Ulster* is getting on in years. This baby will probably take on his title."

Ulster. I couldn't help frowning at that name, full of darkness.

"Blasted convention," I spat out.

"But it's necessary," Adolphus chided. "Just like Castiel is necessary."

I had seen that troubled smile of his countless times over the years. When I remained silent, he adopted a brighter tone. "I can't wait to meet the baby. Sarah promised me that if her next child was a boy, she would make me his namesake."

"If that happens, your darling Lewain will surely cry."

"Oh, didn't you know? Sarah and I have formed a league whose sole aim is to make adorable little Lew cry. We haven't succeeded lately, so this will be the perfect opportunity."

He grinned like the handsome devil he was. I felt very sorry for the poor lamb Lewain.

Coos filled the room as a chubby little hand reached out toward a huge man with a sharp face. The man cried out in delight.

"Pretty girl! She's not even scared of me!"

The man rubbed his own rough cheek against the baby's soft one, a rapt smile on his face. The baby fussed, probably because his beard had scratched her.

"Duran! Don't touch her. She might catch your idiocy," Adolphus scolded sharply.

"That was uncalled for!" the man shouted back in shock. Duran Belsford was a friend of Adolphus's. He was also the youngest child of the Belsford family, which oversaw a domain on the border with Faris. He was currently working in the Royal Security Force headquarters, and while his language was foul, his work ethic was good. I'd known him for ten years myself.

"Your Highness, did you hear that?! This man is brutal!"

"I did indeed. I'm worried, too. Hurry up and give him back sweet little Scarlett."

"What, have I no friends here? Pretty girl, you'll be my friend, won't you?" Duran peered into his arms, and for some reason the baby chortled. "You too?!"

I burst out laughing at his exaggerated despair. Adolphus was laughing, too.

Now that I think back on it, that may have been one of the last times we were able to laugh together so freely. Perhaps that is why the scene appears often in my dreams, even now.

It has become a symbol of the happiness of bygone days.

Aliénore died when Scarlett was seven years old. She had always been frail, and the doctors had told her she wouldn't live long. She had recovered poorly after childbirth and was scarcely able to get out of bed in the years before her death.

When Adolphus told me she was gone, he appeared the same as always. In fact, though I have known him since we were infants, I have never once seen the man get emotional.

"...Do you feel all right?" I asked.

Although our relationship was not as unconstrained as it had been in younger years, I still thought of him as a brother.

"About what?"

Nevertheless, I couldn't guess what was in his heart.

"Just...," I said, unable to put words to my thoughts.

Adolphus blinked, then smiled as always, as if to say I was a hopeless case.

Bad news always comes in threes.

"Sarah and Lewain, both?"

There had been a carriage accident. I couldn't remember the last time I had seen the two of them. Unable to fully absorb what had happened, I stared off in a daze.

Adolphus's cool voice interrupted my thoughts. "Until their heir, Owen, comes of age, Lewain's younger brother, Davis, will oversee the domain in his stead."

I suddenly thought of the younger child.

"...What about Randolph?"

"Simon Ulster says he'll take him in. That was the plan to begin with. It's a little earlier than expected, but I don't think it will be a problem. Anyhow, Earl Ulster is getting older."

In other words, the poor boy would soon begin his *education* with his Great-Uncle Ulster.

I felt a pang in my heart but pretended not to notice.

Little did I imagine then that, in a few years, Owen, too, would be dead.

Owen's funeral took place not in the domain but instead in a neighborhood church in the capital. That was at the request of Randolph, who lived in the capital with his great-uncle.

By the time I'd managed to make it to the church, the guests were already gone, leaving young Randolph alone on a bench gazing at the altar.

When I saw him sitting there looking so lost, I realized that he had been left truly alone in the world.

"...You're not crying."

Lewain had cried easily, despite his intimidating appearance. I thought of that as I spoke to his son. He turned slowly in my direction, but his answer seemed directed toward himself.

"Ulsters don't need emotions," he muttered. His eyes were like still pools of water. Somehow they reminded me of Adolphus Castiel's.

When was it that the gears of fate slipped off track, I wonder.

"Juda Notre has been dismissed?" I couldn't help asking. A former lawyer from a powerful noble family, Notre was a talented civil servant rumored to be the top candidate for next controller-general of finance. "Whatever could he have done wrong?"

Adolphus shrugged.

"Embezzlement, apparently. Comptroller-General Colbert is furious. Says the dog has bitten the hand that feeds him."

"Was it an anonymous tip?"

"No, someone came forward. Simon Daniel—or rather Darkian, I believe. I forgot he took his wife's name."

"The fellow who was doing the books for the army? All I remember about him is that he's Deborah Darkian's husband, but with this, he's sure to have caught Colbert's attention. A lucky man indeed."

Unfortunately, the House of Darkian had not been blessed with many children. There had been several older boys, but Deborah was the only heir to survive to adulthood. Several years earlier, she had married and taken on the family title, but I imagine choosing a husband for such a coddled girl was not easy.

Simon Daniel was the third son of a marquess on the verge of ruin. The boy himself had no remarkable characteristics and wasn't much to look at. But perhaps that was for the best. It would be difficult for his family to meddle, and he himself lacked all sign of ambition.

This ruined noble had been chosen by a duke's family and was now on the road to success via a post as comptroller-general of the treasury. Life is always unpredictable.

As I was reflecting sentimentally on this turn of events, Adolphus changed the subject.

"By the way, some kind of strange hallucinogen seems to be going around lately."

"Hallucinogen?" I asked, flipping through a stack of papers with finance data.

"Yes. Apparently, it's popular among the younger nobles. It's not especially strong, but I wonder how people are getting it. It's only the higher nobles who have it."

"They're not getting it on Rosenkreuz Street?"

"I asked O'Brian, but he said he hadn't seen any sign of it. Lady Audrey keeps a close watch over there, so I believe him."

I shivered involuntarily, recalling the elderly woman who could strike fear in the bravest of hearts. "What's it called?"

"Jackal's Paradise. I've heard people call it J."

"Is that so? A drug named after a foreign beast. Sounds dangerous. I'll tell my sons to stay away from it," I joked, but in truth, I wasn't all that concerned. After all, it was just another hallucinogen. Or so I thought.

It was several months afterward that events took another turn.

"Duran, accused of treason?"

Earl Solms, who held the domain next to that of the Belsfords, had informed on him. The claim was that Duran Belsford was secretly raising an army to revolt against the king.

By that point, I already knew that an organization called Daeg Gallus was involved in the distribution of Jackal's Paradise. The criminal group had members all across the continent. I had ordered Duran to investigate it. Given how busy he was chasing down information, there was no way he would have had time to plan a rebellion.

All the same, he'd been convicted.

"How idiotic," I muttered as I read the report from the Ministry of

Justice, which stated that he'd already been arrested and would be executed in six months.

No matter how you looked at it, things were moving far too fast.

"It certainly is," Adolphus answered. "But I believe you and I are the real idiots."

"...What do you mean?"

"This is the work of Faris. They're pulling the strings."

I blinked, confused. "Faris?"

"Yes. Their aim is to start a war and make us a vassal state."

I slowly took in his words. As far as I knew, we had been cultivating a friendly relationship with our neighbors ever since Adelbide became independent from the old Faris Empire.

I looked at Adolphus in disbelief.

He sighed, sounding exhausted. "I've finally figured out their plans... although it's too late. Duran's already been locked up."

He threw a bundle of papers at me, a pained expression on his face. As I scrambled to catch them, I saw the words scrawled on top.

"'The Holy Grail of Eris'...?"

He laughed self-mockingly. "It seems our kingdom is not so popular after all."

The papers laid out Faris's financial situation and its scheme to wage a war to take over Adelbide for its economic resources. To top it off, Scarlett, descendent of Cornelia Faris, was to be their pretext.

"...So Duran's imprisonment is the work of Faris, too?" I muttered, trying to hide my panic over the information I'd just received.

"Yes," Adolphus replied. "The Belsford domain is on the border with Faris. Its defense is impregnable. They haven't been chasing off the northern tribes all these years for nothing. I have no doubt Faris's goal in the Duran affair is to weaken that stronghold. Most likely, they intend to take advantage of the chaos following Duran's death to attack the border."

How could this happen? I raised my eyes to the ceiling.

"In other words, the reason he was sentenced to death so quickly—"

"Is because there's a rat in our midst."

"...So Solms is a pawn."

"He and Duran were always at loggerheads anyway, so I'm sure they had no trouble manipulating him."

"Then that hallucinogen is a way for them to raise funds?"

"No doubt that's part of it, but considering how popular it is among the higher nobles, the real goal seems to be to erode our kingdom's strength. And if we think about which nobles are close with Solms, who has soared to prominence with such stunning speed..."

I widened my eyes. "Simon Darkian...!"

The unremarkable man who had married into the Darkian family.

In that case, the dismissal of Juda Notre must be related as well. Although I wasn't sure if it was the will of Deborah, current head of the Darkian family, or Simon's own decision.

"We must question Simon immediately—"

"He would just claim total ignorance. And we have no evidence. Our priority must be saving Duran. Most likely, his death will be the trigger for war."

"Unbelievable..."

The very survival of our kingdom was at risk.

The enemy had spent years perfecting their plan. Digging only turned up more damning evidence against Duran, while not a single trace of Simon Darkian's wrongdoings could be found.

We had taken peace for granted, and now we had no chance of winning.

That was the situation when the Security Force named Scarlett Castiel a suspect in the failed assassination attempt against Cecilia Luze. They said an earring that appeared to be hers had been found at the scene of the crime.

I groaned when I heard the news. "Do you think framing Scarlett is part of their plan, too?"

"Most likely it's a coincidence. They have no reason to harm Scarlett."

Adolphus was right. I thought over the military strategy called the Holy Grail of Eris.

According to that plan, Scarlett, who carried the blood of Cornelia Faris in her veins, was to be installed as the new queen. It seemed unlikely that they would intentionally expose her to danger. Without Scarlett, it would be hard for them to achieve their ideal takeover of Adelbide.

At that point, I realized something. Something very disturbing.

Without Scarlett—

Goose pimples rose on my arm. The horror of it made me want to vomit. I was disgusted with myself for even thinking such a thing. But I could not erase the thought from my mind. Many lives would be lost in a war. And as things stood now, Adelbide had no chance of winning. What would become of the people if Adelbide became a vassal state of Faris? As ruler, I had to do everything I possibly could to avoid that.

And yet, sweet smiles from happy days long ago flickered across my mind. The innocent laughter. The little palm. The warmth of a little body.

I couldn't do it.

I couldn't make the decision. I clasped my hands and looked up, searching for something to cling to.

Our eyes met.

Adolphus Castiel narrowed his eyes, those eyes that were the same color as mine, and formed his lips into a troubled smile.

As if to say I was a hopeless case.

"Your Highness," he said quietly.

Not Ern, but Your Highness. When he addressed me in that way, it was always to speak as a loyal subject of the king.

"Let's make use of Scarlett."

Oh Gods, I silently screamed. If it might have led to my forgiveness, I would have kneeled on the ground then and there and repented. If not that, I at least wanted the gods to punish my folly as quickly as possible.

Because it should have been *me* giving the order. It was my duty to speak those words.

I sinned in hesitating. I let myself be carried away by my own emotions. I should never have weighed one human life against the fate of my kingdom. Not if I were a proper king.

I should never have made this man say something so cruel.

"Their plan can only succeed if someone with the blood of Faris's imperial family is involved. So surely, if Scarlett is executed—"

I could listen to no more. "Instead of executing her, we can banish her to Soldita or somewhere like that and then later bring her back…!"

Adolphus smiled.

A gentle smile, as if he were soothing the temper of a difficult little brother.

But his tone did not waver.

"Your Highness, I'm sure you understand the situation. If Duran is executed and the Belsford domain crumbles, the same thing will happen. Faris has a way to invade and conquer Adelbide even without Scarlett. We absolutely must free Duran Belsford. To prove his innocence, we need time. Scarlett's execution will without a doubt attract the attention of the public. In which case, all we need to do is convince them that public executions are savage, primitive affairs. We can instruct Kimberly Smith at the Violet Association to lead the protest movement. She is a student of Simon Ulster's. She will do her job well."

Although it wasn't known to the public, the Violet Association served as a safety valve to diffuse anger toward the royal family and nobles. The majority of its members were commoners who knew nothing of this, but those in leadership roles were specially trained undercover agents.

"If there is an outcry calling for a halt to public executions, Duran's will have to be put off. In the meantime, we can collect evidence proving his innocence."

"Wait, there must be some other way—"

There was but a moment of silence.

"…Unfortunately, we have no time. And this is a better opportunity than we could have hoped for."

I knew that. I knew it all too well. I looked down and covered my face with my hands. I felt unbearably wretched for seeing no way forward aside from sacrificing Scarlett. I was also sad. Sad that even at a moment like this, Adolphus showed no emotion. Sad that under no circumstance would he lay the blame on me.

"Your Highness." His terribly even voice broke the silence. "Remember well who begs you to save Scarlett's life. Most likely the enemy's operatives will be among them."

I was utterly helpless. I bit my lip so hard, it bled. As it was, I couldn't take down a single Darkian.

"I'm certain they will eventually bare their teeth again. But by then—"

If Scarlett was executed and Duran Belsford was freed, Faris would no doubt be forced to retreat. But that would not be the end. They would sharpen their claws and watch vigilantly for the next chance to expand their territory. Exactly like a wild beast scavenging for carrion.

However, we would not be waiting passively while they did so. No matter how many years it took, we would take down Simon Darkian and every last one of the other traitors.

When Adolphus spoke again, his voice was like a spark reigniting the flame that had gone out in my heart.

"We'll have the last laugh, and then we'll rub their noses in it."

©Yu-nagi

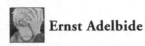 **Ernst Adelbide**

Like father, like son—both screwed up. DNA is no joke.

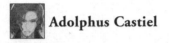 **Adolphus Castiel**

Hasn't been able to smile for the past ten years.

Lately, Talbott's boss had been acting strangely.

Talbott was a greenhorn investigator at the Royal Security Force headquarters.

His direct superior was Randolph Ulster, otherwise known as His Excellency the Grim Reaper, a man Talbott had looked up to ever since he'd entered the agency. He was exceedingly serious and stern, but his approach to work was the definition of fair. Despite his frightening appearance, he was an excellent man, and it went without saying that he never judged a person by their rank...

"Talbott, you look pale. Are you getting enough sleep?"

...And occasionally, he was so kind, Talbott's heart skipped a beat.

"The lieutenant commander, being kind...? That's odd...," Talbott mumbled as he stared at a piece of honey candy.

"What's up with Lieutenant Commander Ulster?" a coworker asked, peering curiously into Talbott's hand. "Oh, he gave you some candy?"

"Yeah. He said it's good for sore throats," Talbot answered, then realized what he had just said and hurriedly added, "N-not that the lieutenant commander is normally mean or anything...!"

"What are you so worked up about? I know what you mean. He's a scary man. It's like he forgot how to smile or something."

It was true. Randolph Ulster was normally so intimidating, a one-word greeting from him was enough to send sweat running down a man's back.

"But recently he seems to have thawed a little..."

Of course, Ulster had taken notice of Talbott before. It was just that when he asked after his health with that stony face of his, Talbott felt like he was being reprimanded for not taking good enough care of himself.

And he'd never given him candy before.

Talbott wasn't sure, but his expression seemed a little gentler this time, too.

"I don't quite know how to put this, but he seems more human... I mean, he was a human to start with, but..."

"I know what you mean," Talbott's coworker said before casually dropping a bomb.

"That girl must be amazing. Man, I'd love to have someone like that to help me relax after work..."

"What?"

"Huh?"

The man blinked at Talbott's confused look.

"What, you didn't know? The reason the lieutenant commander changed is—"

Just then, they were interrupted by a loud voice.

"A date? You're going on a date?"

They turned in the direction of the voice. Kyle Hughes, deputy of Ulster's team, was standing there slack-jawed. Even with that dopey expression on his face, he was still stunningly handsome, but his subordinates—or in Talbott's case, his underlings—knew well that the man behind the mask was a fearsome workaholic.

Ulster lifted his eyes from his stack of documents and shook his head mildly.

"No, we're just meeting to go over some information about the incident ten years ago. I wouldn't call it a date."

Hughes scowled. "Don't tell me you've never once taken her out since you got engaged! Unbelievable."

"I have not... Is there something wrong with that?"

"Is there ever! A man who can't arrange dates is announcing his incompetence. Anyhow, if the two of you are going out alone, how is that not a date?"

"It's not just the two of us, it's the thr—two of us."

"As I suspected. A date."

"...Fine, call it whatever you want," Ulster said with a resigned sigh.

The boss had recently gotten engaged. If Talbott recalled correctly, the girl was a viscount's daughter. She was still in her teens, and though she was a noble, her rank was much lower than his. Talbott had been surprised when he heard the news, considering the pair didn't seem to have anything whatsoever in common.

He remembered what his coworker had said just a few minutes earlier. *That girl must be amazing.*

Which reminded him, the commander had been unusually terrifying on the banks of Lake Bernadia. If he wasn't mistaken, the goal of that mission had been to rescue this same fiancée and her friend.

In other words, the reason His Excellency the Grim Reaper had changed was—

"So the cold fish is finally going on a proper date...," Hughes muttered, sounding impressed. Suddenly, however, he seemed to snap back to reality, pressing Ulster. "And where will you meet with dear little Connie? Are you choosing the spot?"

"I am."

"You ought to avoid anywhere too fashionable; it'll be overly crowded. You'll both wind up exhausted. And don't go anywhere too noisy. It will be depressing if the conversation dries up. And then plays depend too much on preference… Yes, I do think your best option would be a nice quiet place with a good view. How about the lakeside, or maybe a park?"

"I see." Ulster took in this rapid-fire barrage of advice from well-known playboy Hughes with a blank face. "To summarize, I'd do best to choose somewhere quiet, natural—where we don't normally go," he said as if he were reviewing an assignment.

Hughes gave him a skeptical look, which appeared to confuse Ulster.

"Did I get that wrong?" he asked.

"No, not exactly…but do you understand what all this means? You're not choosing the location for a training drill, you know."

Ulster nodded with an unperturbed expression, as if to say, *Yes, and?*

"That shouldn't be a problem," he replied.

※

"That's a huge problem…!"

Several days had passed since the conversation between Hughes and Ulster.

Hughes's exclamation came in response to His Excellency's account of the date with his fiancée. Hughes was actually trembling, likely with fury.

"In fact, the whole thing is nothing but problems! You took her to the history museum on your first date?! What in the world is wrong with you?!"

Ulster blinked in confusion, then pressed his forehead like he had a headache, staring at Hughes.

After a moment, he replied.

"But you said I ought to choose somewhere quiet, natural—where I didn't normally go…"

He tilted his head like he couldn't fathom Hughes's fury.

"Didn't you say that?"

"That's not what I meant!!" Hughes howled. "And wasn't your former wife the one who took you there in the first place…?!"

"She was," Ulster answered simply.

Perhaps overwhelmed by this unexpected response, Hughes finally crumbled. "That's what I'm talking about!"

Talbott watched the drama unfold before him with a dubious gaze. Suddenly, Ulster's sky-blue eyes turned in his direction.

Any other day, they would probably have kept right on moving, but for some reason today, they stopped on him.

"Talbott."

"Y-y-y-y-yes?!"

"…Do you think it was really such a bad choice?"

Don't ask me!!!

After all, the look on Ulster's face was utterly inscrutable. Talbott didn't want to offend the boss he revered. He glanced away awkwardly, putting on an ingratiating smile as he tried to come up with the most harmless words possible.

"Uh, um… Was the date enjoyable?"

"It yielded a number of positive outcomes."

"…Positive outcomes…?"

Those were not words one normally used to describe a date. The smile froze on Talbott's face. He was bewildered.

"Oh yes," Ulster continued, as if he'd just remembered something. "Rather a lot of food was consumed."

He didn't say by whom, but his voice was tinged with amusement.

"She must have been quite hungry. She seemed to like the sandwich I ordered, because she demolished it."

Talbot looked up.

Ulster's face was as stony as ever. But when he looked very closely, he noticed that the corners of his mouth seemed to be slightly—

Before he knew what he was doing, Talbott was talking.

"Lieutenant Commander."

"Yes?"

"It's wonderful that your fiancée had a good time."

Ulster's eyes widened slightly. "…Yes."

The look on his face—like he was surprised or confused by his own feelings—was undeniably human.

Talbott was filled with warmth. He grinned.

"It really does feel great to make someone else happy! I completely understand! Finding a place your date will love really is the most important thing when you're going out! You shouldn't think too hard about these th—"

Suddenly, Talbott felt a hand descend onto his shoulder, interrupting his happy little monologue.

Silence.

The blood drained from Talbott's face. He had a bad feeling about this.

Steeling his will, he looked stiffly over his shoulder. Yes, as he'd feared—the absurdly handsome deputy was standing behind him.

"In other words, my advice wasn't any good?" he asked in a rumbling voice, smiling demonically.

Talbott froze.

※

Constance Grail widened her green eyes and glanced around in surprise.

"What's this…?"

A vibrant, colorful scene surrounded her. There were baskets of vegetables and fruits, hanging cuts of meat, jars of pickles, bundles of dried herbs…

Just the day before, her fiancé had contacted her to say there was a place he wanted to take her. For some reason, they had to go early in the morning. He had come to fetch her at dawn, leading her through the still-quiet streets of the castle district to an intersection near the port.

The streets were lined with the stalls of an enormous central market.

"This is the biggest morning market in the capital. Lots of food here," Randolph said.

"Yes, I see that…"

That wasn't what she'd meant to ask. She nodded, holding back her confusion.

They were at the Alslain Central Market. It was famous as the "people's kitchen," and of course Connie knew about it, though she'd never been there before. That wasn't the point. The point was, why had Randolph brought her here?

"You can eat whatever you want."

"…What?"

She peered around, gaping. Mixed in with the stalls selling groceries were others offering cooked food and local specialties.

"Here I thought he was taking you on a date for once, and then he brings you to the least romantic place in the city," Scarlett said with an exasperated eye roll, her arms crossed.

"…Did I get it wrong again?"

Connie looked up. Randolph's blue eyes were looking down at her with a vaguely embarrassed expression.

"I got it wrong last time, didn't I? This time I was determined to choose a place you'd like, but…I'm just no good at this," he concluded, mumbling the last bit like he was talking to himself.

Connie looked back at the market. Speaking of the morning market, she'd heard that the sandwiches made with crusty fresh-baked bread, slow-cooked pork shank, tangy sour cream, and crisp vegetables were out of this world. That must be what people were lining up for a little ways away. She'd never expected to have a chance to try it herself…

So, in other words, this was their second date.

Connie didn't know why Randolph had chosen this particular place, but she did understand he was trying to make her happy.

"…I like it," she said, smiling voraciously. Randolph let out a relieved sigh.

"You do?"

"Yes!"

She felt herself getting excited. The air was filled with the appetizing smells of breakfast cooking, and she was starving. There were so many delicious-looking foods, she couldn't decide which to try first.

"Do you see something you want?"

"Yes, um, first that pork sandwich, and then the lamb kebabs from the stall next door, and the fried whitefish and potatoes, and the candied fruit, and the molasses-nut cookies—"

"That's a little too much, don't you think?"

"That's a little too much, isn't it?" added Scarlett. They had spoken completely in sync.

Connie blinked. "Well, for now...I think I'll try the sandwich," she announced.

Randolph smiled very, very slightly, as if he'd remembered something. "Ah."

"What is it?" Connie asked. The unusual expression vanished from his face. But she was certain she'd seen it.

"...Nothing. I'm just excited to eat because I'm hungry."

"Oh."

His words were straightforward, but there was something gentle about the look on his face...

Filled with a mysterious happiness, Connie smiled.

©Yu-nagi

AFTERWORD

It happened one cold day.

I was in my first year of high school. The future was full of dreams and hopes, and my skin was glowing with firmness and sheen. Sadly, both are unrecognizable today. Time is cruel.

"This cold is brutal! I can't stand it."

However, my habit of complaining about everything remains unchanged, and on that particular day, I was grumbling away to my friend A.

"Really? I think the cold is wonderful."

Incidentally, A was a cool, intellectual beauty whom you'd never expect to be friends with someone like me, who takes three steps forward and can't remember what they were talking about.

"No way, this feels like some kind of punishment."

"Of course. No pain, no gain."

"I didn't know you were into that kind of thing…"

"Seriously, it's like a warning to us so we don't die."

*   *   *

I threw her a questioning look. She continued as if her point were completely obvious.

"What I mean is, this system has been set up so human beings can survive. And since you just complain about it without doing anything, that means you're no longer human."

She was right. I didn't have the heart to crack a sarcastic joke about how Osamu Dazai would be rolling over in his grave if he could hear her, so I simply stopped into a convenience store and picked up a *nikuman* bun to use as a makeshift hand warmer.

I got in the habit of buying *nikuman* after school, and my midriff started to show it.

Around that time, when the flu was going around school like some sort of winter rite of passage, A came up to me with a deeply mystified look on her face.

"I've been thinking about this for a while," she began. "Why does the flu virus weaken its host? All living organisms instinctively try to proliferate, don't they? And if something happens to the host, then the virus won't be able to survive, right? So doesn't that make their strategy a failure for a living creature?"

What the hell are you talking about?
Sadly enough, that was my response at the time.

If she had asked my current self, who still lacks intellectual knowledge but has at least been pummeled by the rough waves of the world enough to gain some communication skills, I would have diverted the conversation by saying something sensible like, "I think we have to start by asking the eternal question—is a virus even a living thing?" Or if she had asked my university-aged self, who was a great admirer of Richard Dawkins, I would have pretended to know way more than I actually did by saying something like, "It must be a case of the selfish gene."

To make yet another embarrassing confession, my dream at the time—albeit a hazy one—was to become a biologist or something. "Biologist" sounded really cool. That was the only reason. (Looking back, the "or something" should have been a tip-off that my interest wasn't that deep.)

That's probably why my friend's words hit me so hard. She embodied my vision of the "ideal researcher," and I realized then that no matter what I did, I would never have that sort of perspective on life. That was the moment my frail, unrealistic dream crumbled.

I think that was the first time I ever learned something about myself through another person. I was surprised by how much my world changed in that moment, but I remember that, for some reason, it felt incredibly refreshing.

Many years have passed since then, but I am grateful to be able to say that this novel has given me the same experience. Although I've leaned on many people for help, received much encouragement from my readers, and occasionally flailed in the unexpectedly huge ocean of this project, I secretly hope that one day I, too, will become an "ideal researcher."

I'm still being twisted around the finger of a certain Miss C on a daily basis, but more than that, I'm humbled by the awareness that I would never have been able to do this work without the support of so many people. I'd like to yell "Thank you!" from the rooftops to all those people, and to be honest, I'm already yelling it in my own head. They might not hear me, but I'm yelling it.

The truth is, it's thanks to them that I managed to finish this second volume of this story. I am deeply grateful. Once again, my editor guided me straight to my destination (with headlamp strapped on, of course), Yu-nagi provided illustrations that capture the reader's heart at a glance, and Momoyama did such a fabulous job with the comic version, it makes me cry.

Finally, I'd like to tell all my readers who have stuck with me through the second volume that I think of us as "one team." I hope you don't mind! (And as usual, I'm behind the curve on my use of buzzwords.)

I look forward to seeing you all again next time.

Kujira Tokiwa